The Transmigration of Cora Riley

A FORGOTTEN RELICS NOVEL

Ellie Di Julio

ELLE BELLE MEDIA

The Transmigration of Cora Riley

A Forgotten Relics Novel

First Edition

Content © 2013 Ellie Di Julio

Cover image © 2013 Desiree Kern

Back cover image © Rachel Towne

All rights reserved.

ISBN-13: 9780993629013

Published by Elle Belle Media

for jess –
we escaped

PART I
WICKED LITTLE TOWN

ONE

You never know what the final straw will be, do you? Which day will change your life forever? You can be the best mathematician or artist or psychic in the world, but mere humans don't get to see that far ahead. All you can know is that things have been building for weeks or months or years, the pressure on your heart constantly increasing. Someday it'll be too much. Somebody says the right combination of words. Something tips you from "I can handle this" to "not anymore," and it's over. You're done. You're gone. Things will never be the same.

All in just one day.

Sweet Jesus, please go away. Maybe if I close my eyes, he'll disappear.

I squeeze my eyes shut for a moment out of sheer wishful thinking, but when I open them, he's still there, pursing his lips impatiently under the little waxed mustache no one's told him makes him look like Hitler. Comes in every damn day with the same order. Won't let anyone else take it because I'm the only one that gets it right. Lucky me.

But instead of flipping everyone in this place the bird and stomping out the door like I want to do, I say, "Morning, Mr. Johns!" and flash him a brand-mandated smile. "The usual?"

I'd have already started making it when he walked in, but the last time I did that, he had a meltdown about how "you kids today think you know everything." We had to call a rent-a-cop from the electronics store on the next block to calm him down. And I'm freshly thirty, thank you very much.

"Hrm..." he murmurs, pondering the menu as if today might be different as the morning rush piles up behind him. You'd think they'd get a second barista for the early shift, but no. Town's too small, money's too tight. Understatements, both of them.

"I'll have a mocha cappuccino, soy milk, half-caf, no whip, with a shot of mint. But only one - otherwise it tastes like toothpaste. And your smallest blueberry scone. To go."

"Sounds great!" I chime. "I'll get that right out." Should've been an actress.

He's not a bad customer, really. It's just that he's so damn fussy. All self-important in this spit stain on the Missouri map.

I finish the drink and ignore the muffled lowing from the crowd as I hand it off. Johns quirks a half-smile like a stroke and heads out the door. No "thank you" or a tip. Not that I get them from anyone else.

I turn my attention to the next customer, then the next, then the next for the rest of my six-hour shift. I wonder if anyone notices how easily I check out while carrying on inane conversations about the weather, people's kids, who's sleeping around, who didn't come to church, and all the other gossip that sustains a town with one stoplight. I vaguely recall hearing that Einstein's theory of relativity explains why time crawls when you're bored; all I know is that noon can never come fast enough.

When the skinny clock hands finally twitch together, I'm in the parking lot before my green apron hits the floor. I hop into my baby-blue 84' longbed truck, crank the key, jam it into first, and I'm gone.

Instead of hitting the side street that takes me home, I cross the railroad tracks into town for a little decompression drive. The city wouldn't let a chain like the one I work for into the business loop for fear it'd shut down the local start-ups. Smart move, honestly – no way the "Dairy King" or the scuzzy gas stations could keep up. I pass houses that could be historical monuments but are buckled and moldy after being abandoned to urban development. I peek briefly into their familiar windows and wonder if the families that left them behind found something better out there. A richer life than a town where what matters most is who you're related to and if you made the varsity basketball team.

I take a deep breath as I idle at a stop sign. All

the free coffee I drink at work makes my brain buzz crazily, and it's too easy to wander into a philosophical no man's land as I drive through town.

Besides, this place isn't all depressive decay. There's a kind of overgrown beauty here. I can't imagine living somewhere without green trees and blue skies. Spring makes the town itself burst into life; fall sets it on fire. The plethora of churches adds a touch of the divine to the scenery, even though I'm not a regular. And it's quiet. For my twenty-fifth birthday, I spent two weeks in New York City as a gift to myself, but I hid in my hotel for the first three days; I couldn't stand the noise and press of humanity after growing up in endless fields and wild woods. Here in the heart of town, you can still hear yourself breathe, at least. Even if sometimes you think you're suffocating.

I wave to Junior in his truck as I come up to the stoplight. We cross paths nearly every day as I go from work to my folks' house and he goes from the pasture to the bar. He's a grizzled old redneck that grazes his mules on Mom and Dad's property in exchange for odd jobs like servicing the well pump, mending fences, and sharing the dandelion wine that he makes in his basement according to a secret recipe that I'm pretty sure involves wood alcohol. The finest in beverages that make you blind.

Two minutes later, I'm rounding the bend past an ex-boyfriend's house and coming up on the high school. It's a low-slung brick thing cut carefully out of the surrounding woods with an enormous tumor of a gym protruding from its side. Three hundred students, seventh through twelfth grades. Graduation's coming up soon. Somebody will get to write "valedictorian" on their college applications and compete with other number ones from schools ten times as big. Like I did. Unlike me, though, maybe they'll actually go when they get accepted.

I make a mental note to dip into Junior's rocket fuel stash when I get home. It's gearing up to be one of those nights.

I whizz past the city limits doing fifteen over, and I swing my attention back to the drive. Ozark roads are wily. Forget about one hairpin turn and you're down a gulley, into the river, splattered on the rocks. But I learned to drive on these serpentine back roads; I know where to squeeze the gas and where to tickle the brakes. My trusty Toyota leans into the s-curves and bounces high when I hit the bump by the Sherman place at speed.

Despite my pessimistic hangover from work, it's hard to have an existential crisis out here. The warm almost-summer breeze rushes through my hair, whipping through the short ginger strands like a forest fire. I smile, letting the heady cocktail of speed, wind, and sun seep into my bloodstream. If the thrill of driving had a face, I'd kiss it breathless.

At the crest of the junction, I'm fizzing with the need to keep driving. Just go. Get away from this tiny life with these tiny people and their tiny dreams and land somewhere big enough for me to unfold. I want to drive until I find the end of the road, wind up at the oceanfront somewhere in

Texas or Louisiana with nothing but what's in my pockets and the glove compartment. Figure it out from there.

But I do stop. Eventually. Turn left. Surf a few more road-waves, crunch up the gravel drive, park next to a cherry-red Escort, and push open the rusty gate. A knot of feral cats bolts under the fence separating the tiny white farmhouse and garden from the overgrown fields and mule pasture, chasing a rabbit. I make a note to check the bunny pens later in case someone escaped.

I knock gently on the right-hand door of the house. I never did understand why the original owners gave it two living rooms and two front doors. When we moved in, every room was a different eye-searing color, the carpet was piled three layers deep, and the attic was a yawning cavern of raw boards and tetanus. It took three years to make it look halfway normal, but the twin doors stayed. I like having the option of coming into the wood-paneled library or the shabby-chic sitting room, depending on what kind of day I've had.

"Hey, sweetie!" Mom chirps as she pulls open the door. She's drying her hands on a dishtowel. "How was work?"

I one-shoulder shrug and step across the creaky floor to plop into the pile of lacy throw pillows on the couch.

Mom eyeballs me, but she doesn't press. Instead, she falls back to her refrain of the last several weeks. "You don't have to knock, Cora. You live here; you've got a key."

And there goes my driving high.

Moving back in with your parents as an adult is mortally fucking embarrassing, even if it is only temporary. I'm not ready to give up the separation between my grownup life and being treated like a kid again. Six months ago, I was subbing middle school English, planning a family with my boyfriend, having bonfire parties with my friends, and fishing on the weekends. Life was great.

Until it wasn't.

After being off for nearly a decade, my inner lights came on abruptly in the middle of my thirtieth birthday party. I looked around at the run-down bar filled with smiling people I'd known for twenty years, all there to drunkenly celebrate my tiny, mundane life, and I had what felt like my first clear thought since childhood.

How the fuck did I get here?

Trying to answer sent me into a tailspin I'm still recovering from.

It wasn't long before the boyfriend spooked and ran. I stopped getting calls to sub and had to hump it at the coffee shop instead. Friends dried up. There wasn't anything left but to come home, whiplashed and displaced. Like a prodigal housecat that's discovered the wild has unacceptably irregular mealtimes.

How do you explain that to your mom?

Looking up at her from under my nearly invisible eyebrows, I want to say, *It's not you, it's me.* But that would be weird, so I don't.

"I know, I know," I say instead. "I'll remember

next time."

A whiff of something garlicky and rich floats out from the kitchen. "What's for dinner?" I ask. I don't have much of an appetite after months on the depression diet, but maybe a change of subject will take the focus off my weirdness.

"Whatever was in the fridge thrown in the crockpot. Mostly leftover pork roast and some bendy carrots."

I follow her to the kitchen. Bright yellow curtains clash with black-and-red floor tiles, but I like it in here. Warm in the winter, cool in the summer. Great view of the back forty and mule pen. It's where we always wind up talking, especially in the morning as the antique percolator does its thing. I perch on a low worktable against the side windows as Mom turns her attention to the unfinished dishes and talks over her shoulder.

"So, I was thinking maybe you and I could run down to Wal-Mart later to pick up some new sheets and whatnot for your room? It's probably a little too kiddy for you now. Would've done it sooner, but I had to wait for your dad's check to hit the bank."

"Yeah, that'd be great," I say absentmindedly.

I'm fiddling with the white fuzz of a fat cactus nestled in the window. It's in bizarre company, flanked by an African violet, a spidery thing, and a riot of basil. For all the quaint farmhouse charm of the place, it's like a jungle is insinuating itself through the walls. Mom's green thumb keeps the house filled with happy little plants, a talent I didn't inherit.

The scrub-scrub-splash of the water makes an easy, quiet backdrop for us to sit in. I realize that I'm watching her do the dishes. Like I haven't seen it a million times before. Or have I? There was a time she was too busy to do them at all.

"Hey, mom, what happened to your nursery biz?"

She keeps washing.

I'm about to pretend I didn't say anything and head upstairs to my room when she says, "What about it?" I'm not sure if it's silverware clanking in the sink or an edge of steel I hear in her voice.

I'm still petting the soft cactus, keeping things nonchalant even as a surge of awkwardness warms my chest. "I just remember you had one when we lived in Kansas City. You were always out there digging in the dirt and talking about seeds and watering and stuff."

I manage to throttle the next sentence before it escapes. *You were always so happy.*

She doesn't turn around or respond. I wonder if she read my mind. If I hurt her feelings just by thinking it.

Eventually, with her refined Southern patience, she says, "Well, you were about to turn thirteen, and we decided it'd be best to get you out of the city. Your dad heard about the library job through the grapevine about the same time, and he needed a change. The timing worked out."

It's the same answer I've gotten to a dozen different questions about how we ended up here. No mention of her feelings, her sacrifices. Last time

I asked, I was barely old enough to vote, much less understand the struggle of being a grown woman trying to juggle family, career, and her own secrets. My mom's struggle. There's a deadness in her voice now, ten years and a hundred little heartbreaks later. The heat in my chest intensifies as I recognize the echoes of my own internal skirmishes.

But this time the old story's not good enough. This time, I push.

"We've got all this land here – why didn't you start again once we got settled?"

The water shuts off. The last plate slots into the rack. The dishtowel comes back out as she turns to face me, leaning against the sink. Blood races in my ears now, and I can feel a shameful blush creeping up my neck. The air between us is so stiff it's holding me in my seat. Mom never spanked me as a kid because all she had to do was give me that special stare filled with disappointment. I'd punish myself for days after, weaving my own hair shirt, vowing to be better. But rather than giving me that look now, her eyes lower to an imaginary scuff on the tile floor, and she takes a deep breath.

"Cora," she says quietly, "there's so much work to do on the farm every day already. Bringing the nursery here didn't make sense. I needed to take care of you and your dad. You both needed so much more support back then."

It's a lie. And it's not a lie.

I push again. Gently.

"It's not like this is a working farm, Mom. It's mostly overgrown woods. The only things that need daily care are mules and rabbits, and Junior takes care of those." I gesture out the window to the vast vegetable patch out back. "You've got the garden and some house stuff, but there's no more teenage Cora throwing hissy fits and smoking weed in the barn and pretending she doesn't need her mom." I falter a little, wondering how that little piece of me got thrown in, but I keep going, recklessly spilling thoughts I've held onto for years. "You had a dream once. I was only a kid, but even then I knew you've got a special gift."

I hesitate.

There's an invisible boundary between mother and grown daughter that you don't cross. You don't ask about what they gave up for you. What they regret or missed out on. What secrets they keep in marriage and motherhood. But I have to know why she gave up the one thing that I know she loved more than Dad, more than me - the evidence is growing in every corner of this house. Maybe it's how I find out what's wrong with me, a teenaged girl in the body of an adult, completely terrified of failing at life.

"Mom," I say, my voice hardly above a whisper, "why'd you do it? Why throw away your chance to be special? Don't you want to leave some kind of legacy, make a mark on the world?"

My scalp is burning with awkwardness. Every one of my muscles is iron-tense, poised to flee her retaliation. She's never smacked me, true, but Southern blood has given her a razor-sharp tongue that she doesn't hesitate to use. And I just challenged her entire life.

But when she looks up, I'm caught off guard by how suddenly old she seems. How defenseless and tired, as if I'd stripped her naked. In a way, I suppose I did.

I start to go to her – to hug her and tell her I'm sorry, I didn't mean to pry, it's not my business – but she holds up a hand and I freeze. She sniffs once and straightens regally.

"Sometimes," she says in unfamiliar, resigned tones, "you have to give up part of yourself to make life work out. When it came time to choose, I could only pick one. Some women give up romance or kids or careers. I did what I had to so I could make a home for my family. For you."

She takes two long strides to stand in front of me, so close I can smell the pink sugar gum she chews all day. She locks my gaze and jabs me in the chest with an arthritic finger.

"But don't you think for one minute I haven't left my mark on the world. Maybe I didn't do it through fame and fortune or winning a Nobel Prize, but goddammit, my legacy is secure." She taps on my breastbone. "Right here."

The light pressure is as good as a punch. I lose my breath. The kitchen smells that made my mouth water earlier turn sour. Pride, anger, and confusion spin me around. The emotions must be rioting across my face because she steps back and composes herself, all strength and serenity again.

"You have to make your own way, Cora," she says, gathering the dirty dishtowels and heading toward the laundry room like nothing's happened. "I've said since you were a baby that there's something extraordinary about you. You've just got to find it for yourself."

Before she closes the door, she locks my eyes again. I'm crisping under her glare like a chicken nugget under a heat lamp.

"But don't question my choices ever again."

The door clicks softly shut, and I'm alone. All I can hear is the heartbeat in my ears mimicking the bubbling of the crockpot.

TWO

The bathroom door doesn't lock, but there's a handy drawer in the vanity that's an effective doorstop. Mom figured that one out quick; no one ever needs a mother's attention more than when she's peeing. I pull out the drawer, turn on the complaining taps, and strip in front of cartoon turtles on the wallpaper as the water heats up.

Running a hand through my fine, red hair, I decide against washing it. It's not gross yet, and I'm enjoying its modest length. It's nice to not get called "sir" anymore. Shaving my head after the breakup had seemed like the perfect way to start fresh. Dad says I look better with it short – it accents the elfin face he passed down to me –but after a couple of weeks, I missed my ponytail and recommitted to growing it out.

I prop myself against the sink on tiptoe to inspect my face in the mirror. Up close, I can see new freckles ripening under my mildly sunburnt skin. The dark circles under my eyes are thankfully fading; the grey irises were clashing with the purple bags, giving me a zombified air. Overall, not bad. I've certainly seen worse in the mirror.

A hand in the chilly shower tells me the water heater is on the fritz, so I fold my clothes while I wait. These haven't fit properly in a long time – from way too tight to so big I need a new belt. Between the first Meow Mix commercial breakdown and this shower, I've gone from a perpetual pizza-and-ice-cream binge to subsisting on black coffee and the occasional cigarette. I can see the aftermath in the steaming mirror. Nearly all my normal softness is gone, replaced with sharp edges. Stripped naked, I realize I sort of look sick. No wonder Mom's been shoveling extra portions on my plate at dinnertime.

The mirror clouding over is a relief.

I hop into the shower and duck under the spray to tweak the nanometer settings between "lava" and "glacier" as my skin turns lobster-red. Temperature resolved, I relax and lather up to scrub off the smell of coffee and humidity.

As is the way of showers, I start thinking deep thoughts.

Another day gone by. One more step away from a life I thought I'd live forever. One that didn't go anywhere. And I made it through without shutting down, freaking out, or giving up. That's a win, right?

But my treacherous brain won't let me sit with

that self-satisfaction and turns my thoughts back to the conversation with Mom. Your parents naturally think you're amazing, so I don't really give a lot of credence to her assertion that I'm somehow extraordinary. But the topic of dreams and finding my way hit me right in the gut. If I was special, wouldn't I have shown some indication by now? I'll be thirty-one goddamn years old in November, and I can't produce even one measly masterpiece.

I did try, though. God, how I tried.

I spent elementary school living out my unwavering belief that I'd grow up to be a famous painter. After placing fourth in a competition, I threw all my work in the trash. Junior high, I decided I wanted to be a bestselling author. I wrote one chapter of a high-fantasy epic that I'd clearly ripped off from David Eddings but couldn't deal with critique. Never wrote again. In high school, it was music, but I've never seen a rock star flutist. I stuck that one out but haven't touched the instrument since graduation. Add to that a dozen wildly different part-time jobs over the last decade, and it yields the same disappointing result: Cora Riley is nothing but average.

If I do have something special in me, I'm the most boring and latest bloomer ever.

I sigh as I crank off the water. How does anyone get to be this age and not know where they're going, what they're all about, why they do things? What's wrong with me that I can't settle into the routine and forget about the scratchiness in my soul?

Okay, that was a little melodramatic.

I slip out of the bathroom, still lost in thought, and tiptoe up the stairs to my room. As I open the door, a mottled grey barn cat ninjas his way inside and tries to rub against me in case I've got some food in my towel, but I leap back just in time. He smells like he rolled in something dead and covered in mud, then ate it.

I let him poke around the milk-crate décor as I dig through the dresser and pull on clean jeans, white tank top, and a white Oxford button-up. It used to be Jeremy's only non-work shirt. I found it in one of my boxes when I moved, and for a while, I kept it in my bed where I could smell him as I fell asleep. I'd wake up with tears on my pillow as I dreamed about his oil-stained hands, his dusty yellow hair, his sweet drawl. How he stopped touching me when I needed it most. But it only took a couple washes to remove the memories; funny how fast that happened. All that's left now is a nicely tailored shirt with a nicotine stain on the left cuff.

Thinking back, I don't blame him for leaving. Not really. If the roles were reversed, I can't say I wouldn't have done the same thing. But it happened to me, so I'm a little bitter.

Jeremy didn't understand. The paralyzing terror I have of never seeing the world has no foothold in him. He's content to work on farm trucks and tractors until he dies, only touching the world through his someday-children.

He was kind about my breakdown at first, though. I'll give him that. He'd heard about depression from health class and vague commercials during *Law & Order*, but after a season of loaded sighs and no sign of things returning to normal, he retreated, too. Started working late at the garage and sleeping on the couch instead of braving my sad space at night. After four years together, that hurt the most.

The last straw came on the heels of yet another one-sided conversation about how I was feeling. His patience snapped. He slammed a dish in the sink, and I gasped, shrinking into the couch. He accused me of not wanting to get better, called me weak and cowardly and frigid. When that storm passed, he sighed and said he was sorry but he couldn't do it anymore.

He wasn't sorry. I could tell.

Desperate questions rushed through my mind. Who would I be without him? Did I even still love him? But instead of sliding further into the darkness, I had a microscopic flash of insight that said, "I'm more than this." It was only a peek through the fog on my mental windshield, but it reminded me of the world outside the dull existence I'd been living.

A curious lightness flooded the sinkhole in my chest. Relief.

"I'm sorry, too," I said.

But I wasn't sorry, either. Not anymore.

Mom's back in the kitchen when I come downstairs, and I help her get dinner together. We chit-chat about the weather and what we need to do tomorrow as we shuffle dishes and construct a salad from her crop of early greens. It's like nothing happened this afternoon. I'm not sure if I'm relieved to forget about it or annoyed that we can't talk woman to woman instead of mother to daughter.

But I don't mention it. I've done enough boundary crossing for one day.

As I lay the last of the silverware on the pockmarked kitchen table, Dad rumbles through the front door on the library side. His side. He ducks his rust-and-salt head to cross the threshold, even though the doorframe is a foot over him. Habit, he says – the house in Kansas City was built for hobbits. Mom meets him as he crosses into the other living room. Her side. She kisses him on a stubbly cheek, and his sharp grey eyes shine as pulls her close. Their bodies fit exactly together, perfectly matched. Average height, average looks, average marriage, average kid. And yet, for a moment, they're the most amazing two people in the world.

My inner child gags dramatically at the display of affection. My inner adult is jealous as hell. I tell both parts to stuff it and wave at Dad from around the corner.

"Hey there, *piskie*," Dad calls out to me in his faint Irish accent. I make an exaggerated sassy face in his direction. *Piskie. Pixie.* Like I don't know I look like a faerie. I get it from him.

He makes the face back at me as he breaks away

from Mom. I smile. He smiles.

"How was work?" he asks, following me into the kitchen.

"Eh, you know. Work."

"You still going to Whelan's for drinks with the girls tonight?"

"Nah. I could use a quiet night at home, I think. Work's been a bitch."

I hate lying to him, but I really don't want to talk about how far I've fallen down the social ladder. What I thought was a tight circle of girlfriends quickly put an arm's length between us after the breakup. They still invite me for our monthly girls' night, but after the weirdness with Mom today, I'm not up to faking friendliness with people who called me a slut in high school and are probably banging my ex.

If Dad picks up on my thoughts, he doesn't show it. Instead, he loosens his tie and says, "Hey, guess what I saw on the way home?"

"I have no idea."

He leans in, checking to make sure Mom's not in earshot. I'm drawn forward in spite of myself. "A fresh faerie ring," he says conspiratorially. "In the Andersons' driveway."

"Really?" I'm trying not to sound interested, but it doesn't work. It's been weeks since he's spotted anything interesting.

"Definitely. Brand new mushrooms, only half an inch high. Want to go check it out after dusk? I'll let you hold the flashlight." He waggles his eyebrows excitedly.

On the surface, this sounds utterly insane at worst and childish at best. But where most logical adults only encourage belief in magical creatures and other worlds until their kids are in middle school, I grew up with a father who never stopped believing himself. He'd regularly take me out gnome spotting, and once we even camped out in the woods listening for banshee wails. I believed in Santa and the Easter Bunny until high school because of him. This faerie ring is only the latest in a long line of supernatural expeditions.

I bought it all as a little kid, but in my teenage years, belief waned to non-existence. He and I fought like wildcats, then. He hated that my faith in the science I was learning at school was outweighing the wonder I'd learned from him. I hated to see a grown man so stupid as to lie to his only child about the true nature of the world.

But I'll be damned if one hot night I didn't see a water nymph in a pond. I know, I know. Sounds crazy. It was there, though – all pointy teeth and huge eyes and reedy hair. I never told anyone else about it except Dad, who smiled and nodded. We made up after that. How could we not?

Every now and then, I'll still see something strange out of the corner of my eye. A glowing wisp or a brownie waving hello. Just enough to keep me believing, if not enough to send to the tabloids. I keep it to myself. I'm already outcast enough in this Bible Belt town without being the crazy lady who sees faeries.

Any other night, I'd jump at the chance to

investigate our new magical neighbors with Dad. It's how we stay tight. But I'm still rankled by all the talk about purpose and specialness. I can feel the depression monster's tentacles probing me for new purchase. That's the last thing I want; better to sequester myself to my room until tomorrow than have a meltdown in the dark while I'm trespassing and carrying a carton of milk.

"I don't know, Dad," I say. "Maybe you can swing this one without me? I'm pretty tired."

The excuse is incredibly lame, and the disappointment I see in his usually cheerful face stings. He doesn't say anything, though, just nods and kisses me on the forehead as he heads to his bedroom to change.

After dinner, Dad and I do the dishes together in relative silence. Mom watches TV on the couch with her feet tucked under her, woman's work done for the day. Twilight is settling over the garden, casting rich orange shadows in the furrows. The weather-beaten shed is particularly spooky. We opened the doors when we first moved in and found heaps of scrap metal. Dad insists a gremlin hides in there and steals pieces for nefarious purposes at night. I laugh and agree to humor him; I don't tell him Junior sells it when the bar calls in his tab.

I slide the last glass into the cabinet and flop the dishtowel over the stove handle. Dad dries his hands and takes a deep, satisfied breath.

"All done for the day," he says to no one in particular.

"Yep."

"You sure you don't want to go with me tonight? The ring will probably be gone in the morning."

"Nah, I'm going to head to bed. Maybe read a little."

There's a hint of concern in his grey eyes, but he lets it slide again. Like maybe he already knows and doesn't need to ask.

"Okay, *piskie*," he says, "whatever you want to do." He reaches over and kisses my forehead. "Sleep sweet. And make sure to check under the bed for monsters."

I pretend to be annoyed with the little kid treatment, but I'm secretly delighted. See, depression monster? Not everyone abandons you when shit gets hard. I fight down the impulse to throw my arms around my father, bury my face in his shoulder, and stay there. Let him protect me from the heartaches and unfairness of being a grownup the way he did when I still had to stand on his shoes to dance. A daddy's girl to the end.

But I don't. I'm way too big for that now.

"Night, Dad," is all I say.

THREE

The world is drenched in blood. Red sky, red ground, red mountains, red sun. At first, I think I'm on Mars, but I can breathe fine. I peer around to get my bearings, but there's nothing except rock for miles. A mini-tornado of dust spins past in a hot wind. I follow it with my eyes and catch sight of a black dot on the horizon. It moves fast, standing out against the sandblasted landscape as it barrels toward me. When I can see it without squinting, I can tell it's a knight on horseback hefting a lance into attack position.

Instinct kicks in. I try to dodge out of the way, but I'm rooted to the spot. I wave my arms, screaming for help. The lance doesn't lift. The horse doesn't turn. The rider is so close I can see that he has no face – just a skeleton in black armor.

I wrap my hands around my head and try to

*crouch down, as if that can protect me. I can
already imagine the wood shoving itself through
my throat. Brace for impact.*

I fling myself out of bed before I'm actually awake.
In a scrabble to get to my desk, I whang my knee on
the futon frame and stumble over my boots
crossing the worn carpet. It sends an alarm of pain
up my thigh, but I manage to put pen to paper
before I forget the dream. *Scribble, scrawl,
squiggle.* A page and a half later, I've managed to
drag myself into the actual chair rather than
kneeling on the floor. I'm definitely going to have a
bruise. Worth it.

This notebook's nearly full. A complete record of
every fucked-up dream I've had since I moved back
home. I don't know if it's the transition from city to
well water or a side effect of the depression
squatting in my brain, but I can't sleep without my
subconscious dodging acid rain, roasting over a
spit, spending time as a tree, or leaping off a cliff
into oblivion. Sometimes I get to kick back with a
golden harp on a cloud or gallop through the forest
on horseback, though. I started keeping the journal
when I realized that, good or bad, all my dreams are
ending the same way: with the realization that
something's wrong, a moment of mortal peril, then
waking up in a cold sweat. They're so vivid and real
that I can't shake feeling like they're supposed to
mean something. Like the universe desperately
wants to tell me something I'm too stupid to

understand.

I scan what I've written as the brain fog clears and the red world slips away, replaced by the urgent need to pee. I sneak downstairs and back up as carefully and quickly as I can, trying not to wake up my parents in their room below.

Just as I'm about to ease my bedroom door shut, a streak of grey flies through the opening. A teetering pile of unopened boxes in the corner sways dramatically as that damn grey cat hurtles into it in hot mousy pursuit. He must've been hiding in the hall. I only have enough time to inhale to shout at him before the boxes lose to gravity and burst on the floor. The cat freaks at the resulting crash and bolts back out the way he came in.

"Dammit, you stupid shit!" I holler after him, nighttime propriety forgotten.

I clap a hand over my mouth as I listen for movement downstairs. Five seconds pass. Nothing.

Damn, I hope I sleep that well when I'm in my fifties.

I shrug, close the door, and turn my attention to the mess. It's mostly papers from high school. Medals, certificates, pins, diplomas, honors, acceptance letters. In retrospect, it seems silly to have moved them around with me, but I never could throw them out. It's the story of my education – my struggle to be somebody before I forgot to keep trying, the academic detritus of an overachiever who never really achieved anything. Maybe someday I won't need these things to remind me that I've got value as a human being.

But this is not that day.

I start to repack the carefully labeled cardboard boxes, when a thick, glossy photo drops out of the pile and lands face-up on the worn carpet.

Class of 2002.

Someone had decided it would be cool to take old-time photos for our senior picture. Always popular with the Ozark crowd. I do have to admit that we're quite a sepia-colored sight in our Western wear and grave stares. A bunch of incredibly white teenagers from the boonies pretending to be cowboy badasses as they prepare to face 21st century adulthood.

I pick up the photo and lightly touch the faces I remember most sharply.

There's Henry Adams. My middle-school crush. He gave me his basketball windbreaker, inflating my social status several points. He was convinced he'd crash in a white pickup and die before age thirty. He didn't.

There's Rebecca Coulter. I told her I might be a lesbian in seventh grade. She spread it around, and I lost all my friends. She stayed in town to marry some hick, then joined the Army and shipped out to Afghanistan.

There's Sarah Fox. Still my best friend. She's the closest thing we had to a minority in this town, although she's the whitest brown person ever. She escaped to Texas to be near the ocean. No husband, no kids – just her and the sea. I wish I'd had her courage to leave.

There are the Graves twins. Brilliant girls we

expected to burn up the music world with their talent. Instead, one joined the Navy and was divorced by twenty-three. The other found Jesus and lost her mind. I was so jealous of them in school. Turns out we all fucked it up pretty badly.

And there's Cora Riley.

I almost missed myself. I hardly recognize the girl sitting on the floor holding a flintlock. No worry lines in her forehead, no hunched shoulders, no haunted look in her eyes. Short, dyed-black hair and a Mona Lisa smile. We were a month away from graduation, and I was flying high on plans to plow through college and become an ad exec, my latest fancy.

But at the last minute, I turned down the full-ride scholarship and stayed. There was a boy. Then Mom's cancer scare. Lust and guilt threw away that letter.

One year, I'd told myself. Then I'll go start my life. But one turned into two, then three. Something always came up. A new job, a baby mule, a community disaster, Mom's relapse. Just one more year, I kept saying. Then it was five years later. Then ten. I'm not sure when I stopped believing I'd leave – when I stopped wanting to.

Did I miss my chance?

A tear slips off my chin and pats onto my own face in the picture. I wipe it away with a flash of anger.

What a goddamn cliché. Look at me, sitting on the floor of my room that hasn't changed since I was eighteen, surrounded by meaningless accolades, pawing through high school photos, making excuses for myself, and crying about my wasted life. All I need to complete the picture is a glass of gin and a string of pearls. Fucking pathetic.

I shove the picture back into its box and slap the old tape over the top. Cram it into the unfinished crawlspace I use as storage and pile dirty laundry in front of it. Wipe my nose on my shirtsleeve, flop onto the unfolded futon, take a deep breath, stare at the ceiling.

What the fuck am I doing here? I had a mental breakdown because my life was stalled, gave up my relationship and my independence, and then wound up back at home like I'd never made it out of high school. Living every day like it was a decade ago. How is that better? It's just treading water. Water from the past – not even the present.

I briefly consider trying to smother myself with a pillow. It's a funny bit of melodrama at first, but there's a quick twinge of the serious around the edges that scares me. A flutter of uncomfortably familiar longing to be done.

Right after Jeremy moved out, I sat on the bathroom floor of our empty apartment with a bottle of Xanax clutched in my fingers, waiting for a moment of courage. The only time I'd gone to the doctor about my depression, he took one look at me and wrote a prescription without even asking how I felt. The pills hadn't helped, but I thought maybe if I took them all at once I'd feel okay. Or feel nothing. I was poised to swallow a fistful but stopped just short of my mouth. What if nobody cared enough to notice I was gone until I was a swollen, runny mess and my mom had to identify me like that?

I let guilt win again. This time, with relief.

I chuck the pillow off the bed as if it might decide to act on my treacherous thought of its own accord. It lands heavily on top of a flattened black duffle bag, a trophy retained from a summer spent at a camp for "gifted kids" when I was freshly sixteen. After an IQ test and a lot of gloating, I spent four weeks at a state college learning Japanese, kissing anyone I wanted, and pretending to be an adult. My blood fizzed like it'd been replaced with Diet Coke as I drenched myself in new people and experiences. I couldn't get enough life that summer, could never be too full.

It all evaporated when I came home, of course; the bright colors of the real world replaced by the washed-out sameness of home. Routine took over, and I somehow forgot everything I'd learned.

Thinking about that month now, though, I can almost smell the cut grass of the university's lawn, can almost remember the taste of boundless possibility on my tongue. Coal-fire urgency rears up, something hesitant but excited, reminding me of how much time I've lost between that bright-eyed girl and this broken-hearted woman.

It's now or never.

And then suddenly I'm standing at my dresser, yanking out the drawers, spilling jeans and underwear and t-shirts and socks everywhere. I peel off my PJs and change hurriedly back into my street clothes. The rest of my meager wardrobe gets stuffed into the duffel by the handful. The coffee can filled with my rainy day fund jangles as I pull it out of the bookshelf along with my jewelry box. I snatch the dream journal and a smattering of precious and necessary things from around the room, then dump it all unceremoniously on top of the clothes and zip the bag.

Tears sting my eyes as I breathlessly scrawl a note to my parents. Courage nearly deserts me then; I can imagine them panicked in the morning, as if I were a teenager running away from home. Again. I even start balling up the paper as I step into the hallway and turn to go back to my room, back to bed, and forget the whole thing. But as I cross to the trash can, my eyes fall on the pile of junk in front of the resealed box containing the photo of all the people I grew up with who are still stuck in this town doing nothing but existing, procreating, and dying.

No.

I smooth the note and pound down the stairs, pausing for a moment to stick it to the fridge with an I Heart NYC magnet and to grab my truck keys from the hook in the kitchen.

Then I'm out the door, running across the yard, duffel pounding on my back, headed anywhere but here.

I have no idea where I'm going. No atlas, no GPS. Even left my phone charging on my desk. I know – it's a stupid move, and I'll probably regret it later, but it's too much temptation right now. Too easy to call home or text Jeremy when I get lost or sad. Too easy to get myself talked into coming back. Doing anything besides driving away from this smotheringly small town might literally kill me right now. I'd die of a disappointed heart behind the wheel.

But despite my frenzied departure from the house, I don't rush once I'm clear of the long gravel driveway and onto blacktop. The intrepid pickup and I swoop along the curves of the rural highway as one creature, riding under the speed limit, savoring the kinetic sensation of progress. A voluptuous country moon illuminates the landscape so brightly I could turn off my headlights and still see perfectly. It guides me down the pine-lined back roads toward the interstate where I'll flow into the never-ending stream of traffic and not emerge until I run out of gas.

Maybe I'll go south. Head to Galveston and hang out with Sarah. Fish every day in the warm gulf, soak up sun until I peel, see what answers the ocean holds for me.

Maybe I'll go west. Explore California and all the glitz and glamour I've lusted after in every movie I've ever seen. Find out if I've got what it takes to be a starlet.

Maybe it's better to leave the country altogether. Fly to some exotic paradise or forgotten city and melt into the background. Study poetry and have a string of lovers.

I roll the possibilities around for a while in

silence, trancing out to the hum of the engine. The little truck is exactly my age, its life lovingly extended by Jeremy.

Oh, hey –

I'm delighted to notice I'm not thinking about him. Not really. Not like that. I'm not even thinking about my folks. Or the town. Or anything, really. It's a blissful moment of nothing but a warm summer night and a deserted stretch of road.

But that gets boring fast. Damn my short attention span. I pop in an antiquated cassette tape of my favorite musical to fill the silence.

> *Lady Luck has led you here.*
> *And they're so twisted up*
> *They'll twist you up, I fear.*

The tinny sounds fill the cab, and I immediately get goosebumps. For a second, I can't seem to find my breath; my lungs and throat tighten at the coincidence of this particular song coming on at this particular moment. But that's all it is, right? Just where I shut it off last time. Coincidence.

> *The pious, hateful, and devout –*
> *You're turning tricks til you're turned out,*
> *The wind so cold it burns,*
> *You're burning out and blowing round.*

As many times as I've heard this song, it's never sunk in until right now how descriptive it is of my own life. The small-minded people I've let twist me up in this shallow town. That understanding combines with the last dregs of my courage to finally leave tips me from action to emotion. I close my eyes against the tears. Just for a second. Just so I can concentrate long enough to swallow the rocks in my throat. They're so heavy they're rattling straight down into my chest. I breathe in deep – once, twice – then I open my eyes again.

It all happens in slow motion, like you always see in movies.

The long bed of the truck flicks out to the side as the tires bite into the ground where a shoulder would be on a better road. I clamp down on the steering wheel, knuckles white, and the flood of adrenaline makes me overcorrect. I remember not to stomp on the brakes, but the body's so light it doesn't matter. Momentum throws the Toyota's weight to the other side, and I skid across the center line. I jerk the wheel again and am immediately punished with a searing tire scream and the stink of burning rubber.

The world blurs and goes sideways as the truck rolls over. I crack my temple against the doorframe, momentarily knocking out my vision. My hands go slack and release the wheel, hovering as the vehicle turns. The rotation is so smooth that I feel like I'm in the space station from *2001*. A ballerina in zero gravity. I can see the trash from the floorboards floating in mid-air as we dance together.

Gravity interrupts the beauty of the moment by shoving the cab to earth.

Once.

Twice.

Three times.

Boom. Boom. Boom.

The crunch of compacting steel is like a bomb going off in my ears. Each landing snaps my head on its delicate stem, underscoring the impact. A detached part of me is screaming with fear and pain, but it's far away; I've slipped into a separate place where it can't reach me. Sparks fly as the roof skates along the blacktop. I absently wonder if my hair will catch on fire.

Everything stops. Time comes back to me.

There's grass in my armpit where the window edge has dug up the turf. A warm, sticky trickle runs up through my scalp. The top of my head rests on the peeling roof of the cab, bending my neck awkwardly as it tries to support the weight of my body.

Somehow I manage to unbuckle myself and release the pressure on my skull by crumpling across the inverted top of the cooling truck. The wheels are still spinning, shaking the whole vehicle gently, like a mother rocking a cranky baby to sleep. There's a clamor of nerves trying to get my attention, but I'm stretching to reach the opposite window. Mine's scrunched so tightly I'd have to starve here for weeks before I'd fit through. My fingers brush the blue velour of the passenger seat.

Thick, hot ooze fills my ear. My vision kaleidoscopes, then goes monochrome. I'm so deeply bone-tired. I'll just close my eyes for a second. Someone will be here soon.

I call out in a faint voice no one could possibly

hear. "Help. Somebody help."

A small miracle: The stereo is still running.

> *And if you've got no other choice,*
> *You know you can follow my voice*
> *Through the dark turns and noise*
> *Of this wicked little town.*

Silence. Darkness.

Dear Mom and Dad:

It's time for me to leave the nest. There's something I need to find. I don't know what it is yet, but it's out there somewhere, and I can't find it if I stay here forever. Mom, you know what I'm talking about. Dad, I hope you never do. Sorry I didn't get to say a proper goodbye, but I had to go, and you were already asleep. I promise I'll call as soon as I land somewhere safe. I love you so much.

Thank you for everything.

Cora

PART II
DOORS TO NOWHERE

FOUR

Ow. Ow. Ow.

Cora's heavy eyelids flutter open against her will, and she tries to focus on the grey blob that's standing over her, jabbing her in the ribs. It must still be night; the light's so low she can't make out anything behind the figure. Another stupid dream.

"Get up!" the blob shouts. A man's voice tossed in a rock tumbler.

"Erngh. Go 'way. 'm tired," Cora replies. *Why is Dad waking me up so freaking early?*

She half-rises and swats at the air with an arm rubbery from sleep. Her hand connects with a rough wooden shaft, and she pulls out of spite, but her antagonist grunts and backs away. Satisfied she's won the battle for extra Z's, she closes her eyes and flumps back down.

Right onto a cold stone floor, cracking her head

on a stray rock.

She yips in pain and scrambles to her feet. "What the hell?!" Putting a hand to her hair shows there's no blood, but there'll be a brilliant goose egg. That'll be fun to explain at work in the morning.

Or will it?

The knock to the head seems to have cleared her brain; her eyes focus sharply as her other senses come online. Her dreams are always vivid, but this one is in high definition.

A darkened sky hangs low over a smooth granite floor and is lit only by an enormous orange moon, giving the place a decidedly cavern-like feeling. Both inside and outside. A massive wall of rough grey bricks extends beyond her vision to the left and right. There's a reinforced wooden door – or is it a drawbridge? It must be twenty feet high and appears to be the only way through the wall; there aren't any windows. There's movement in the two towers that flank the door, but whomever or whatever is up there is too small to see.

On the other hand, the squat armor-wearing thug in front of Cora is clear enough.

He steps forward to menace her with his spear. She can't see his face under the low brow of his helmet, but it's easy enough to tell he doesn't intend anything good.

"Hey, hey, hey. Take it easy, mister," she says.

She retreats a step, hands in front of her in placation. The instant her foot comes down, her shoes flood with icy water. Gasping, she leaps forward again and spins around to see an endless grey ocean stretching out behind her. The water wraps around the little apron of land she's standing on, meeting the wall directly and cutting off any chance for retreat.

An amused chuckle comes from the helmet, and the thug takes another step forward, pinning her in place. "It's either come with me or swim for it, missy. I won't even tell you about all the nasties in the water."

Her eyes flick from the spear to the wall to the ocean and back again, trying to gauge the danger level of the dream. She inhales the tang of the ocean and feels the breeze in her hair. They certainly seem real. And then there are her clothes. In every bizarre dream she's ever had, she's been naked. Dreamers don't get wardrobe budgets; she shouldn't still be wearing the jeans and button-up shirt she put on before leaving the house. She pinches herself hard in the thigh for good measure but all that does is smart. An uneasy feeling of disbelief creeps up her skin as she realizes the creature with the spear and strangely mottled grey skin may actually, factually be real.

As if to underscore his existence, the goon says, "Ain't no good pinching anything. You're here, and the Mistress is waiting. Now get a move on."

He thrusts his weapon at her again, and Cora jumps to the side, allowing herself to be corralled toward the wall of what she's starting to realize is a castle. Once they're closer, she can see a normal-sized door next to the gigantic drawbridge. Her captor's spear nicks her with paper cut precision when she slows to take in the spectacle of the building, and she obediently shuffles on to avoid more of the guard's encouragement.

As they approach, a metal grate in the side door slides open to reveal a pair of glowing yellow eyes and the top of a snout. Cora's guard grabs her wrists behind her in one of his leathery hands, then steps up to the hole.

"The prisoner's been captured," he says. "Lemme in so I can take 'er to the Mistress."

"Friend or foe?" says the guard on the other side.

An annoyed huff. "Friend."

"Password."

"Are you kiddin' me, Larry?" The goon lifts the visor of his helmet to reveal a pair of similar eyes set in a hideously knotty face that reminds Cora of the dried apple heads she made in elementary school for Halloween. "It's me. Hank. I only left five minutes ago, and I was right out front. You saw the whole thing from here."

"Password," sniffs Larry.

Despite the weirdness of the situation, Cora has to bite her lip to avoid giggling at the exchange. Laughing is probably a bad survival strategy.

Another huff from Hank. "Fine. 'Swordfish.'"

"You may pass."

The eyes disappear, and the grate slams shut. There's a moment of shuffling behind the door, then it swings inward on smooth hinges. A glimmer of light comes from inside and silhouettes Larry as he ushers them in. Hank ignores his colleague, but Cora can't help staring. The other guard is a full head shorter than Hank and isn't wearing a helmet, revealing him to be grey-brown, scaly, and vaguely piggy. Cora's mind races to find a label for what she's seeing. *Goblins? Orcs?*

Whatever they are, they march her down a series of ruler-straight corridors lined with jail cells so dark Cora can't tell if anyone's held there or not. Everything from the rusty bars to the pitted stone floor seems on the verge of falling apart. There's a rustle from inside one of the cells as the group passes, but the guards shove Cora forward before she can call out. By the time they reach the staircase at the end of the hall, her lungs are heavy with old hay and mildew, and she's glad when they climb out of the dungeon into clearer air.

At least momentarily.

They emerge in the far corner of a vast, open room that comes across like a King Arthur movie set. Tapestries and antique weapons decorate the walls. The roaring fireplace on the right is big enough to roast an entire cow and casts strange shadows in the corners of the chamber. The smell of wood smoke mingles with the cold earthiness of the unvarnished stone floor, reminding her of nights spent camped beside the river. More of the creatures – orcs, she decides - wearing breastplates and armed to the teeth are posted at the exits and around a broad dais that holds an empty throne. Cora is shuffled forcibly toward it. Derisive laughter ripples around the room when she ducks under a dribbling candle chandelier although it's easily a dozen feet over her head.

Her chuckling captors push her roughly onto the lonely strip of carpet marking the path up to the throne. Hank releases her hands and prods her with the spear to keep moving but doesn't follow. It's not like she can run away.

She does think about it, though. Enough of her otherworldly dreams have covered escaping from enchanted castles that she knows the drill.

Four visible doors, one going to the dungeon. Ten – no, twelve guards. That sword by the fire is pretty low. I could grab it and...

"Come here, girl."

The order is soft and insistent but easily cuts through the cruel laughter of the orcs, silencing the entire chamber. It's used to getting attention, like a lighthouse on a dark sea, and Cora's moving again before she realizes she's heard it.

"A little closer."

Her eyes dart around for the source of the voice. It seems to be coming from the throne, but the echoes of the stone room make it hard to pin down. The guards are all staring at her – she can feel their gaze pressing against her clothes – but she can't see another soul in the room. She takes more tentative steps forward until she's standing near the bottom step of the dais. Curiosity mingles with a slow upwelling of fear, and she absentmindedly chews a thumbnail for comfort.

"Such a filthy habit from such a pretty girl."

Embarrassed, Cora drops her hand and opens her mouth to snark back at the voice, but before any words come out, the air in front of the throne sizzles. Cora's mouth stays open as she watches a tall, elegant woman develop in a shower of sparks. A metallic gold dress edged with glossy black feathers ripples into being, trailing heavy silk down the steps; an instant later, finely-crafted arms and shoulders sprout from the corseted top as hips fill the skirt; next, a head appears on a graceful neck and is crowned with a simple gold circlet entwined in thick, golden hair. The last thing to materialize is the face, a combination of pale skin, sharp cheekbones, and completely black eyes. The end result makes Cora gasp and retreat.

The woman's lips curl into an imperious grin of pleasure. "No need to run away, my sweet. I have no intention of harming you. If I did, you never would have made it through the gates."

Small consolation, Cora thinks.

"I am the mistress of this place," the woman continues, lifting her chin. "You will call me 'my lady' or 'your grace,' Miss..." She trails off, turning her head to look expectantly at a nearby orc without armor. When he fails to respond, she snaps her long fingers sharply. He leaps several inches and flutters the pages of the enormous book he appeared to be writing in moments ago.

"R-r-Riley, M-m-mistress! C-c-Cora Leigh Riley!" he stammers.

She returns her bottomless gaze to Cora and smiles overly sweetly. "Miss Riley. I expect you have many questions, do you not?"

Cora blinks hard and nods warily.

Still smiling, the Mistress gathers the front of

her dress in both hands and makes her dainty way down the handful of steps of the dais to the floor. She paces a wide circle around Cora, scrutinizing her from mussed hair to grimy boots, making alternately approving and disappointed sounds. Eventually she comes to a stop before Cora on the plush carpet. Up close, the bizarre perfection of the Mistress' features is even more startling. Her skin is almost translucent. Her whiteless eyes command Cora's undivided attention. She's unnaturally tall and thin, as if stretched from above, and the air fills with the scent of sun-ripened apples when she speaks.

"You may ask three questions – only three – which I will answer without trickery." A mischievous gold sparkle illuminates her eyes briefly. "And then you will answer mine."

But Cora can't move, speak, or breathe with the Mistress' eyes boring into her. She can only stand frozen in place as she fights down the part of her brain telling her to kneel in the presence of authority. It would be so much easier than standing. In fact, it would be wonderful to forget the questions and let the Mistress tell her what to do. Like Jeremy did.

That does it.

A hot, rebellious voice burns through the litany of dependence, shoving her animal mind back down. She tears her gaze from the Mistress and fixes it on her reassuringly ordinary boots. It's enough to ground her so she can form words around her whirling thoughts.

"Where am I?" she asks.

The question is directed at the floor, and Cora can hear the Mistress' growl of annoyance at the disrespect, but she doesn't dare lift her chin.

"You are standing in the center of the throne room of the Mistress of the Land of the Dead," comes the answer.

The next question tumbles out in a reflexive gasp of shock. "I'm dead?"

A hint of amusement. "Yes."

Cora manages to stifle the "how?" forming on her lips before she wastes the precious last question. Her mind, primed since childhood to believe in fairytales, races to reassess everything she's seen and heard since arriving. The dark castle, the grey ocean, the strange guards, and the ethereal queen – they certainly add up to her mythological expectations of the underworld.

The tingle of recognition ignites a sudden memory of twisted blue steel and uncontrolled speed that smashes into her gut, making her want to retch.

The truck. The accident. I died on the side of the road. No one came to save me.

"Well?" the Mistress demands, cutting through Cora's nightmarish reverie. "What is your final question, girl? It is not polite to keep others waiting."

Now Cora does look up, fists clenched at her sides and fire in her chest. This isn't what she wanted. It's too soon. There's still so much to do, questions that can't go unanswered, wrongs to right. She juts out her chin with a defiance she feels but isn't sure she can maintain when she meets the Mistress' eyes.

The Mistress smirks appreciatively at the show of will, but the smile slides from her face when Cora says, "How do I get back?"

"Back? There is no going back. Once you are here, you must stay." The Mistress raises her head haughtily and peers down her aquiline nose at Cora. "Surely even the dimmest mortals know that to be true."

Years of memorization leap to Cora's rescue to strengthen her resolve with a litany of human heroes who visited the underworld and returned to tell the tale. "What about Lazarus? And Orpheus? And Pwyll? And – "

The slap rings out sharply in the hall, followed by the muffled sound of Cora's body hitting the ground. She catches herself on both hands, jamming her wrists against the solid stone and sending fresh waves of pain up to meet the four brilliant finger marks across her right cheek. She wills herself not to show weakness by crying, but she can't help the panicked tears slipping out when the Mistress presses one long, metal-heeled shoe into the center of her chest. The air around the Mistress crackles, and Cora lets herself be pushed flat to the floor.

"How dare you." It's a condemnation, not a question. "How dare you challenge my authority in my own domain? You have no right to make demands of me. That you throw silly folk tales in my face is laughable proof of your ignorance."

She presses the spike of her heel further into Cora's ribs. They creak alarmingly, and Cora tries to hold her breath for support, her mind racing.

The Mistress leans closer, tilting her head to one side like a bird of prey. "Do you know what happens if you are killed in the underworld, child? Do you know what eternal torments wait for you?"

She turns her black eyes directly to Cora's grey ones, and the remaining breath drains from Cora's lungs. She braces herself to receive images of horrendous deaths and torture, but none come. Instead, warm tendrils of alien thoughts touch her mind, and she can feel the Mistress carefully searching her dark, private spaces, soaking up her essence. Cora's panic rises as ugly memories and shameful desires are churned to the surface, things she's never told another soul, feelings buried out of fear. She's violated, stripped of her defenses.

After a long moment, the Mistress raises one delicate eyebrow and murmurs something under Cora's hearing. Then she laughs without humor. "You are a petty, selfish little girl, Cora Leigh Riley," she says.

The Mistress yanks her foot from Cora's chest and stalks her way back up the dais to perch on the throne, skirts pooling around her feet in a river of gold. Cora gulps air as the world comes back into focus. She doesn't want to die here – she didn't want to die in the first place – and she knows it must be possible to go back. There are too many stories for them not to be true. Her hand gently prods her ribs to make sure nothing's broken, then she gets to her feet.

Face hot with anger, she takes a shaky step forward, looking anywhere but at the eyes that see through her. The orc guards, previously slouching and entertained by the spectacle of her humiliation, become suddenly alert and close rank in front of the dais. The Mistress smirks from behind them, almost daring her to come closer.

"You know I'm right, *my lady*," Cora says, taking another, more determined step. "The legends are all the same. The ruler of the underworld makes a bargain with the hero, sets him some monumental task in exchange for a second chance, and then has to keep their promise when the hero succeeds." She takes another step forward. The guards cross their weapons into a barrier between her and the Mistress. Cora smiles; it widens the split inside her cheek, but she doesn't care. She holds out her arms and gestures grandly around the throne room. "And since I don't see anyone else here asking for a ticket back to civilization, I guess that makes me the hero. And you owe me a quest."

Her words echo strongly but are met with silence. Long seconds drag past. And then the Mistress starts to laugh. It's the bouncing of dice, the rustle of leaves in an orchard. Apple blossom scent bursts through the room. One by one, the orcs join in, their guttural snorts marring the sound. Cora lowers her arms and her face falls as the laughter continues for what seems like an hour.

But it ends abruptly, the Mistress' face suddenly

a mask of seriousness and danger as her hand cuts through the air to silence her minions. She crooks a gold-taloned finger to the corner of the chamber, and Hank rushes to kneel in front of her.

"Take this insolent child to the dungeon. Perhaps a night in the cells will smooth her rough edges. Tomorrow, I will determine her fate."

"Yes, Mistress."

Hank pops up and rushes to Cora's side. She's so dumbstruck that she doesn't struggle when he seizes her elbow and marches her back the way she came only minutes ago.

Dammit. That should have worked.

FIVE

If she's honest, she's been in worse jail cells. Not that anyone but she and the New York City judiciary system know about that. And besides, spending a night curled up in the corner of a crowded drunk tank doesn't really count, does it?

The stone under Cora is reassuringly solid, and the organic smell of the hay she's laying on is familiar enough to tug at memories of home. This isn't a dream, she decides. There's been no indication of the paralysis or sudden onset of superpowers that usually mark her adventures in the dreamscape. The fact that she's definitely got a physical body is also strong evidence in reality's favor; the throbbing in her mouth, face, and ribs is too strong to be imaginary, and she's been shoved out of sleep for less painful things. In fact, she feels even stronger and more alert than she has in months – almost normal.

Well, as normal as can be expected after her encounter with actual orcs and the bizarre Mistress.

The Mistress. There's something hyper-real about her, Cora thinks. It's almost like she's superimposed on a green screen in a special-effects movie – more solid than everything around her. Cora can't suppress a shudder as she remembers the woman's touch on her mind. It left behind a fever chill, like the warmth of a sunburn. The phantom fingers lifted the lid off her memories and peeked inside places even Cora hasn't touched in years. There wasn't anything she could do to hide from it, no defense against the intrusion, no telling what demons have been released. Even her worst nightmares don't unsettle her this deeply.

But she shakes herself and sets her jaw before she sinks too far into those thoughts. The dungeon of the underworld isn't exactly the best place for a pity party.

The idea that this castle is the entrance to the land of the dead does feel wrong somehow, though. Isn't the ruler of the afterlife usually a guy? And what happened to fluffy-cloud heaven or burning-inferno hell or a river of souls? Not that she ever seriously believed in those things, but still; there has to be more to what she's seeing.

A rustle of hay somewhere down the corridor plucks her senses into high alert. Listening hard, Cora tries to pick out any sign of life from the ambient noises of the dungeon. The skitter of rodent paws and a steady drip in a far corner don't suggest anything sentient, so she presses her face to the iron bars of her cell for a peek around. Down to the left are another dozen or so identical cells and slick cobblestones. Cora whispers, "Hello?" in her tiniest voice but only hears her echo in return. She huffs, then looks down the right side of the hall.

"Holy shit!" she shouts and shoves herself backwards.

Two cells down on the opposite side, someone is silently staring at her, eyes intensely wide in a wan, pinched face half hidden behind filthy blonde hair.

Cora puts a hand to her chest and gulps air to calm down. *How long has she been watching me? Was she here when they brought me through before?*

The other prisoner doesn't move, doesn't blink. Just waits.

Once her heart isn't in danger of exploding, Cora creeps back up to the door and puts on her best you-didn't-scare-me-at-all face. "Uh, hi. I'm Cora. I didn't know you were there." *Duh.*

The woman doesn't react.

Cora tries again. "What are you in for?"

"I am here at Her Grace's pleasure." There's a twitch of a smile. "And Her Grace is seldom pleased." Her voice is strangely clipped and high, more girl than woman.

"What did you do to get in here?"

"I was in the way."

"In the way of what?"

In response, the other prisoner withdraws into the shadows of her own cell.

"Wait! Don't go. Sorry if I offended you," Cora

pleads. "I'm just sort of freaked out. I had this car crash, and then I'm being assaulted by extras from *Lord of the Rings,* and then they tell me I'm dead, and then the Mistress flips out, and now I'm down here. I don't know what's happening."

A hopeful pause.

Nothing.

Cora gives a resigned sigh and scoots back to her makeshift bed to try puzzling it out on her own. Maybe she can trick Hank or Larry or some other stupid guard into letting her out. But where to go after that? There's no escaping through the front door, and from what she saw outside, there's no chance she can navigate the maze of the castle fast enough to avoid being caught again. The Mistress hadn't said specifically what happens if you die in the underworld, but if this place is where you go the first time, she doesn't want to think about the second time.

"I cannot help you," comes the voice from the other cell, weak and distant. "I am no one. I have no power here anymore."

Cora slides back to the bars, but the woman hasn't reappeared. "If you can tell me anything about what this place is or who our jailers are," she says, "that would be plenty of help. The more information I have, the better."

A low chuckle. "Information can be more precious than valor, but all aid comes at a price in this place. If I tell you what you want to know, what will you provide me in return?"

That's a stumper. Cora searches her pockets for

anything valuable or interesting but comes up empty. Apparently death not only steals your soul, it takes your wallet, too. And the only treasure the cell has to offer is what the rats have left behind.

"Shit. I don't have anything to give you."

"I never said your payment need be in treasure."

Cora ponders this for a moment, and soon another snippet of fairytale rises up to fill the gap. Mysteriously imprisoned people usually only want one thing.

"I don't suppose you'd be interested in me breaking you out of this joint, would you?" she says hopefully.

And then the face is back at the cell door, eyelids narrowed in shrewd evaluation, hands gripping the bars tightly. Her matted hair is swept back now, and Cora can see that she's split down the center, half jet-black and half snow-white.

"Do you mean it?" the woman demands. Her voice is sharp and clear with no hint of the weariness it carried only moments before. "Will you set me free?"

Cora hesitates. Maybe she should have asked more questions about her new friend before making that offer. What if she's an axe murder or a demon or something else regrettable? Is it a promise Cora can even keep? She couldn't avoid getting locked up here in the first place – what makes her think she can rescue them both?

But the excitement in the woman's eyes tells Cora it's too late to back out now. Information for freedom. That's the deal.

She nods. "I'll do my best."

"Swear."

"What?"

The woman presses against the bars of her cell insistently. "Without an oath, a promise means nothing. You must swear to me that you will keep true to your word or there will be no bargain."

Eyebrows raised in confusion, Cora slowly makes the promise. "I swear that I will do everything in my power to free you from this dungeon."

Relief floods over the woman's face. "And I swear to give you the information you require about this place and those who hold us."

There's a delicate chiming sound in the air between them, and an oozing sensation runs down Cora's scalp as if someone cracked an egg over her head.

"So sworn, so sealed," the other prisoner says. "May those who break their oath be punished in the fires of hell."

"Oookay. Yeah. Hell."

"Now," says the woman, straightening her shoulders into a more authoritative posture and ignoring the hesitancy in Cora's voice. "What would you ask of me, child?"

Cora huffs in spite of herself. "Why does everyone keep calling me 'child' and 'girl'? I'm clearly an adult. I'm getting sick of this being talked down to bullshit."

The woman grins lopsidedly. "You are still young to our eyes, my dear. So very insignificantly young."

"Whose eyes?"

For a moment, the woman appears offended, but her expression switches quickly to one usually reserved for lost puppies and tourists. "The gods', of course."

"Gods? Plural? As in pantheons and burnt sacrifices?" Cora bursts out laughing. "You can't be serious, lady. I mean, sure, I'll buy pixies and gremlins and even a literal underworld, but gods? I don't think so."

There's a subtle sink in the pressure of the dungeon that makes Cora's ears pop twice. She looks over at her cellmate and sees her eyes have turned from a clear blue to a fiery ruby red. The air around the woman's head begins to crackle with black sparks. Pieces of straw littered in the corridor whisk around in a breeze that picks up out of nowhere. Cora's eyes widen as she's struck with waves of longing, the sort the night has to see the day, an unending desire that makes her feel cosmically insignificant.

"Oh my god, I'm sorry," she says. "I'm sorry, ma'am. Jesus Christ... I mean, uh, um, please don't smite me. I've never, you know, believed in gods." She holds up her hands defensively and braces for a lightning bolt.

The wind dies down. The pressure returns to normal. The red eyes change back to blue. The bottomless ache dissipates.

The caged goddess sighs bitterly as she slumps against the bars. "It is not your fault, child. No one believes any longer. At least, not many." She gestures at her surroundings. "How do you think I ended up here?"

Cora shakes her head mutely. The day's been too full of surprises, and her brain simply refuses to process any more impossible information right now. Stories her father told her as a child are butting up against what she learned in school and what she's convinced herself to forget. They fight for control of a mind that wanted to be rational and detached but could never quite say goodbye to fairytales. It's a wonder smoke isn't pouring out of Cora's ears as the machinery grinds against itself.

The woman watches her face intently, seeming to be far away. There's a gentle knock, then a tug, at the door of Cora's mind. She gasps, remembering the Mistress' intrusion, and pulls her thoughts back as the first touch lands in her memories. The woman seems surprised at losing the thread but only for a moment. Her eyes narrow in contemplation as she re-evaluates her cellmate. Several minutes pass, neither woman moving, before the goddess speaks.

"I will tell you what I can while upholding my part of our bargain," she says slowly, "but you know more than you should for a mortal. That changes things somewhat, even if you are not fully aware of the knowledge you possess."

Cora surfaces from her mental battle enough to protest. "Wait, that's not fair. How am I supposed to know what I don't know?"

"You must believe that you know it."

"What the hell kind of sense does that make?"

The woman winces but rallies directly into icy pride. She lifts her chin and asks, "Do we still have an accord? Or will you refuse my help and leave me to rot in this prison?"

Cora huffs. She's only been in the land of the dead for a couple of hours, and she's already tired of being jerked around by weirdos. Why does everything have to be trickery and half-truths? Can't anyone give a straight answer? Then again, there isn't a single legend she can remember without a puzzle or a riddle for the hero to work out before they finish their quest. If she's going to be the hero of this story, she's got to play by the rules. But it doesn't mean she has to like it.

"No, we're still on," she says sulkily. "I may have started the day being dead, but I probably shouldn't end it by being a liar. Tell me whatever you can. I'll work out the rest."

"I have no doubt of that," the woman says, nodding. She glances furtively down the corridor, then continues in a hurried whisper that Cora has to strain to hear. "The sphere of the underworld is under siege. The Mistress has overthrown the true ruler and uses the power of the throne to her own monstrous ends. But both deposed regent and usurper are dying slowly, and time runs short for the Mistress to find the object she seeks within the fields of the dead. If she cannot locate it soon, I fear for the fate of this world. If she does, I fear for the fate of yours."

The pair lapse into silence as Cora chews over the information. A thought occurs.

"Who's supposed to be in charge here?" she asks. "The Mistress seems pretty tough, but I figured someone like Hades or Satan could fight her off."

The woman's face splits into a horrible grin, and the black and white mottling across her skin slides into a firm division down the center of her face.

"I am."

Cora takes in the filthy hair, ragged clothes, and borderline insane expression. "You?" she scoffs. "And who are you?"

"The most called-upon regent of the underworld. But I cannot tell you more without securing your belief and risking the Mistress' wrath."

"My belief? In what? What does that have to do with anything?"

She sighs. "The trouble with belief –"

At that moment, the door at the end of the hall bangs open, and a particularly portly orc in ill-fitting armor appears in the hallway. He levels his rusty spear at the woman's cell as he storms toward it.

"Hey, you!" he barks. "You know yer not allowed to talk to the prisoners – Mistress' orders! Don't make me toss yer worthless bones into the oubliette again."

The woman shrinks back and disappears into her cell. A hurried noise later and she reappears, tossing what appears to be a rock into the middle of the open floor. The smell of cured meat entices to the guard forward. After a furtive look around, he stabs the lump with his spear, then grunts appreciatively.

"Harumph. Well, I'll let you slide this time. Just keep it down. Last thing I need's the Mistress finding out. Steve still walks on an angle."

And then he's gone.

Cora waits until the clang of the closing door dies behind him before saying, "What was that all about?"

"The Mistress is understandably fearful of her secrets being uncovered. Thus I am often relegated to the darker parts of my own dungeons. I must horde my provisions. Fortunately, they are useful for other purposes on occasion."

"Do I want to know what kind of meat that was?"

"No."

After the guard's interruption, though, no amount of cajoling will convince the goddess to tell Cora more about herself, the underworld, or the Mistress. She hazes and flickers, like the effort of fulfilling her end of the bargain has literally drained her, and she melts back into the shadows.

Back in her own cell, Cora cranks the wheels of her imagination as she huddles on her straw bed, trying to figure out what it all means. Gods can overthrow each other? Where are the other underworld regents? And what was that last thing about belief? Even for a supernatural world, it all seems so far-fetched. She briefly considers trying to question her cellmate again but abandons the idea. If what the woman said is true – that Cora knows more than she thinks – the pieces should start falling into place soon.

She falls asleep waiting for it to happen.

The dream isn't like anything she's dreamt before. There's no mad landscape, no bizarre creatures, no disembodied viewer. Instead, she sees through her own eyes into a tiny room she doesn't recognize but is clearly normal. A small window lets in afternoon sunlight. A cheery buzz of electricity floats by. A voice in the hall says her name, but nothing comes out when she tries to answer. When she tries to sit up, she's held fast. And suddenly she's cold and hungry and utterly exhausted. She sinks back and drops her head to the side. On a table beside her is a vase full of daisies, her favorite.

How nice. Someone remembered, she thinks before she slips away.

SIX

"Wake up, you!"

Cora leaps to standing from a dead sleep, erupting in hay, and throwing an errant punch through the air just in case. Her eyes eventually focus on a pair of orcs standing in the open door of her cell. One of them has a spear leveled at her.

"Mother*fucker*! Don't you guys know any other way to wake up a person? Jesus Christ..."

The guards snuffle a laugh. "The Mistress wants to see yer," says the one on the left. "Get yer pink hide out here on the double, or Greg'll pull you out himself."

Greg waggles his spear suggestively.

"Okay, okay, I'm coming. Keep your helmet on."

Cora steps out into the marginally less musty air of the hall and positions herself between the guards. She tries to peer into the ousted goddess' cell as they pass by, but she can't see anything inside. When they start walking away from the door to the throne room, she knocks on Greg's helmet from behind.

"Hey, you're going the wrong way. Throne room's behind us."

"Who says that's where we're going?"

The guard behind her laughs menacingly, and Greg joins in. Clearly there's some hilarious joke that she's not in on.

One of the drawbacks of castles is that everything pretty much looks the same inside. You've seen one iron-reinforced door or threadbare wall tapestry, you've seen them all. This castle in particular seems to be missing interesting diversions like portraits or sconces or anything but more orcs. It seems to Cora like they're walking on a treadmill, opening and closing doors into the same empty hall for hours.

Walking does help to shake the last of the sleep from Cora's mind, though, and she starts applying herself to how she'll defend against whatever punishment the Mistress has in mind after her outburst yesterday. There's a pang of regret for making demands of someone who turns out to be a kingdom-usurper; could've gone way worse than a night in the dungeon. Maybe contrition is the way to go, even if it chafes her sense of pride.

Before she can concoct lines to try out, the escort party stops abruptly in front of another unremarkable door. Cora doesn't have time to make a snarky comment about it before it's pushed aside and her mouth drops open in surprise.

They're standing on the edge of what looks like the African veldt, a plain of knee-high brown grass stretching as far behind the castle as the grey ocean does in front of it. The same low sky and fat pumpkin moon hang overhead, reinforcing the inside-outside feeling of the place. A lazy breeze heavy with ozone and earth drifts by. But where scrubby trees or ancient boulders would dot the landscape in the real world, there are neat rows of freestanding doors, each painted cottage white with a brass knob and a number plate. No frames, no walls, no nothing – just doors in a field. They're so far apart that Cora can only see a scattered few from where she's standing. She cranes her neck and stands on tiptoe to try to spot others.

And then the Mistress is in front of her in a rustle of golden skirts.

"Hello, my darling," she hisses sweetly. "I trust you slept well."

Cora rocks back on her heels and trains her gaze on the Mistress' mouth to avoid the terrible eyes. "Not bad. Could've used a pillow, though."

Stupid, stupid, stupid.

The Mistress' mouth curls disdainfully. "Next time, perhaps."

Without warning, long fingers dart out and seize Cora's elbow in a grip like tree roots around stones. The orc guards, having successfully turned over the prisoner, hustle back inside the castle and slam the door behind them. There's an audible click that tells Cora she's stuck out here in the literal hands of a madwoman.

The Mistress half-drags, half-leads Cora to the doors. As they get closer, a second row becomes vaguely visible, as if they're a long way off. But Cora doesn't get a chance to investigate further as she's spun around and released in front of door with a brass number one in its center.

"Now," says the Mistress, her eyes pressing down on the top of Cora's head. "I am going to speak, and you are going to listen. You will answer when I ask you a question, and you will not ask any of your own. If you do not do as I say, I will strike you down where you stand, and you will discover what it means to truly die. Do you understand?"

A glimpse of sharp silver in the Mistress' hand forces Cora to nod her consent.

"Good. You learn quickly, I see. This lesson should be simple enough." She lifts Cora's chin with a single red talon. The black eyes caress Cora's mind enough to threaten but not enough to intrude. "You have challenged me to give you a quest," she says, "one which I am obligated to give according to the unwritten laws of order and which I give unwillingly. Fortunately, the terms of that quest are entirely up to me. Which is most unfortunate for you."

The Mistress takes a step back and holds out an arm to indicate the field of doors. "Here is your quest, Cora Leigh Riley. You are tasked with returning to the castle through the thirteenth door within three days. You must begin at the beginning, and anything you bring with you on your return is forfeit to me. Should you succeed, I will release you back into the mortal world as you have asked. Should you fail to return by the appointed time in the appointed way, your soul will forever rest where it stands in that moment." She grins with wicked satisfaction. "Those are the terms of your quest. Do you accept?"

A million questions chase each other through Cora's mind, but a quiet, calm voice pushes aside any panic she feels.

This is my only way out. The only way I'll ever get to have a chance at making a life worth living. I already wasted so much time being safe and small. There can't possibly be a better time to risk it.

She takes a slow, deep breath and considers the gently swaying grassy field. How hard can it be to find a door, anyway? Six are practically visible from right here. Thirteen should be a piece of cake.

Turning back to the Mistress, she squares her shoulders and nods. "I accept."

A rushing breeze nearly knocks Cora to the ground with the smell of apples, and a chord of metallic chimes peals across the sky. The Mistress inclines her head in acknowledgement, somehow more regal and imposing. The same oozing sensation she felt in the dungeons creeps down over Cora's scalp in what she's come to recognize as the sealing of a deal.

Two mystical oaths in twenty-four hours —not the best idea I've ever had.

There's a tense moment long enough that Cora starts to feel awkward. An expectation is hanging there, but she's at a loss to name it, so she decides to get moving, as unstorylike as it seems to stroll away.

"So, uh, I'm going to go ahead and get started on that, then," she says.

She makes a little wave to the Mistress and starts down the aisle between the first two doors, heading toward double digits.

Three steps is as far as she gets.

Before her foot falls for the fourth, she's yanked violently backwards by an iron hand digging into her collarbone. Her boots drag in the grass, tearing up a skid as the high, echoing laughter of the Mistress fills the air. There's a blur of brown, gold, and white as the first door is flung wide, blowing damp-smelling air into the dry field, and Cora is thrust bodily through the frame. She keeps her feet but wobbles as her boots sink into soft, loamy soil, the shift from soft yellow light to near darkness making her head spin. The sound of the Mistress' laughter behind her makes Cora whip around. There's a stark divide between where she stands in damp darkness and the bright, dry field where the Mistress stands, like a hole cut from a landscape painting and replaced with another scene. Cora makes a grab for the door's frame to pull herself back through to the field but is easily shoved down by one of the Mistress' fingers against her forehead. Cora totters backwards from the remarkable pressure and trips over a gnarled tree root, landing hard on her tailbone.

Even through the flashbulbs of pain going off in

her brain, Cora sees the Mistress framed in a rectangle of warm light cut from the dark greenery of her own surroundings, clearly enjoying the sight of Cora thrown off balance and confused.

"Did you think it would be that easy, foolish girl?" she chuckles.

Sort of, Cora thinks.

"Remember, you have three days. If you can survive that long."

And with that the door slams shut, erasing the edges of the doorway until there's no hint there was ever anything in that spot besides the massive oak looming over Cora like an executioner sharpening his axe.

SEVEN

Trapped in a world inside a world. Scared and alone. On a deadline.

So of course it starts raining.

Thunder and lightning rumble and flash high above the forest's thick canopy mere moments after the Mistress' face disappears from view. Cora jumps up and presses her back against the oak tree as fat raindrops pat the ground faster and harder, turning the soft earth into slippery mud. The wide circle of foliage keeps her relatively dry, though, and she thanks whatever providence is watching for that small mercy. She leans against the trunk for a while to study her new surroundings as the throbbing in her tailbone dies down.

Even peering through the veil of rain, things seem oddly familiar. At first, she assumes it reminds her of the Ozark woods she knows so well, but the more she stares, the more she realizes she hasn't just seen something like it – she's been here before. That shouldn't be possible. But the riot of wildflowers running through the dark green grass, the lightning-bruised clouds, and the smattering of boulders suggesting mountains nearby tug at her memory. Details of the landscape rush to fill a mental map she didn't know she'd been carrying. It's a valley ringed by a low mountain range that starts north of here, and there's a wide-open meadow somewhere to the east with a huge clear pond on the other side. She knows it all so clearly that she starts to feel nostalgic for this place it's impossible for her to have ever been. It has to be from one of her strange dreams.

Are they more than dreams?

Curiosity begs her to duck out from under the shelter of oak branches to confirm her theory, but the storm is only getting started. She steps toward the edge of the leaves to squint around, but there doesn't seem to be a better place to ride out the storm. No stately trees big enough to keep her dry, no mysterious cabins or nomad tents, nothing. A crash of thunder makes her yelp with surprise and sends her darting back to the safety of the trunk. She sighs, annoyed at her skittishness.

"Great," she grumbles to herself. "Guess I'm stuck here until this blows over."

"You say that like it's a bad thing."

Had it been any other time or any other place besides her first day in the actual-factual underworld after challenging a goddess for the right to come back from the dead, the voice would've scared the bejesus out of her. Instead, she takes a deep breath, peels herself off the tree trunk, and carefully peers around, up, even behind the tree itself for the speaker. But it's only her standing there, white shirt becoming more see-through by the minute.

A tug at her ankles makes her look down in alarm. There's a fat red squirrel sitting by her boot, prodding her experimentally with both forefeet as if testing her solidity. Its ears are so full of fur they appear to be tiny mohawks.

"How come you're still human-shaped?" comes the voice again. It's got a soft, skittering quality that seems to match the curious eyes looking up at her from the ground.

A talking squirrel.

She shrugs. Why not? It's the least bizarre thing that's happened to her today.

"Am I not supposed to be human-shaped?" she says, feeling silly.

The creature shakes its head so vehemently Cora wonders if it's communication or a bug in its ear. "No humans here," it says, poking her in the calf again.

"At all?"

Another violent headshake.

"Why not?"

"The Ladies. They make everyone right."

Cora scans the vicinity again, her danger sense creeping up an octave. The last thing she needs is to get on the bad side of more power-hungry goddesses, but there's still no movement in the downpour. She relaxes slightly.

"There's nobody here, dude."

"No one except me."

Cora spins around at the sound of the new voice, nearly punting her squirrel friend in the process as he flees the scene, and comes face to face with a pair of tawny yellow eyes. She takes a step back, and there's a flash in her peripheral vision as a hand lands on her shoulder. The grip is light but firm, and it stops Cora's retreat before it can begin. She freezes there at arm's length and evaluates who got the jump on her. The girl can't be more than sixteen, is shorter than Cora, and appears to be completely naked. And green. Her hair, skin, and nails are the color of new leaves – everything except her eyes, which make Cora feel like she's being pinned by a particularly patient cat.

"You are trespassing here," the girl says after a moment or two. "There are no living humans in this place."

"I'm not staying, if that's any consolation. I only stopped here because of the rain," Cora explains. "And I need to get going, or I'll run out of time."

The girl's brow furrows. "Time? You are already out of time if you have arrived here. This is the end of your journey."

"Is this Door Thirteen?" There's a tinge of hope in her voice, buried in doubt. Surely it couldn't have been that easy.

The mossy eyebrows furrow, and the green girl shakes her head. "This is the Garden. And while I admit you are a strange case to have come to us still wearing mortal flesh, it is no trouble for us to help you take your place among us. I promise you will feel no pain."

Alarm bells go off in Cora's mind. Isn't there a story about dryads pulling humans into their trees for eternity? Or turning mortals into reeds? That sounds like an excellent way to be stuck here forever.

Gently, she takes another step back, and the dryad lets her hand fall from her shoulder. "That sounds, uh, nice, thank you," she says, slowly backing away from the tree. "But I really need to get moving. Things to do, quests to fulfill. You know how it is."

"I do," the girl says solemnly, her words soft and almost swept away under a roar of thunder. "And I do not intend to shirk my duties by allowing you to stay in my domain without undergoing the necessary change. You must become part of the greater whole; it is my charge to oversee your assimilation."

Every ounce of survival instinct in Cora's body stands to attention. But when she turns to bolt free of the oak tree's canopy, there are two more identical dryads standing at the edge of the sheltered space. And two more. And two more. Cora turns in place, taking in the semicircle of green young women moving steadily toward her. They're not armed, but they probably don't need to be. Who knows what they can do on their home turf against a puny mortal with no magic of her own?

Cora turns back to the original dryad with panic

rising, her mind filling with images of an afterlife spent as a thistle or geode. "You don't understand," she pleads. "I'm not supposed to be dead. I can't stay here. I have to find the way out so I can go back to my real life."

The girl half-smirks without any pity. She lifts a thin hand and snaps her fingers with the sound like a twig breaking, accompanied by the excited giggling of her sisters. Behind her, the air shimmers on the oak trunk where the edges of the first door disappeared earlier. A golden cloud puffs into the air and swirls past the dryad to settle around Cora. Her eyelids flutter as she tries to blink away the sweet pollen that clings to her hair, face, and clothes. The scent of green wood sings in her bones, urging her to take things slowly and put down roots.

Sleep, child of the earth, and stay here with us. Let your first mother take you back into her arms. Wouldn't it be nice to stay planted here for a century or two?

The lullaby is all she can hear. She sways gently in the rainstorm's winds, and her muscles relax with acceptance. She can feel the semicircle of dryads closing in slowly around her, eager to take their new sister home to their tree.

No. I stayed put for thirty years. I can't do it anymore.

It's a simple thought dredged up from sleepy recesses, an automatic last defense that's enough to jolt Cora out of the trance. She shakes herself like a wet dog, swatting pollen off her clothes and coughing it out of her lungs. She rubs her eyes and sees the dryads standing within ten feet of her, some with arms outstretched, ready to pounce.

This time, self-preservation wins. Muscles contract and shove Cora into a run straight through a swiftly-closing gap between bodies, barreling toward the nearby meadow. While she's never been a great long-distance runner, she did hold the sprinting record at school for three years. She disappears into the storm before the dryads can react.

They're not surprised for long, though. A shriek of rage pierces the air as Cora's boots pound the squelching ground trying to put as much distance as possible between her and the massive oak. She's soaked clear through to her underwear in less than a minute, but the rain seems to be letting up as she goes. Which is either helpful because she can see better or will get her caught because her pursuers can see better, too. Pursuers that are getting closer on silent feet; their snarling is the only thing giving them away. Dryads surely must be faster than humans, and it's only be a matter of time before Cora's lungs start to fail and burning muscles force her to stop. Then she'll be screwed.

For now, adrenaline keeps her dodging roots and leaping over fallen branches without pausing to look behind her. But as her attention splits between the immediacy of escape and finding a place to hide, a cleverly disguised stone slick with moss tangles her feet. She sprawls face-first into the mud, bloodying her shin on the insulting rock and skidding into a clearing.

A cackle of exultant laughter erupts behind her, and she tucks herself into a defensive ball to wait for the scratching nails and grabbing hands of the tree spirits who want to change her into a sapling. As much as she despises the idea of going down without a fight, the sprint through the woods has exhausted her reserves. Until she gets her breath back, there's nothing for it but to hope for a second chance to break away.

But seconds pass and no blows come. Cora peeks out from between her fingers expecting to see proud green faces and sees only grey skies above her. She slowly uncurls and sits up to check back the way she came. There they are – half a dozen willowy girls gathered at the tree line staring menacingly at her. And not moving.

Confused, Cora glances around to see if there's some other, bigger threat trained on her that would keep the dryads at bay. Thunder rolls overhead and a nearby flash of lightning illuminates the clearing to reveal that it's actually a broad green pasture dotted with dandelions and clover. No sign of hideous monsters or more murderous nature spirits whatsoever. She looks back at the dryads trying desperately to break through the tree line and into the meadow to chase her.

And then she breaks out into a ridiculous grin.

Of course. They can't leave their trees.

She pushes herself up to standing and yells across the space separating her from her would-be captors. "Sorry, Ladies! You'll have to turn me into a newt some other day. I don't think I'll be coming back to visit your little enchanted forest any time soon, though. Hospitality could use some work."

More snarls that sound like creaking branches from the peanut gallery. But the leader just stares, yellow eyes blazing. She holds Cora's gaze for a long moment, and Cora can't tell if she's pissed, amused, or worried.

Right before Cora turns away, though, the green girl calls out in a mocking tone. "A word of advice, mortal: Watch your step in the field. I hope you dodge faster than you run." Then she turns and stalks away, followed by her entourage. Two by two, they dissolve into the forest as silently as they appeared.

Cora makes a show of shrugging off the warning in case they can still see her, then starts walking. The sky is still an angry purple, and the humid air tells her the storm hasn't quite finished yet, so she starts hunting for new shelter. She'd like to dry out a little before continuing her journey. If this really is one of the places she's visited in her dreams, there should be a pond on the other side of this pasture with a fishing shack next to it. It's as good a spot as any to ride out the rest of the storm. And maybe find something to eat, her stomach interjects.

With a quiet minute to herself, she tries to make sense of the time since she left the castle. It must be spring here; it seemed to be autumn back in the doorfield. Maybe all the doors are different worlds with their own seasons and landscapes and terrifying things trying to absorb you into the collective. Although, the dryads didn't seem to be aware of any other doors or worlds. What if there's no way back to the doorfield? What if she's stuck here, doomed to be the only human in the Garden for eternity? Goosebumps rise on her arms as she walks, not just from the brisk wind picking up around her.

She's about halfway through the meadow when the first lightning bolt slams into the earth a hundred yards ahead. The tang of electricity mixes with the smell of burning grass, filling the air and sending Cora's heart into overdrive. With no trees or bushes in the area, she's the tallest thing in the vicinity, and she's heard enough old wives' tales about lightning to know she should be worried.

Another bolt plows into the dirt as she weighs her options, closer this time, forcing her to make a decision. She drops into a crouch and starts to wrestle with her shoelaces. If she can get these size eight grounding devices off her feet, she might stand a chance of surviving if she does get hit.

It costs her precious seconds. Two more bolts crash to the ground, seeming to get closer each time and followed by a sonic boom of thunder directly overhead. Divots of grass and dirt fly through the air with startling force as Cora tugs off one boot, then the other, fingers clumsy under pressure. The next lightning strike is less than fifty yards away from her, the sound of pure power cutting through the atmosphere like a knife through silk.

It takes a million years, but eventually she has

the boots off and is on her feet calling on the last of her strength to make a suicide run through the field. Part of the mountain range that forms the valley's bowl stretches off to her right, and she heads toward it, hoping to veer into a geographic safe zone.

But the lightning doesn't seem to notice. In fact, as the next bolt slams down only twenty yards away, it seems to be chasing her. And laughing. Another one comes in at fifteen yards, and Cora *knows* she hears giggling – it's hidden in the sizzle of electricity and the sonorous thunder, but she's so close that it sounds human.

"You can't ruuun! There'sss no hiding from usss!"

Another bolt comes down, then another, and another, closing the gap with every successive assault. Ten yards, five yards. Ten feet, five feet. The lightning flirts with disaster, dancing her across the field as she evades being blasted. She feints toward the mountainside or in the direction of the fisherman's shack that's now visible, but she's corralled back each time. Even the thunder seems to be enjoying itself, laughing in its booming voice whenever she screams. Her stomach lurches as she tries to dodge, duck, dip, and dive out of the way, but she isn't fast enough to keep it up. The hair on her arms is singed, and the tops of her feet feel like they've been hit with a blowtorch. There aren't any reserves left for her to call on. It'll be over soon.

Static charge builds up in a localized bubble, dropping the air pressure in a private depression around her. Cora freezes as her short hair gently starts to lift away from her scalp. Briefly, she remembers a friend describing this exact sensation before he was zapped off a tree root on a float trip. She drops her boots, squeezes her eyes tight, and holds her breath. If she's lucky, she'll survive. Although, with anthropomorphic lightning, who knows if it'll strike twice in the same place. There's a crackle of electrical laughter, and she tenses for the blow.

But rather than the jolt through the head she's expecting, she's bulldozed sideways like a quarterback at the Superbowl. Strong arms wrap around her middle, and she's hoisted bodily away a fraction of a second before a lightning bolt three times the size of the rest crashes into the earth, digging up a crater big enough to bury a small car.

"Run!" comes a husky voice from behind her.

And then they're running together, Cora and her unseen rescuer, headed for a dark smear on the side of the mountain.

Sheer survival takes over and floods Cora's system with the last of her adrenaline, pushing her on, almost making it to the mouth of the cave. But the moment her battered feet touch solid stone instead of wet earth, her lights go out and she collapses forward into exhausted sleep. At least this time someone's there to catch her.

EIGHT

An eavesdropper would wonder about the sanity of the man sitting with his back to the cave wall. He's talking to a red squirrel in his lap.

Then again, the eavesdropper might well wonder about their own sanity: the squirrel is talking back.

"What do we do now?" it says.

"I'm not sure, Geoff," the man replies, looking out over the meadow. "Xavier will be back soon, and we need to get moving, but she's sleeping too heavily to leave her."

"Maybe she's dead."

"She isn't."

"Are you sure? She's all pale and sweaty."

"Feel free to check for yourself. I'm sure the sensation of tiny, sharp claws on her throat would be a welcome wake-up call."

"Oh, har, har. Your sense of humor is getting better, I'll give you that, but you've still got a long way to go, buddy."

The pair sits in silent contemplation for a while.

"Maybe she's insane."

"Perhaps. We can't determine that until she wakes up, however."

"How do you think she got here?"

"Another excellent question that will have to wait, I'm afraid. She seems solid enough, and the Ladies weren't able to change her."

The man unfolds his long limbs to stand in the mouth of the cave, dumping the red squirrel unceremoniously onto the ground. The sleeping woman near the fire may be unconscious, but he keeps a respectful distance. The last thing he needs is a misunderstanding inside a complication. He's certainly in trouble for interfering with the absorption of a spirit into the Garden, but he couldn't watch her be disintegrated by idiotic weather sprites.

"Well done, by the way," he says out loud to the squirrel. "If you hadn't reached me when you did, she certainly would've been evaporated."

"Just trying to do the right thing, boss. It was pretty obvious she had no idea what she was doing." Geoff scoots closer to the man's feet. "Although, I wasn't sure you'd be around. It's been a while since we've seen you."

"I'm sorry about that. I was convinced to take my substantially built-up leave after the last case."

Quirking his head, Geoff says, "Probably for the best. You know, I wasn't sure you'd come even if I could find you. Time was not long ago you wouldn't have bothered."

Where another man might wince at the condemnation of character, this one furrows his brow thoughtfully as he weighs the statement.

Five years ago, it's questionable – maybe, maybe not, depending on orders and circumstance. He'd certainly been known to go rogue as a younger man. One year ago, though, absolutely not. This stranger isn't important to his mission, and if she were a high-priority asset, he'd have been informed. There's no objective reason to involve himself in her situation, putting his life and the fate of his charge at risk.

Or that's how he used to think.

"Things are...different now," he says.

He peels his watchful gaze from the field outside and turns it toward the woman lying curled on her side nearby. The fire highlights the red of her hair and ruddies her freckled cheeks. She's peaceful as she rests, with no hint of the sort of frenzy and fury of the girl he encountered last year, the one that ruined everything he'd built so carefully. Another case, another cave, another set of choices. He finds himself wondering what strangeness this new woman has brought into his life and what it will mean for him.

Geoff tugs on the cuff of his khakis, bringing him out of the reverie, then points his tail at the girl insistently. She's waking up. Before the man can react, though, the squirrel is bounding across the cave floor right up to her fluttering eyelids.

"Welcome back, crazy human!" he squeaks,

waving a paw at her.

When her eyes open to the squirrel inches from her nose, she doesn't scream. She doesn't even jump back in surprise. She simply says, "Oh, it's you again," and sits up, rubbing life back into her arms and legs.

The man can't help but be a little impressed. A quick adapter, this one.

But when she sees him standing in the broad cave mouth, it's a different story. Now she does cry out and scramble back. She even does a speedy inventory of her damp clothes to make sure they're all in place.

Dammit.

He knows what she sees. How imposing he is when people meet him for the first time, even without knowing his reputation. Tall enough to have been courted by basketball scouts in high school, intense brown eyes, severely-cropped black hair, skin dark enough to give him trouble in airports, posture like a military cadet. Easily mistaken for an attacker rather than the protector he's sworn to be.

He looks down at the ground to avoid any threatening eye contact, then raises his arms to show her that the inside of his brown leather jacket is empty. "I'm not armed," he says. "I promise nothing untoward happened to you while you slept."

Her eyes are all over him, trying to read his body language for any sign of untruth or hidden motives. It's pointless – years of training have erased those telltale signals – and he waits impatiently. He's telling the truth and is on a timetable; she clearly has no idea where she is, and he doesn't have time to babysit another charge. But he knows better than to jump to conclusions in this place. She could be capable of anything, and he needs more information before making a final plan.

She doesn't speak for a long time, so he tries again. Arms still out to his sides, he raises his gaze from the floor and does his best to be nonthreatening. His eyes meet hers, and he's struck by their color – the only people he knows with grey irises are certainly not random humans lost in the underworld. He tucks the information away for later. Right now, he needs to secure her trust, not wonder about her heritage.

"My name is Jack Alexander," he says, then points a thin finger at the squirrel. "This is Geoff. He told me you ran into the Ladies and might need some help."

She narrows her eyes at him and pats herself down again to be sure. Jack doesn't move. Geoff helpfully drags her discarded boots over one at a time from their place by the fire. After a long moment, seemingly satisfied that everything's in order, she starts to lace them up. They make a squelching noise in the echoing cave, stubbornly wet from the rainstorm that's still rising and falling outside. Her jeans didn't fare much better, but at least her white shirt isn't see-through anymore.

"Thanks for the rescue, mister, but I need to get going," she says. "I'm on a bit of a deadline."

That gets his attention. "Deadline? What kind of deadline?"

"Like I'm going to tell you, a strange man who talks to squirrels in the middle of a magical forest."

Jack lowers his arms slowly. "You talk to the squirrel, too."

"Hey! I have a name. I'm sitting right here, you guys."

Cora ignores Geoff's protests. "Good point, but still. I don't have time to sit around getting to know each other over a cup of tea in your lovely dank cave."

She finishes with her shoes and pops up to standing. She cross the cave, careful to stay close to the opposite wall from Jack, and sticks her hand out into the open to check the rain. A flicker of lighting zooms across the sky far above them, making her flinch.

"I wouldn't try it until after the storm is fully past," he warns. "The lightning sprites think everything is a game, and they don't like losing. They'll be twice as vicious if you go back out there."

The girl groans and slumps against the cool rock wall.

Now that she's closer, he can see she's faintly outlined, like heat over asphalt in the summer. Curious. Eyes half-closed, he inhales as deeply as he can without alerting her. A breeze rises over the meadow and brings him the smell of her skin: cotton and leather and what he can only label as "blue." The last comes with a primal pull of recognition; he's only ever caught that undertone in his own scent, and even then only in brief flashes. An unfamiliar prickling sensation blooms in his chest that memory reminds him is hope. The scent, the outline, the eyes – is it possible?

But the emotion vanishes as easily as it arrived. The weather could easily be playing tricks with his senses; thunderstorms collect the strangest smells in the Garden. Logic overrides the excitement of possible discovery, and he clears his throat to explore a more reasonable, obvious solution.

"Did you get lost on the way to your heaven?" he asks.

"My heaven?" She gawps at him like he's grown a third arm. "What the hell are you talking about?"

He sighs, crestfallen. "I suppose we can start at the top. But can you at least tell me your name before we continue? You have the advantage over me."

She purses her lips and tries to read his face again. He's careful to appear interested in her but not overly so.

Eventually, she says, "I suppose it can't hurt," and sticks out her hand. "I'm Cora. Cora Riley."

There's an awkward moment where her hand is out and he's staring at it trying to decide if it's a good idea to shake it. Touching strangers in the underworld has led to more than one injury, but there's something in the set of her jaw that tells him there's nothing to be worried about – yet. Maybe they could both use an ally right now.

He reaches out and takes her hand.

You can tell a lot about someone by the way they

shake. A limp bunch of fingers with a sweaty palm isn't someone you want to trust; they're usually slimy in more ways than one. Cora's grip is firm and strong, though, and she only pumps his arm twice. The mark of a country person who puts stock in the value of a good, solid handshake. He mimics the style and is rewarded with a brief smile.

"Nice to meet you, Cora Riley," he says, releasing her hand. "Although I'm sorry it had to be under these circumstances."

She nods in acknowledgement, the smile souring on her lips. "I'm sorry to have to meet anyone under these circumstances. Dead isn't exactly what I wanted to be when I grew up." She laughs sarcastically, and there's a flicker of disappointment when he doesn't join in.

He lets it go. Can't win them all.

"Do you mind telling me how you ended up here?" he says. "I can see you're unfamiliar with this place, which is remarkable for someone who made it through a door they don't belong to. And the mention of a deadline is stranger still."

He can see her hesitation before she even speaks, and he wonders briefly if she knows how easy she is to read. He smiles a little to himself, pleased to be able to notice things like that again.

She crosses her arms protectively and diverts her eyes. "I died," she says. "I woke up in front of the castle, and the Mistress wasn't happy about it. She gave me three days to find the thirteenth door and come back to her. Some kind of test, I guess. It seemed simple enough at first, but I started walking between the rows and she grabbed me and chucked me in here. Now I have to get back to the field so I can finish the job, but I don't see any way back."

The calm in Cora's face lets Jack know he's hidden his confusion perfectly. Most of what she's saying doesn't make any sense. He's never heard of a Mistress or a thirteenth door in the field. The ruler he's familiar with certainly doesn't go by such a cliché name, and there are only the dozen different worlds.

At least, as far as he knows. Could things have changed so much in the six months he's been absent? With his extensive experience doing this work, the idea he may have missed something so vitally important nags at his pride.

Something else is bothering him, too, he realizes. While her suggestion of a quest rings true, everything he can sense says she's not dead. But if she's physically present *and* doesn't know the mechanics of the interconnected worlds? That complicates things. There's less than a one percent chance he's right, and if she doesn't know what she is...

He's about to ask a clarifying question when he's interrupted by the appearance of a child running toward them. The little boy is a streak of delighted laughter in the rain. He keeps close to the mountain until he plows into the cave at top speed. He hits Jack at the knees, causing himself to flicker momentarily, then wraps his chubby arms around Jack's legs, nearly knocking them both to the ground.

"I seen a goldfish in the pond!" he exclaims. His sapphire-blue eyes are even more startling in contrast with the deep ebony of his skin. "This big!" He spreads his hands and extends every finger for maximum effect.

Jack throws his arms out to keep his balance, and Cora laughs.

The boy immediately switches his attention to her. "Hi! My name's Xavier. What's your name?"

She squats down to eye level with the boy. "My name's Cora. Nice to meet you, little man."

"I'm six and a half," he says, holding out six fingers. "How old are you?"

"Old enough that I don't answer that question," she says, trying to keep a straight face.

"Aw, come on. Please?" He half-turns and points to Jack. "Mr. Jack is thirty-six! I bet you're not even *close* to that old."

"That's quite enough, Xavier," Jack says with exaggerated patience as Cora rights herself. "Miss Cora doesn't need to tell you how old she is."

Xavier pouts at being chastised but only for a few seconds. He quickly spots Geoff sprawled out on top of a small boulder near the back of the cave and trots off to play. Cora watches him harass the squirrel for awhile, then turns back to Jack who's contemplating the meadow again.

"You want to tell me what *that's* all about?"

He almost does. Turning to look into those penetrating grey eyes and pulled by the feeling he knows who and what she is, he wants to tell her everything. His assignment, his unique talents, his history, his struggle. There's an understanding under her spikiness that encourages honesty, and he's taken refuge in harsh truths for so long that honesty is practically automatic. She accepted Geoff and the Ladies so easily. Perhaps it's safe.

But he stops himself as the first word starts to leave his lips. It's her first time here, and she clearly has no clue what's actually happening. Throwing too much reality at her at once might be a bad idea. Instead, he decides to tell her part of the truth, enough to answer her questions, not enough to scare her; the rest can wait.

"Xavier is my charge," he says. "He died last week in a car accident in New Orleans. I'm taking him to his heaven so he can be at peace."

Cora stares, first at him, then over at the boy chasing a red streak near the fire and laughing when he falls down. The disbelief on her face is slowly overtaken by sad acceptance as she turns back to Jack.

"That's the second time you've mentioned a personal heaven. I always assumed it was fluffy white clouds or eternal damnation or nothing at all, but you talk about heaven in lowercase letters. Like there are options."

He nods appreciatively. "That's exactly what I mean." When she doesn't respond, he takes it as encouragement to continue. "In the mortal world, there are hundreds, maybe thousands of different ideas about what happens after you die, but they're synthesized down to a dozen basic ideas in the actual underworld. It's belief in the concept of the afterlife that matters." He nods to indicate the field outside. "The Garden houses all the different structures of belief where you return to the earth and become part of nature. Every blade of grass and speck of dirt here represents a human soul."

Cora leaps and tries to keep her feet off the souls making up the floor of the cave. Jack puts his hands into his jacket pockets and watches impassively until she gradually calms down.

"I guess they don't actually mind, do they?" she says sheepishly.

"Not in the slightest."

"Hey, wait a minute – that means those fuckers trying to electrocute me are ghosts screwing around?"

He nods.

"Bastards!" A pause. "I can't believe you let Xavier run around out there in this storm. They almost killed me a second time; that's cruel to wish on a kid."

He hesitates for a fraction of a second. "His circumstances are different than yours. They can't hurt him."

It's the truth but not the whole truth.

"And the dryads?"

"Also formerly humans. They're tasked with overseeing the transformation required for souls to integrate into the Garden."

There's a long pause as Cora looks out toward the forest she narrowly escaped. Jack can almost hear her mind whirring. He watches her in profile and is startled to notice that he's appreciating what he's seeing. He shakes himself mentally. The last case may have changed him, but it's far too soon for that.

"Where are you taking Xavier?" she asks after a while.

"To be with his family. He got lost in transit from the mortal world, and it's part of my job to guide special cases like his back to where they belong."

"So," she says slowly, "you're a guardian angel."

Jack laughs, smiling in spite of himself. It's a strange feeling but a good one. "Something like that," he says.

NINE

The rain stops soon enough, but the rest of the storm takes its sweet time moving on. Xavier plays with Geoff until they pass out together next to the fire. Cora and Jack stand on opposite sides of the cave mouth for a while, quietly thinking their private thoughts.

She's pretty sure the guy's an angel. She's never heard of one with no wings who wears combat boots and smells like Old Spice, and he does talk a little weird, but Xavier seems to love him without question. And she can't think of any other way you'd be able to visit alternate afterlives, knowing there is such a thing. He seems legit. Watching Jack out of the corner of her eye, she grudgingly admits he's also sort of handsome in that standoffish-guy-in-a-biker-jacket sort of way. But she doesn't entertain the thought longer than a moment. She's here to win her life back, not hit on mythological creatures.

So, what next? That's the question that keeps popping into Cora's mind. She's running out of time. She could try going back to the oak tree where she came in, but the thought of another run-in with the Ladies seems even more deadly than the lightning field. And there's no guarantee she could open the door even if she did survive in human shape. There has to be another way.

"How do I get out of here?" she asks, keeping her voice low to avoid waking Xavier.

Jack seems far away, lost in his own thoughts, and it takes him a moment to answer. "It's more complicated than it should be," he eventually says. "There's only one entrance and one exit for each world. Unfortunately, the exits only lead to other afterlives; they don't go back to the doorfield directly." He smiles a little sardonically. "The doors are also magically hidden to avoid accidental visitors. And they move."

Well, there goes the oak tree plan. Good thing she asked first.

"Great. So, what you're telling me is that I'm totally fucked." She huffs and rubs her eyes with a free hand.

"Not necessarily."

He's staring directly at her, his face carefully blank. Even years of reading Sherlock Holmes and watching too many police procedural TV shows aren't helping her read him. Another point in favor of the angel theory. They're supposed to be unknowable, right?

"Go on…" she prompts.

"One of my skills is the ability to detect the doors and open them. It's part of how I do my job. If you think you can keep up, I can take you as far as Xavier's heaven at Door Twelve. An additional person on the journey is only minimal trouble."

Cora raises her eyebrows. That's nearly to the end of her quest - a generous offer and nothing to sneeze at. But…

"And then what, exactly?" she says. "You dump me there? I'm already stuck here; I'll just be stuck in a different place and still doomed for eternity. Plus, I don't actually know you. It sounds like the plot of a bad horror movie." She holds up her hands to frame the imaginary tagline. "'Young woman trusts strange man with kid, ends up in a ditch covered in petrol on fire.'"

He doesn't flinch. "I can only reassure you that my sole intention is to offer help. You're not obligated to accept." He shrugs. "But if you prefer to work out the puzzle on your own, I wish you the best of luck – returning to the castle in three days will be extremely challenging without a guide. However, Xavier and I need to be on our way."

Cora watches him cross to Xavier and crouch down to wake him. The boy smiles when he sees Jack and hugs his neck. There's a whispered conversation she can't hear, but the ease between them is clear enough.

She gnaws thoughtfully on her thumbnail as she weighs what she's seeing against every ounce of "don't get raped" training she's ever been through at school, at work, and at home. On the one hand, he's a powerfully built stranger who looks at her a bit too intensely for her liking. On the other, he's been nothing but respectful and helpful, and even the dorky talking squirrel trusts him.

Switching her gaze outside, she realizes how vast the Garden is without the haze of rain over it. In her dreams, she always chalked up the endless feeling of the place to dream physics, but now she can see that it really does stretch out for miles in every direction. Going back out there without a guide, searching for a door that leads into another alien landscape filled with who knows what – a door she may not be able to open even if she could find it – seems like an increasingly stupid idea.

As she's thinking, Jack stands, takes Xavier's small hand in his large one, and the two of them walk past her. Jack dips his head to her in acknowledgement, and Xavier waves exuberantly, shouting "Bye!" as they step into the fresh air. They veer off to the right, heading toward the pond. She watches them cross the meadow at Xavier's little-boy pace. He's chattering the whole time, an unfiltered litany of what he sees and thinks. Jack says nothing. But when they hit the edge of the water and start to curve around to the fisherman's shack, she can see he's smiling.

That does it.

"Wait!" Cora calls out, running to join them.

The pair stops immediately and waits for her to catch up. Her mind is still fighting the decision, reminding her to stay on her guard, that she doesn't need another guy telling her what to do, but every stride makes her heart feel a bit lighter. Stubborn pride may well get her killed here; what she needs now is help. And besides, she didn't spend four years taking martial arts for nothing. She can handle it if things go sour.

"You're a fast runner, Miss Cora!" Xavier says as she pulls up.

She smiles at him. "Only in little bits, I'm afraid." To Jack, she says, "Take me as far as you can. Maybe I can figure out the trick on my own and go from there."

Jack nods. "I certainly hope so," he says. Something about the tone makes her wonder what he actually means, but she doesn't ask.

What she does say is: "None of this white knight bullshit, though, understand? I pay my debts. You saved my ass back there, and now you're playing Boy Scout, and I'm thankful. But now I owe you, and I don't like that. I *will* make this square somehow. Got it?" She keeps her voice low out of habit. You don't swear around kids where she's from, but sometimes cuss words are needed to make a point.

He meets her eyes, and for a moment, they're locked together, assessing and reassessing each other.

Then the moment ends, and he says, "Understood."

There it is again – the sensation of an egg cracked on her scalp. She can feel the layers of oaths in her hair and has a sudden burning desire for a shower. How did she wind up owing so many people?

Jack starts walking, and Cora falls in on the other side of Xavier. She's only half surprised when she feels his warm little hand slip into hers. It's oddly light. She tries not to think too hard about the fact that he's a ghost. It does make her wonder about her own corporeality, though. She holds up her free hand and stares at it. Seems solid enough. Maybe you always seem normal to yourself even when you're dead.

As if reading her mind, Xavier asks, "Miss Cora, are you an angel, too?"

"If I am, someone seriously screwed up," she laughs. Xavier doesn't get it, so she says, "No, sweetie. Just another lost soul like you."

Xavier squeezes her hand. He doesn't say anything more about it, but he doesn't stop talking, either. It's the sort of childish blather that's endearing rather than annoying. In the five minutes it takes them to reach the fisherman's shack, he's told her everything he knows about the goldfish in the pond, explained why the sky is blue, and named every dinosaur he can think of. Cora listens and nods and smiles, feeling oddly maternal. Funny, she never wanted kids – another reason she and Jeremy were probably doomed from the start – but walking through this sunny meadow with this adorable little boy and his guardian angel, she can see the attraction.

She glances over to Jack, who's been silent since their exchange. He's watching the terrain, scanning for something Cora can't see, pretending he's not listening. But there's a hint of amusement at the corners of his eyes makes her wonder.

When they reach the decrepit wooden building at the edge of the pond, Jack lets go of Xavier's hand and motions for them to stay put. Cora nods and finds a broad tree stump nearby where she plops the boy into her lap to wait. She'd assumed that the fisherman's shack would be the natural place for an exit since it has a door of its own, but Jack doesn't go in. Instead, he slips behind the building and starts walking methodically around the curve of the water, one hand shading his eyes, head on a swivel. The way he moves sets off her admittedly scanty tracking experience as being completely wrong, all switchbacks and telltale noises. If he'd been hunting a deer and not a door, she'd say something. As it is, she turns her attention the riveting game of "spot the fish" Xavier has been playing without her.

"Whoa," she says.

There are over a dozen fat fish crowded in the shallows by their feet. Which makes sense, seeing as it's afternoon and the roots of the tree stump make a great hiding spot. But they're not hiding. They're staring up at Cora and Xavier like they're waiting.

"Uh, sorry, I don't have any food for you guys," she says.

Xavier rips up a fistful of grass from the bank, and Cora winces, thinking about all the souls he's uprooted. He waddles almost into the water and flings the grass, shouting, "Here, fishies!" None of them moves. Not even a feint at the prospect of food. It gives Cora the willies.

"Ooh, ooh! There he is! Told you!" Xavier shouts, bouncing and pointing.

A massive, shiny body shoulders its way between the fish half his size to eyeball the humans at the edge of what he surely thinks of as *his pond*. He's even bigger than Xavier said, worthy to be the adversary of any angler. Bright gold scales reflect the sunlight, and Cora has to squint and turn her head to avoid being dazzled.

When she peers up the shoreline trying to spot Jack, he's not there. This only worries her a bit more than the crowd of wild rabbits that have gathered at a stone's throw from where she and Xavier are sitting. They're staring, motionless, just like the fish. And more animals are coming. A family of deer step out of the forest at the far edge of the pond, followed by a badger and a clutch of possums. Crows and sparrows land on top of the fisherman's shack one by one. Cora pulls Xavier to her.

"I want to pet the fishes," he whines. But when he sees the growing mob of forest creatures, he loses interest and focuses on them. "Ooh, bunnies!"

She's not prepared for how strong he is. Xavier shimmers faintly, then twists and pops out of her grip, making a beeline for the deathly still watchers. Warning bells go off in Cora's mind. Back in the world, these animals are fairly harmless, but she has no idea what could happen if he touches one here. She stands to go after him, then stops short as a flash of brown passes in front of her.

Jack appears from behind the fisherman's shack, moving fast. His long arms snatch Xavier up from the ground, pulling the protesting boy expertly to his chest.

"Hey! I want to play with the bunnies! Put me down!"

Fat tears start to well up in Xavier's huge blue eyes. It tugs at Cora's heartstrings, but Jack is unfazed. He lets the boy throw the tantrum, taking a couple kicks to the midsection, without taking his eyes off the eerily silent crowd.

"Cora," he says quietly, "we need to get in the water. Walk very slowly, and don't turn your back on them."

"Why? They're not moving. Just staring."

"For now, yes, but we don't belong here. They're attracted to the scent of mortals. It won't be long before –"

There's the lonesome sound of a single branch snapping nearby, and the tension breaks. Animals scatter everywhere, fleeing for the meadow or the forest, peeling off around the three humans they'd been so anxiously watching. The area is empty in seconds. Even Xavier stops bawling in surprise. Cora exhales loudly, glad not to be the subject of scrutiny, but Jack hasn't moved. She follows his gaze and sees an enormous brown bear lumbering out from between the evergreen trees.

"Oh. My. Fuck," she breathes.

With exaggerated care, Jack lowers Xavier to the

ground, eyes still on the bear. He walks backwards slowly, past Cora and still holding the boy's hand, until he's up to his ankles in scummy pond water. Xavier splashes in, and Cora winces at the noise.

"Cora. Back up. You need to get into the water."

The bear stalks its way toward them. Its jaws hang open loosely, drool dotting the grass as it moves, ears pitched forward. It almost seems friendly. Except for the rows of sharp, yellow teeth.

"Maybe it'll go away," she says weakly.

"We smell wrong to him. He's going to walk right up to us and attack."

Cora half-turns toward Jack, now knee-deep in the pond. His forehead is creased and his jaw is set. He's probably not used to having to argue with his charges, she figures. Xavier looks unperturbed, even though the water is up to his shoulders.

Jack stares hard at Cora for a second and then turns his back to her. She watches as he dips a single finger into the water at a seemingly arbitrary spot and traces out a wide semicircle in front of him. There's a sound like an airlock being released, and the edge of the doorway appears exactly where he drew it, extending into a perfect circle ten feet across. He leans down and whispers something to Xavier. The little boy's face floods with fear, but Jack puts a reassuring hand on his head. Xavier nods, then takes a deep breath and dives into the outlined section of water.

Ten seconds go by, but Xavier doesn't reappear. Where Cora is now intensely worried for the kid, Jack's face is calm as he turns to her and makes a "come on" gesture. She looks back at the bear, now substantially closer and looking more agitated by the second. Its ears are flattening, and a low rumble boils out of its muzzle.

You'd think it'd be an easy choice. Trust Jack and jump in the water and live or don't trust him and take your chances with a ton of bear. If only she hadn't almost drowned in a pond exactly like this during a party when she was eighteen. If only someone had taught her to swim properly as a kid. If only she wasn't such an untrusting chickenshit after being dumped for having feelings.

"Cora..."

"Okay, okay, I'm coming," she hisses.

The slavering bear closes the distance as she retreats, its huge, black claws biting into the soft earth of the waterfront where she stood moments ago. She grits her teeth and walks backwards. Waves of panic rise up her throat as cold water rises up her legs. Memories of darkness and burning lungs make her gasp for breath when she sinks up to her waist. Every thought she has is of getting out of the pond as fast as possible. She can try to outrun the bear wading into the shallows; there's no fighting when you're sinking like a stone.

When she reaches the edge of the doorway in the water, her resolve gives out.

"I can't do it," she groans through gritted teeth. "I can't swim. You'll have to go without me."

Jack looks from her to the bear. "We don't have time for this," he says. He reaches out one arm as if he's going to grab her around the waist. "You need to trust me that you're going to be okay." He waves her toward him, eyes flicking occasionally toward the bear that's making waves around them and closing fast.

As Cora watches him standing there waiting, just moments from being eaten himself, some detached part of her brain reaches back to high school English and pulls up the only piece of Hemingway she's ever been able to remember.

The best way to find out if you trust somebody is to trust them.

She reaches out and closes the distance, wrapping both arms around his middle, squeezing far too tightly, and jamming her eyes closed.

"Deep breath!" Jack shouts.

She inhales sharply and gets a lungful of warm, foul air as the bear bellows from inches behind them. There's a sharp sensation of claws whistling toward her as she's lifted up, then plunged below the surface of the pond.

Back into the darkness.

TEN

There's a heart-seizing moment where the darkness they're standing in is indistinguishable from the darkness they've left. Memories he's tried to bury remind Jack of the consequences of missing his target. If they're stuck in the Gauntlet, the treacherous gap between worlds, there's no assurance he can protect his charges. Or himself. Uncertainty turns to the beginnings of panic, the emotions overly strong with newness. He should never have attempted a carryalong sidestep in the field. Not after being away for so long. Not with a stranger.

But when Cora peels his arms from around her waist, the tide of anxiety subsides. She's not frightened. Their surroundings are decidedly neither wet nor endless void. The air is close, stuffy, and dry. They made it.

Jack lets out his held breath and stretches up to

his full height. He senses Cora move away in the darkness, passing in front of a thin streak of yellowish light that extends from floor to ceiling. He bounces on the balls of his feet to test the ground. Wood? Cheerful voices nearby call out to each other in rapid fire, overlaid with a single sharp voice in the unmistakable tones of someone in charge. A deep breath brings him the warm brown smells of baking bread, cooking fires, and cedar wood. A picture begins to form, along with an exit strategy.

And that's when he realizes they're missing someone.

"Xavier?" he whispers.

No answer.

"Is he with you?" he asks Cora.

Her nervous voice whispers back, "You don't have him?"

Jacks curses in three different languages. Of all the places to lose a small child.

"He must have wandered off while we were wasting time in the pond," he growls. "We'll have to search for him."

"You can't track him? Don't you have some sort of magical kid-locating device?"

He grits his teeth in the dark, bending his frustration into the comforts of logic. This is not her fault. She doesn't know how dangerous it is.

Doubt has never been in his emotional repertoire, but it's rearing its head now. If he'd just trusted the instinct to tell her the whole truth up front maybe this wouldn't have happened. He makes a mental note to correct his mistake as soon as possible. Even if she can't accept it all at once, she's tangled up in this now, and she's got a right to know what's going on.

For the moment, though, they have to find Xavier before the Hunters realize he doesn't belong here.

"It doesn't work like that," he says. "We'll have to find him the old-fashioned way. Fortunately, opening interworld doors is a rather specialized skill, so he can't have gotten far on his own."

He steps forward to join Cora next to the intricately carved doorjamb. An eye applied to the crack of light confirms his suspicions as to their location, and he sighs. This might be harder than he thought.

"That can't be good," Cora says. "Angel huffing is never a good sign."

"No. We've arrived at the Hunting Hall," he says, turning to face her. They've been standing in the dark long enough that he can make out the details of their surroundings. He gestures to the shelves. "Luckily, we turned up in a closed pantry closet."

"You sound surprised."

Again, he wrestles with how much to say. The shortness of time forces him to keep it brief, and he redoubles his resolve to be completely transparent with her once they're not in mortal peril.

"The laws of the underworld are guided by idiosyncratic magic, meaning exits don't always open to the same place. You could exit Door Seven and end up at Door Eleven or Door One. A solitary, inexperienced traveler could be lost in an infinite loop."

"Is it possible to make it through without getting lost?"

He nods. "You can influence the direction you move by knowing what number you're heading for. It takes a tremendous force of will, however, and you can only travel down the rows. Three, Six, Nine, Twelve – that sort of thing. You often visit undesired worlds before you arrive at your intended destination."

"So you can't take Xavier straight home."

"Correct."

Cora mulls this over for a moment. Then she says, "Why don't you go back to the doorfield and walk to the right one?"

Jack gives a rueful laugh. "No doors go back there directly once you're inside. All official transport is done from the castle and Door Twelve; one rarely comes through the doorfield itself. And since all my charges are already in an afterlife, my work is always done the hard way."

A jiggle on the door handle keeps Cora from asking a follow-up question. The narrow strip of light widens and reveals a medieval kitchen bustling with activity. A wide man with hairy arms wearing a blood-streaked apron is breaking away from the work, apparently to get himself a snack from the pantry.

"What are you *doing*?!" screams a blonde man near the main fire pit. "Get your indolent arse back to turning this pig or it'll be *your* carcass we serve at the high table!"

The man jumps and hollers, "Yes, Chef!" as he sprints back to his post.

Jack and Cora stand statue-still. The door is hanging wide open, exposing them to the entire kitchen. But no one's looking in their direction. Dozens of cooks in a multitude of shapes and sizes are attending to their duties, each chopping, stirring, tenderizing, and frying as if it's all that matters. The only one even glancing up from their hands is the angry supervisor who's issuing a sustained tongue-lashing without seeming to breathe. And his back is to them.

Jack puts his finger to his lips to signal for silence and then holds out his hand to Cora. She takes it gingerly after a fraction of a second's hesitation. The roughness of her palm in his is reassuring; she's not entirely unused to hard work. The Hunting Hall might be easier for her to navigate than the Garden.

The supervising chef continues screaming. "This ostrich is so raw it's trying to eat the parsley it's sitting on! Put it back in the pan, you great drooling oaf!" He storms over to the far counter to confront the unfortunate cook.

It's their only chance.

As one person, Jack and Cora bolt for the swinging double doors on the other side of the kitchen. Both crouch automatically to lower their profile, and the sound of their footsteps is easily hidden under the head chef's tirade. Every set of eyes is too focused on not getting dressed down to notice the commotion. It's a miraculously clear shot between the high islands and the rows of hanging pots and pans. Seconds after leaving the pantry, they're pushing through heavy doors and slipping out. Momentum carries them down a long hallway bristling with mounted antlers before they come to a stop under a large torch. They press against the rough wooden walls, and Jack counts the seconds, his whole body tensed for a pursuit.

One...

Two...

Three...

All that follows them is the faint sound of shouting from the kitchen.

"I can't believe it was that easy," Cora pants, dropping her hand.

"Sometimes it is. Most of the time it's not."

She glances up and down the corridor, then says, "This place is just as confusing as the castle. I only see three doors out of here, and everything looks the same. Which way do we go to find Xavier?"

He peers around to get his bearings, but there's no trace of the boy, not even his peppery scent in the air. He'd have to guess. He hates guessing.

"I don't know," he admits.

Whatever progress he's made with his emotional vocabulary isn't enough to interpret the look she gives him. Something like confusion mixed with anger. But he shoves it aside. Much more important issues need dealing with before he has time to process something so inconsequential.

Cora's eyes narrow, and she says, "Do you even know where we are?"

He nods. "Going right takes us to the feasting hall," he tells her. "Going left takes us to the training hall. The door in the middle opens into the courtyard."

"And where's the door to the next heaven or whatever?"

Jack closes his eyes and takes a deep breath to ground him. Reaching out with his mind, he searches the ether for the familiar signature of a doorway. When the tingle of recognition does come, he manages to keep his face serene, if only just. Seems like they're going to pay for their easy escape from the kitchen.

"It's in the feasting hall," he says, opening his eyes.

"Then let's go to the training hall first."

He stares blankly at her.

"We need to get out of here fast, right? Better to start searching on the opposite side so we don't waste time doubling back."

A slow nod. "That seems logical."

She rolls her eyes and laughs. "Thanks, Spock."

"Who?"

"Nevermind."

Cora starts toward the training hall, and Jack stands alone for a moment, surprised by his own lack of response. She's carefully alert in this unfamiliar place but moves with a confidence he didn't have the first time he came here. Natural talent, eagerness to help, and a sharp, open mind. He adds these qualities to his growing assessment of her, then closes the mental file for now. It's time to stop thinking of her as a lost little girl and start treating her like the ally she clearly is.

In four long strides, he's caught up with her. The heavily reinforced wooden doors are closed, and Cora eases them open far enough to peek inside. No guards are posted at the entrance, so they slip in undetected, standing in a high gallery overlooking an open room.

The sight that greets them seems lifted directly from ancient woodcuts of Viking life. A long, narrow hall lined with crackling torches, racks of gleaming weapons, and training dummies is filled with easily a hundred warriors in various states of armor or undress. No one is sparring, however, and the mood seems artificially muted. Everyone stands near the center of the hall, talking excitedly and facing the back wall where space has been cleared for wooden statues depicting six different deities. A handful of burly men and two blonde women the size of horses are positioned to create a natural barrier between the statues and the waiting warriors.

"Looks like we've arrived in time for the dedication ceremony," Jack murmurs to himself.

"Is that good or bad?"

Instead of answering, he steps to the railing and casts his eyes over the crowd, searching for a tiny dark speck in the sea of bodies. The warriors have spread out along the length of the south wall and mingle indiscriminately. Cora comes up beside him to look, and her brow wrinkles as she notices the variety of races.

"I thought this was Valhalla," she whispers. "All the hunting trophies and wooden beams and such. Don't the different cultures have their own warrior heavens to go to?"

Jack doesn't take his eyes off the training hall. "The Happy Hunting Ground, the Hall of the Slain, Valhalla – it all amounts to the same thing under the laws of belief. If you died bravely in battle and believed you'd be rewarded with endless fighting and feasting, you come here."

There he is.

Terrified blue eyes stare directly up at Jack and Cora from a dark corner behind a statue on the floor below. Even from this far away, it's clear Xavier has been crying. When Jack's eyes find him, the little boy's face lights up, and he almost calls out, but Jack waves him into silence. Xavier puts both hands over his mouth and nods obediently.

Cora grips the handrail of the balcony. "How are we supposed to get to him?"

"The only way to the ground floor is through the courtyard. We can get into the hall, but I'm not confident we'll be able to extract him without being caught. There are too many people, and the presence of those two valkyries makes stealth practically impossible."

"Valkyries?" she starts, then shakes her head. "You know what, nevermind. If you say they're valkyries, I'll take your word for it." She looks from Jack to Xavier and back again, face worried but voice cool. "Is there any way to, like, camouflage ourselves long enough to snatch him? If you already know where the door is, we should be able to make a run for it."

Jack rolls the idea around for a moment. "In theory, it could work. But I don't know enough about the ceremony to determine if it's worth the risk." He narrows his eyes at the mass of people. "I need more information. I don't want you or Xavier to be put in jeopardy due to a miscalculation."

Down below, one of the buxom women steps to the center of the room.

"I think you just got your wish," Cora says.

The valkyrie spreads her arms like an eagle flexing its wings and booms, "WARRIORS, YOUR ATTENTION TO ME, IF YOU PLEASE."

Deafening silence follows and all eyes turn toward her.

She doesn't lower her volume as she continues. "YOU ARE ALL HEREBY OFFICIALLY WELCOMED TO THE HUNTING HALL. TODAY, YOU SHALL RECEIVE YOUR JUST REWARD FOR YOUR LOYALTY AND HEROISM. YOUR DEATH IS THE PRICE YOU HAVE PAID FOR YOUR SEAT AT THE TABLE; THIS CEREMONY IS THE KEY WITH WHICH YOU WILL ENTER THE HALL."

There's an explosion of applause under a roaring wave of cheers and stomping feet. The woman raises her fist in salute. A broad-faced man with a bushy black beard joins her on the floor as the echoes die away.

"Thank you, Sister Helga," he says to the valkyrie. To the accumulated warriors, he says,

"Brothers and Sisters! You see before you statues of the six rulers of the Hunting Hall. To enter into the eternal halls of battle and feasting, you must give your blood one final time to the deity who has loved and protected you most during your short, glorious lives."

Sister Helga steps in before the applause can resume. "PLEASE FORM AN ORDERLY LINE BEFORE THE GOD OR GODDESS OF YOUR CHOICE. BLADES WILL BE PROVIDED ONCE YOU REACH THE FRONT SHOULD YOU REQUIRE ONE."

The crowd begins to part as the assorted souls arrange themselves into rough estimations of lines, organization not being their strong suit. Jack checks on Xavier, who thankfully hasn't moved but is standing close to where the warriors will leave the training hall once they've sworn their oath. As uncomfortable as it makes him, there's no time to think through a logical plan. He's got to act. Right now.

"Whoa, what are you doing?" Cora exclaims as he hands her his leather jacket.

He peels off his black T-shirt and offers it to her. She takes it, but with some reluctance. "I'm going down to get Xavier."

"Naked?"

"Of course not. That would be ridiculous. But I need to look at least passingly like a fallen warrior, and modern street clothes aren't acceptable here."

"Okay..."

Jack strips off his white undershirt and adds it to

the pile, now bare to the waist. It takes a moment, but he does eventually feel her eyes on him, examining the four dark scars that run diagonally from his collarbone over his ribs. How long as it been since anyone else has seen them? The self-consciousness is so foreign as to be completely new. There are unspoken questions in her searching grey eyes, but there's no time. There doesn't seem to be time for anything he wants to tell her.

Cora coughs lightly to break the spell, then rolls up the wad of clothes and sticks it under her arm. "What do you need me to do?" she asks, eyes purposefully trained on his face.

"Wait for me in the courtyard. I'll circle back with Xavier, and then we can head for the feasting hall to take the doorway to the next stop."

"Are you sure you don't need me in there with you? I'm no slouch in a fight."

He shakes his head. "I know how to act here. They'll be able to tell you're out of place more quickly than they can spot me. Although I'm sure you're more than capable, if this comes down to a fight, it'll be too late."

Jack starts to walk away, keenly aware of the other strange sight on his back, when she calls out. "What happens if you don't make it?"

He half-turns and says, "Then it's up to you to get him to where he belongs."

The door closes quietly behind him, muffling her confused protest, and he takes off at a jog toward the courtyard, hoping he doesn't need to put her in that position. But he can only see one way over this particular obstacle, and you never know what will happen when you're making a blood sacrifice to a vengeful god.

ELEVEN

I'll have to take him? And how exactly am I supposed to do that, Mister Angel Man?

Cora's eyes stay trained on Xavier from her perch in the upper gallery. He's fidgeting in all the excitement, and that's got her nervous. What if someone spots him before Jack gets there? What if he darts out into the ceremony? But thankfully he hasn't moved from his hiding spot, making him far more patient than Cora was at his age. More patient than she is right now, too. Funny, when she considers how long she waited to take control of her life.

Come to think of it, everything is sort of upside down right now. The overall lack of weirdness in her current situation is weird in itself. Normal people don't talk to goddesses, escape from dryads, and make friends with angels, right? But once she got over the initial shock, she's felt right at home. Maybe it's Dad's faerie training or all the gnomes she found in the woods or the dream adventures that have turned out to be real. Those certainly aren't normal either. Whatever the underlying preparations, standing in Valhalla overlooking a throng of dead heroes being directed by valkyries to swear final allegiance to definitely-existing gods isn't melting her brain. In fact, she's kind of digging this whole magical quest thing.

Oh fuck, the quest.

The reminder jars her, forcing her mind into trying to calculate how long she's been away from the castle. It feels like hours, but it could easily be days for all she knows. Panic rises in her throat, and she's suddenly aching to run.

But before she can take off in pursuit of her future, an abrupt commotion in the crowd below brings her back to the present. Two warriors dressed in furs are wrestling in a decidedly unfriendly way while shouting what can only be curses. A circle opens around them, and the chant goes up. The cadence transcends the language barrier: *Fight! Fight! Fight!*

It doesn't last long.

"BREAK UP THIS SHAMEFUL DISPLAY AT ONCE! HAVE YOU NO SENSE OF DECORUM?"

Everyone freezes as Sister Helga stomps through the parting bodies, waving her broadsword in one hand like a conductor's baton.

"THIS IS A SOLEMN OCCASION," she booms, "AND HERE YOU ARE SCRAPPING LIKE

CHILDREN. PULL YOURSELVES TOGETHER AND ACT LIKE THE PARAGONS OF VALOR YOU ARE SUPPOSED TO BE!"

A dead silence follows, punctuated by shuffling feet as the combatants stand to hang their heads in appropriate deference. There are muttered apologies. Sister Helga nods, and chastisement satisfactorily issued, stomps back to the front of the room.

Cora suppresses a giggle and sees Xavier in the corner doing the same. She has a momentary pang of guilt for not keeping her eyes glued to him. Not that she could do much about it from up here in the gallery. She raises her hand to remind him she's watching, hoping to keep him reassured for a few more precious minutes.

And then she spots Jack at the edge of the dissolving fight circle. Men and women stream past him back to their lines, but he's standing still, staring right at her. Their eyes meet briefly, and then he's gone, blending into the crowd with eerie ease. Cora wonders for the first time if maybe there's more to Jack than she thinks.

He's a little impressed that the distraction worked so well. He'd anticipated a mild tussle after whispering to the Viking at the back that a Cherokee warrior had insulted his honor, and he'd been rewarded with an all-out brawl. All the better to cover his entrance into the hall. Coming through the main door wasn't the best tactic, but he's working on the fly, and not everything can be perfect. At least, that's what he keeps telling himself.

Thankfully, Cora's got eyes on Xavier; from where he's standing, the boy isn't visible. Jack mentally chastises himself for letting his charge out of his sight in the first place. While it may have been Cora's somewhat understandable reluctance to trust him that caused the gap between their arrivals, it's his duty to ensure Xavier's safety, no one else's. Only the least experienced handlers lose their charges, and he's a veteran in his field. A treacherous and too-familiar part of his mind suggests that his time away has made him soft, that his steely edge has been weakened by unnecessary emotion. If he fails to retrieve the boy and get him home...

Jack shakes his head to clear it. No use thinking about that now. He's getting close to the head of his line of warriors, and it's going to require all of his considerable willpower to make it through what comes next.

Logic dictated the statue he's chosen; it's the last in the row of idols, which puts him closest to Xavier, assuming the boy hasn't moved. The plan is deceptively simple: accept the blade, cut his hand, mime the blood sacrifice, duck behind the statue as if making to leave, collect Xavier, quietly move back to the main doors, exit into the courtyard to meet Cora. It sounds so easy that he knows it will go wrong. The only question is how.

When the dark woman in leather standing in

front of him steps up to make her dedication, Jack is relieved to see Xavier still in his hiding spot.

He can also clearly see which deity he's facing.

It's a goddess with a familiar face. The delicate carving stirs faint memories of sitting by a fireplace at the feet of an old woman, listening in rapt attention to stories about a burning country ruled by a long-forgotten people whose gods walked among them. The name floats through his mind like ash in a hot wind.

Ishtar.

Someone nearby clears their throat, and Jack sees Sister Helga looming nearby, staring at him with narrowed eyes. He isn't cowed. One of the benefits he's reaped from years of detached functioning is a thousand-yard stare that can turn blood into ice. He returns her look with equal disdain and half-smiles in victory when she blinks first. But it's never that easy when you're dealing with valkyries.

"Don't I know you?" she says in a low enough roar to be disguised in the ambient sound of the bustling hall.

Jack squares his shoulders and pulls himself to his full height, standing almost as tall as the warrior woman. Lifting his chin proudly, he declares, "You have likely heard of my conquests from the many souls I have sent here before me. My deeds are known across many lands."

Her eyes fall from his defiant face to the scars on his chest. "How came you here?"

"I perished in glorious battle," he scoffs,

gesturing meaningfully at his wounds. "Is there another path I could have taken to this realm?"

Sister Helga's eyes narrow even further, her voice lowering to rock-concert decibels. "That is a strange question for one who claims to be one of the honored dead."

What Cora sees from her spot in the high gallery is this: Jack stopped and interrogated by one of the giant, formidable women; her looking smug; him seeming deflated. Their voices are too low to hear, but the body language is clear. He's been caught.

Fuckfuckfuck.

She looks to Xavier, who's practically leaping in anticipation now that Jack's within eyesight. He keeps weaving around the base of the last statue like he's winning at hide and seek. It's only a matter of time before someone spots him and it's all over.

There's got to be something she can do. Standing by and watching the disaster unfold like she's some helpless princess in a tower is not an option. But she's not an angel or a valkyrie or warrior. What can a measly human intruder do?

Before she can even start to form a plan, the scent of bay and cinnamon hooks her attention. She'd nearly forgotten about the bundle of Jack's clothes she's holding. All of the sudden, it's all too obvious what she needs to do.

The door to the gallery slams behind her as she takes off down the hallway, pulling on the leather jacket with one hand and smoothing down her hair with the other.

Jack gauges the danger in Sister Helga's voice and opts for a modicum of deference. Better to play it straight and avoid a scene that might get Xavier discovered prematurely.

He bows his head in a show of deference. "Do you wish for me to prove my worthiness, O Chooser of the Slain?"

The valkyrie's full mouth curls in a wicked grin. "You do not have to prove anything to me, hero. You must prove yourself to your god."

A long, thin dagger is pressed into his left hand, still warm from use and wiped clean on the thigh of Sister Helga's robes. He grips the handle, certainty rising that he can't mime the ritual. The watchful valkyrie is too suspicious to let him through with anything less than full participation, including blood sacrifice and oath. There's an unsettling moment of hesitation as he wrestles with the consequences. Is it worth the price he'll pay for making the oath? Is his life worth the cost of Xavier's afterlife? But he clamps down on the doubt, gritting his teeth at the effort; he's got no right to sacrifice Xavier for his own sake. He's only failed to complete his mission on two occasions in over a decade of service. He refuses to make it three, even if he pays dearly for it later.

The blade is sharp and smooth across his right palm, opening a neat line of crimson to the air. Sister Helga's face is a strange mask of emotions

Jack doesn't quite recognize, but she nods, takes the dagger, and waves him forward.

Xavier is frantic as he approaches, and Jack does his best to signal for patience. The boy is no more than two feet from the foot of Ishtar's statue, and Jack has to resist the urge to simply scoop him up and run. Whatever danger they're in right now will only be worse if he breaks character.

"Stay," he whispers, lips not moving.

Xavier nods and crouches down.

Raising his cut hand to the already stained statue, blood oozing down his forearm, Jack can feel Sister Helga's eyes on his back. There's no faking it. All in.

"Hail, Ishtar!" he proclaims loud enough for her to hear. "You have watched over me in life and now collect my soul in death. I spill my blood for you one final time in offering. Allow me passage to your realm so that I may honor you ever after in the halls of the valiant dead among my ancestors."

He reaches out and dramatically smears his blood on the wooden face of the goddess. A flash of agonizing heat shoots through the fresh wound on contact, making him cry out in pain. He crumples halfway to the ground and tries to remove his hand from the statue but can't. Other warriors turn to stare at him – no other supplicant has been affected that way.

Just as Jack's vision starts to fill with sparks of pain, a soft voice speaks directly into his mind.

You are mine now, Jack Robert Gregory Alexander, as you have been since before you were born. Leave this place and attend to your duty knowing that I will call upon you one day to collect the service you have offered.

His hand comes free with an audible tearing sound that makes the onlookers gasp. Clutching his ruined palm to his bare chest, Jack stumbles forward, mind reeling from the goddess' touch. Sister Helga steps forward to steady him, but he waves her away, trying to conceal Xavier and hide his own weakness at the same time. Dignity quickly takes over. He straightens with some difficulty and strides around Ishtar's statue toward the exit through which other sworn warriors are disappearing.

The instant the valkyrie's gaze lifts, he darts to the corner where Xavier is waiting. Tear tracks down the boy's cheeks wipe clean as he clamps onto Jack's legs. Jack tries to avoid touching him with his bloody hand, but when he checks his palm, there's nothing there. No blood, no wound – not even a scar. All that's left is sense of impending doom.

There'll be plenty of time to ponder the onus laid on him by the goddess once they're safely away from the Hunting Hall. The trick now is to get his charge to the courtyard doors past the mob of warriors all facing their direction.

"Xavier," he whispers, "we're going to play the quiet game."

In Cora's ideal world, she'd be able to lie here in the

courtyard for hours, sunning herself by the three-tiered fountain and reading under this shady willow tree. In reality, or whatever she's currently experiencing, she's standing at the doors to the training hall, wearing Jack's leather jacket and black shirt with her hair slicked back, clutching heavy short sword she found hanging in the corridor, and psyching herself up to go in after Jack and Xavier.

It's a bad idea. She knows it's a bad idea. Everything about it screams bad idea. But it's the only one that makes a lick of sense if she wants to live up to her claim to the Mistress that she's the hero of this story. Her friends are in trouble, and she's the only one who can help them. It won't be the first time she's barged into a fight to rescue someone. She hopes Jack will appreciate it as much as Sarah did.

"Okay, Cora, this is your moment," she says to herself, taking a massive deep breath. "Let's do this before we realize we might get killed."

Choking up on the sword she doesn't know how to use, her pulse in her throat, she reaches for the door handle. But before she can close her fingers, it swings open, shoving her backwards as a tall figure rushes out. Reflexes learned from diffusing drunken brawls as a bartender impels her to spring into the attack rather than run away. She hefts the sword like a baseball bat and starts to bring it around, resigned to fighting her way into the hall, but a solid hit to her elbow easily knocks the weapon out of her hands. The following strike sends her to the ground, then there's a foot on the side of her face, pressing her head into the grass. She closes her eyes and waits for the killing blow, flashes of remorse and embarrassing high school memories taunting her with her failure. At least she can take solace knowing she died trying to do the right thing.

And then, suddenly, the pressure is released.

She rolls over to see Jack, his normally placid face wild with the fight. He's physically the same as when they parted ways in the gallery, but the grim threat coiled in him now makes her flinch. Recognition takes over, and she starts to shake as her protective adrenaline evaporates. She curses herself for being so easy to overpower. Is this what she gets for trusting an angel?

But that thought is shamefully dismissed when Cora sees his face. Her own distress is clearly mirrored there, his usual careful mask temporarily stripped away. She can see both the raw power hidden under the surface and the equally powerful fear of hurting her. It's only there for a second. Then he's closed again and retreating.

"Oh my god, Cora," he says, voice husky. "I'm so sorry. I didn't know it was you. I just reacted. I could've..."

"But you didn't."

It's a simple statement that brings him up short. An apology, forgiveness, and a subtle reminder that she's not the delicate flower he may think she is. Not forgive and forget; more acknowledge and move on. It hangs between them, diffusing the tension.

A sound slowly filters through their silence. Xavier is standing near the fountain, sobbing and terrified. Jack starts to go to him, but Cora interrupts.

"Xavier, sweetheart, be a dear and come help me up, would you?" she says, waving a hand for assistance. "Someone seems to have bruised my tailbone."

The boy eyes her warily as if trying to decide if it's safe. She smiles as sweetly as she can manage through the new aches in her body. "It's okay. Mister Jack was protecting you, and we didn't recognize each other right away. I'm sorry if we scared you."

Xavier looks to Jack for confirmation.

Under her breath, and without taking her eyes off the boy, she says to Jack, "Help me up and be really nice about it. If he doesn't trust me, I can't travel with you, and then I'm fucked."

He doesn't hesitate. They lock arms, and he hoists her gracefully to her feet. But it doesn't stop there. Cora pulls him into a light embrace, her forehead touching his collarbone. The smell of his cologne mingled with her cotton and leather puffs upwards and encircles them. He's clearly confused and still on edge, but he doesn't break away.

"What are you doing?" he whispers, wrapping his arms around her shoulders.

"Making sure Xavier doesn't think I'm scary so I don't have to leave."

"I meant with the sword and my clothes."

"Oh. Uh, I was going to rescue you."

"...really?"

"What, you think I couldn't do it?" She tightens her grip, squeezing a breath out of him before he can answer. Then she laughs and lets go. "It's cool. I'll get it right next time."

Xavier, apparently satisfied that his protectors aren't going to kill each other, runs over and attaches himself to Jack's leg. Cora smiles down at him and runs a hand over the boy's bald head. For a moment, they're a weird little family, standing in a beautiful park, happy to be together.

And then a valkyrie throws back the massive door to the training room and shouts, "THERE HE IS! AFTER HIM, GIRLS!" and they're off and running again.

TWELVE

There's only time for the briefest of directions before four broadsword-wielding women will be on top of them. Approximately sixteen seconds, Jack judges. His tactical training and logistical mind make it more time than he needs.

"Take him through there and wait for me," he says to Cora, pointing to a set of double doors on the opposite side of the courtyard.

"But..."

"Look for the exit and stay hidden. I'll meet you there."

She doesn't argue, just pulls Xavier to her side and nods her understanding. He nods back and takes off in the direction of the long hallway, valkyries close on his heels.

"DON'T LET HIM GET AWAY, GIRLS! NO MAN ESCAPES THE FATE HE'S DIED TO!"

All four warriors rush past the woman and child, completely ignoring them in hot pursuit of their quarry. Jack dodges through the doorway Cora thankfully left propped open and darts right, heading for the training hall. He's got to buy some time, and a lap or two around the high gallery before leading them into the feasting hall should do the trick. Besides, he's reasonably sure valkyrie diets aren't the sort that make for good runners. To the best of his rushed calculations, he'll easily outpace them.

Probably.

Cora and Xavier burst into the feasting hall from the courtyard, poised to dart away from more threats at any second, but they come through the side door to find the room empty. Six massive wooden tables cram the hall, each with an intricately carved chair at the head and benches down the sides. Boughs of greenery, floral wreaths, and hunting trophies decorate the walls and mantle over a fireplace the size of an SUV. Steaming platters and bowls burden every table and waft their alluring aromas through the air.

Xavier's stomach growls angrily. He tugs on her jacket, eyes fixed on the unattended banquet, and says, "Miss Cora, I'm hungry."

"Me, too, sweetie, but we need to find a good place to hide first. After that, we can snag a roll or something. Nobody'll miss that."

The boy looks like he's about to cry but keeps his

protests to himself. It seems practiced and resigned. Cora wonders how often he's been told there isn't anything for dinner. She takes him by the hand, and they cautiously start to walk toward the fireplace, hunting for a spot to conceal them.

Jack said to look for the doorway out, but unless there's a giant neon sign hanging over it, she's clueless. She even tries to push out her consciousness with her mind the way books about psychics describe, but it only makes her eyeballs hurt. Whatever minor talent she developed for spotting creatures that shouldn't exist in the real world doesn't extend to locating invisible magical portals in space-time.

Then again...

As they get closer to the ludicrously huge fireplace, the hall takes on a sense of the familiar. The carvings along the mantle's timbers, the intense heat from half trees burning, the strange horned creature mounted overhead. Like back in the Garden, she's getting the unsettling feeling that she's been here before.

The details come back in a torrent.

She's sitting at the head of a long table, eating what appears to be an entire chicken as warriors and heroes toast her good health. Her back is to the bone-warming fire after a day in the bitter cold. The feast is in full swing when she stands to give her speech, congratulations for a battle won through glorious deeds. But as she raises her goblet, someone shouts for her to duck. She looks around to see a man with a double-headed axe running directly toward her, murder in his eyes. In slow motion, he flings the weapon at her head with deadly accuracy. Her reflexes force her to duck, but she loses her balance against her chair and topples backwards into the fireplace.

Cora gasps to catch her breath at the memory of the terror of the dream. Xavier pulls his hand away and wipes her sweat off on his shirt, making a "you're gross" face. She smiles weakly, knowing it isn't very reassuring, and her eyes fix on the crackling fireplace. Could that be the doorway?

"And that's how I got here. Who knew lions could wake up so fast?"

Cora whips around to see a handful of warriors coming into the hall from the courtyard. They're talking and laughing amongst themselves as dozens more people stream in behind them. Without a word, she hustles Xavier under the nearest table to hide. The dedication ceremony must be over; it's time for the celebration banquet. Xavier whines softly, and Cora hugs him to her. Whatever Jack has planned, now would be a good time.

Excited shouts and the clatter of armored feet against bare stones brings curious faces to the porthole windows of the kitchen as Jack tears past, leading the pack of valkyries. He appears to have underestimated their endurance. What was supposed to have been a merry chase to wear them down only seems to have enraged them further.

Fortunately, he's still faster, if only by genetic

lottery. It took him longer than most boys to grow into his frame due to his height, but now his lean muscles and quick reflexes give him unusually fluid movement. As the warrior women hurl themselves and the occasional handy object in his direction, he dodges easily out of the way and continues on, which only gives them more incentive to catch up. They've been shouting assorted insults for the last five minutes. Mothers have been brought into it.

The entrance to the feasting hall is coming up quickly, and Jack has a flash of worry before hitting the doors. Any doubts he had about Cora's ability to take care of Xavier or herself are gone, but the banquet tables hold special dangers. He hopes whatever mythological knowledge she has includes the most basic of underworld rules: Don't eat or drink. That's how you end up cursed.

That's all the time he has to think about it before he bursts past the double doors into the far end of the feasting hall. He skitters to a stop, panting and hastily taking in the situation. There's a frozen moment where he's framed in the open doorway as a hundred heads turn toward him. He searches frantically in the crowd for red hair or blue eyes but comes up with nothing.

"WE'VE GOT HIM THIS TIME! CHARGE!"

Sister Helga, face flushed and blonde hair streaming, barrels directly into Jack from behind. He stumbles forward without falling, but Helga's three companions aren't far behind, and they plow forward into a pileup of breastplates and swearing. They tip his fragile balance and everyone crashes together. Jack, propelled like a bullet by the momentum, sprawls over the end of one of the long tables. An entire roasted pig tumbles to the floor with a greasy splat directly onto the feet of a group of Amazons. Jack skids past them on his sweat-slicked back, ending his ignoble entrance parked before a surprised-looking man in heavy face paint.

No one moves or speaks for several seconds. Then a whisper of steel draws Jack's attention to a man in samurai armor drawing a sword very slowly.

"Praise be to the Gods – a little entertainment before dinner!" bellows a nearby Viking.

And the battle begins.

Every man and woman in the hall erupts to their feet and draws what weapons they have. A dozen different war chants turn into a deafening roar of joy. This is the eternal paradise of the glorious slain, after all. Vikings clash axes with Scottish claymores. Arrows from Celtic longbows ping harmlessly off Zulu cowhide shields. Friends who arrived to the Hunting Hall together fight each other, then their neighbors and anyone else who feels like cracking a some heads before appetizers. Even the valkyries forget their quarry and join in, singing what sound like operatic arias as they wade into the swarm of bodies. Laughter and appreciative exclamations punctuate the air as often as the ring of metal.

Jack barely has time to catch his breath before he has to spin off the table to avoid a bone club smashing into the table where he head should've been. He lands on all fours in a sticky pile of destroyed grapes. The Maori warrior grins at him with every sign of friendliness, then moves on to engage the samurai.

Stray kicks from passing boots encourage Jack to take shelter under the table where he can take a moment to get his bearings. Not that he doesn't enjoy a good fight as much as the next guy, but he's on a deadline. Two of them, in fact.

He closes his eyes and takes a grounding breath to start feeling for the doorway. The edges of his will slowly expand into the hall. It's in here somewhere, he can tell, but it's playing hard to get. And the ham that hit him in the back hasn't helped.

Right at the point where frustration starts to dim his focus, someone calls his name.

"Jack! Over here!"

His eyes snap open.

Cora.

Her voice cuts easily through the din, landing directly in a disused part of his mind that he has no time to analyze. All that's important is finding her and Xavier and getting them out of here before something horrendous happens.

"Cora, keep talking! I'm coming!" he shouts.

He orients himself toward the sound of her voice, and starts crawling forward, careful to stick to the relative safety of the table. Shuffling feet knock over the long benches and send ruined food flying past him. Occasionally, he's forced to grab an ankle and trip someone as they try to pull him bodily into the fight. The table seems to go on forever, but Cora's voice gets steadily louder and he presses on.

Then there she is, huddled behind the oversized head chair near the fireplace, all flaming hair and freckles, calling his name and waving him forward. But there's no sign of Xavier.

Fear slaps him hard, driving the air from his lungs. The chaos of the surrounding fight juxtaposed with the intensity of such an unfamiliar emotion pushes him into panic. He spins around frantically and ignores Cora's cries to hurry. Heedless of danger, he scuttles from under the table and stands in the rout, calling the boy's name at the top of his voice.

I can't lose another one.

A dark flash in the corner of his vision pulls his head around, and Xavier comes into view. Waves of relief spill over him then freeze in his veins.

"Xavier, don't!"

The child is poised on his tiptoes at the corner of the table with a trident-like fork in one hand, reaching eagerly for a turkey leg the size of his head. His bright white grin would be cause for Jack to smile in any other circumstance; instead, he lunges forcefully at his charge, fear giving him an extra boost of speed. The food is halfway to Xavier's mouth when Jack slaps it away. Xavier stares at his empty fork for a stunned moment and then bursts into tears.

Cora appears from underneath the table as he starts to cry. She glares accusingly at Jack who scoops up the boy to comfort him.

"What the hell did you do that for?!" she shouts

over the din. "He's just hungry!"

Jack shouts back, "He only thinks he is! You can't eat anything here!"

"Why not?!"

"We don't have time – "

The sheer horror that suddenly appears on Cora's face makes him lose his train of thought. What did he do to deserve that? By the time he realizes she's looking over his shoulder, things are already happening.

Cora's small hands snatch a gravy boat big enough to bathe a dog off the table. Jack barely hears her yell "duck!" before he's doing it, clamping Xavier tighter to his chest. Thick clouds of steam rise off the liquid as she hefts it high over his head in a shining brown ribbon. There's a terrific scream in Greek and a heavy thud as a double-headed axe falls to the floor behind Jack. Cora drops the empty tureen and shouts "move!" as she slides back into the relative safety of the underside of the table. He immediately follows suit.

"See?" Cora says between breaths. She flashes Jack a satisfied grin. "Told you I'd get it right next time."

Despite the crying child prodding him in the ribs with a fork, he can't help but give a small chuckle. "I'd say so."

"Good. Now we're square." She surveys the hundreds of feet stomping and running around them. "I think it's about time we got out of here, don't you?"

Jack's brow furrows. "The door's nearby, but I

can't concentrate long enough to find it with all this chaos."

"Shit, really? I thought you had some kind of divine GPS to find them."

He shakes his head, annoyed at himself, and absentmindedly pats Xavier's back. The boy's calming down, which helps, but it's not enough to let him focus the way he needs to. A hubcap-sized platter of meat pies splashes to the floor nearby as if to underscore the insanity of the situation.

"Have you tried looking for the door yourself?" he asks.

Cora huffs. "Yeah, but I'm not magic. I don't know what to look for." She hesitates for a moment, considering something. "But I did have this dream once that went an awful lot like this. Almost threw myself out of bed after I fell into the fire."

He narrows his eyes at her. A dreamer? It could be possible, but why didn't they know about her before now?

"Is that bad?" she asks.

The concern in her face brings him back to the present. "No," he says without further explanation. "I need to try again. I think you're on to something. Can you take him?"

Xavier, still clutching his fork defiantly, is shuffled into Cora's lap. Jack closes his eyes and guides his consciousness toward the fireplace. The door reveals itself almost instantly – directly in the heart of the blaze.

"Shit."

Cora covers Xavier's ears and shoots Jack a dirty

look. "Hey, language."

He points at the fire. "You were right. It's in there."

"Shit," says Cora.

"Shit!" says Xavier, laughing.

Cora grimaces and drops her hands. "Do you think we can make it before someone sees us?"

"That's not the problem," Jack says slowly. "Someone will definitely see us, but there's a forty-three percent chance I'm interrupted before the portal's fully open."

"What happens then?"

He ticks off the three options on his long fingers. "We could lose the connection and be consumed by the fire. Or we could be stuck between worlds forever. Or we could make it through safely."

The color drains out of Cora's ruddy cheeks. "Isn't there anything we can do to make it safer?"

"No."

But even as he says it, there's a thought rising up to negate it. It's only a story, something he read a long time ago in a dusty book given to him by his mentor. He watches Cora sweltering in his clothes as she talks quietly with Xavier. They're both relying on him, trusting that he knows what's right. He's got to try. The carryalong worked fine; perhaps his luck will carry over to an even riskier move.

"There's one thing we can try," he says slowly. Cora looks up at him with hope written in her face clear enough that even he can see it. "It hasn't been done in living memory, but the logic is sound. It'll substantially decrease the chances of interruption."

There's a loud twang of reverberating steel as a machete embeds itself into the floorboards mere inches from Jack's knee.

"Let's do it," Cora says firmly.

Jack nods and scoots out from underneath the table. The three of them stay huddled close together, dodging people and projectiles as they cross the dozen yards to the hearth. Xavier's hoisted into Jack's arms, and he offers his free hand to Cora.

"Aren't you going to trace the outline?" she says, barely audible in the crowded air.

He shakes his head. "It's a one-step jump." He offers his hand again.

"OH, NO YOU DON'T! I SEE YOU THERE, OATH BREAKER!"

The sound of Sister Helga's booming seals it. Cora slaps her palm into Jack's.

"I need you to concentrate," he says, holding her gaze. "Take the energy from your fear and push it through your hand into mine. That's how we're going to get out of here."

"I don't know how to do that."

"YOU'VE MADE A MOCKERY OF THIS PLACE! YOU WILL BE HELD TO ACCOUNT!"

"Yes, you do." He squeezes her hand in what he hopes is a convincing way.

Uncertain eyes search his face, but she nods and squeezes back.

"KARA, BRUNHILDA! TO THE FIRE! DON'T LET HIM SLIP AWAY AGAIN!"

"On my count."

Cora grips his hand so hard his bones grind together. He winces but almost immediately feels blue sparks of electricity rocketing through his skin. Of course she could do it.

"One..."

The floorboards beneath their feet rock as two valkyries storm toward them through the mass of fighters.

"Two..."

Jack closes his eyes and takes a deep breath. His will, strengthened by Cora's donated energy, sweeps around them in a protective bubble. It's not much, but it'll have to hold.

"WE'VE GOT YOU NOW!"

"Three!"

In perfect concert, they leap into the fireplace. Flames lick their clothes and hair, trying to find purchase on such willing prey. A cerulean burst of energy erupts from their clasped hands as Jack drains their joint reserve of power and opens the portal at the apex of their jump. Surprised exclamations from the feasting hall follow them into the darkness as they disappear, heading wherever this new door might lead.

THIRTEEN

Eyelids like tomb slabs inch open to let in a sliver of light. The chilly, sparse room is lit by electric bulbs, the blinds on the windows down against the night and patter of summer rain. Someone is singing quietly.

> The faeries changed him in her arms,
> a burning coal of fire,
> but Janet held him to her breast
> to be her heart's desire.

Daddy?

She tries to speak, but nothing comes out. With titanic effort, she turns her head. And there he is, his face strained and wet with tears. He seems so much smaller than she remembers. The bigness of his presence has been sucked out of him somehow. She wills her voice to make a sound, any sound that will comfort him.

The faeries changed him in her arms,
 a wolf and then a snake,
but Janet held him to her breast,
all for her true love's sake.

It's okay, Daddy. Look, I'm right here.
But he doesn't hear. When the song ends, he starts again.

It's the raging headache that wakes her up, a cross between a red-wine hangover and allergies. Cora moans and leans over to roll out of bed in desperate need of a shower, a cup of black coffee, and a fried-egg sandwich. But instead of the squishy futon, her hands and feet only find hard dirt. Turns out she's not at home after all.

Strangely, this doesn't bother her. She reaches out and runs her hands sensuously over the ground with her eyes closed. The grass is lush and thick – almost a better mattress than her usual bed – and it soothes her tense muscles, all her fear and stress seeping into the earth. Even the energy-drain headache is already dissipating. No one's chasing her. No one's asking her to do the impossible. No one's even talking to her. For the first time in what seems like years, she's safe. Relaxed. Calm. Taking a deep breath of fresh air, she feels like she could rest here forever.

Too bad it can't last.

Steady, metallic creaking floats to her ears, filling her imagination with mace-swinging valkyries waiting for her to move wrong. Survival barges its way back into the driver's seat and throws her to her feet.

There aren't any valkyries, but she is standing woozily in the most beautiful garden she's ever seen. She turns in a slow circle, eyes wide, taking it all in. It's nothing she's ever dreamed but somehow it's everything she'd love to plant if she didn't have a black thumb. Well-tended rose bushes line the front yard's dark-stained wooden fence, interspersed with low beds of daisies. Blossoms from fruit trees litter the side yard like confetti. Fat lilacs flank the wide steps up to the two-story brick house.

Where a little black boy with startling blue eyes is playing happily on a wooden porch swing, the chains creaking in time to his kicks.

Xavier.

The jolt of remembering ratchets up her headache to a dull roar. She pinches her temples and starts to call him when she remembers her other traveling companion.

Where's Jack?

Her eyes dart around frantically. There's the house, the garden, and a toolshed but no sign of another person. A sensible voice under the mounting worry reminds her to look down. She does.

Jack is sprawled maybe three feet from where she lay a moment ago. She feels a little stupid; she could have reached out and taken his hand.

But he's not moving. Is he even breathing?

Cora drops to her knees beside him, wishing she'd taken CPR training when she'd had the chance. She hesitates for a moment, then presses a hand to his still-bare chest. There's the faintest of movements, the barest of heartbeats. She releases a breath she didn't realize she'd been holding. He's alive. Passed out and probably drained but alive.

"Xavier," she calls out over her shoulder. "Come help me."

There's a clatter and creak followed by the staccato thumps of short legs running down the pathway toward her.

"Did you see anybody while you were playing?" she asks. The last thing she needs right now is some angry troll or banshee or faerie on their case. She's confident she can get herself and Xavier to safety but an unconscious full-grown man is another story.

"Nope. Nobody's home."

Whew. "Okay, good. Hopefully, it'll stay that way."

Xavier goes around to Jack's other side and eyeballs him curiously. "Why's Mister Jack still sleeping?"

Her brow furrows. "I don't know. But we should probably get him inside." She leans down to double-check his breathing. It sounds shallow but regular. To Xavier, she says, "I'm going to try to wake him up, okay? He might be upset or scared, so be ready."

"Okay," he says, taking a step back.

There are a dozen things she could do to rouse

him. A shout. A slap in the face. A light shake. A poke in the ribs. A splash of cold water from the creek she can hear nearby. Gently running the back of her hand along his cheek isn't something she would've put on that list. But it's what she does.

Jack stirs. Cora stretches her fingers and cradles his head in her hand. "Hey," she whispers. "It's me. You still in there?"

In response, he leans into her palm and whispers back. "I'm still here."

A sigh of relief. She gestures with her other hand for Xavier to come over. The boy trundles back warily and plops down at Jack's shoulder.

"You okay, Mister Jack?"

He turns his head to face Xavier. "Yeah. I'll be okay. Just tired, that's all."

The smile he gives the boy tells Cora that Jack may be awake, but he's not totally alright. When his eyes turn up to her, she's acutely aware of the affectionate nature of her position. She pulls her hand away from his face as a blush rises at her throat. What made her do that in the first place? Talk about being too intimate.

"Let's get you up," she says, forcing casualness into her voice. "Xavier, take his other arm."

Working together, the two of them help Jack up to sitting. Cora peels off the brown leather jacket she's been wearing and gingerly drapes it over Jack's shoulders. He takes a moment to get his bearings, and then Cora pulls him fully to his feet.

"You sure you're okay?" she asks.

His eyes don't quite focus on her when he says,

"I'm always okay."

"Sure you are."

He doesn't protest when she wraps an arm around his middle and throws one of his arms over her shoulders. They move slowly up the pathway to the house together as Xavier runs ahead.

"Is anyone inside?" Jack asks, warily surveying the building.

"Xavier says there isn't. That's good enough for me right now."

He stands a little straighter and tries to shake her grip. "I should go in first to investigate." But he winces and leans heavily against her again.

She can't think of anything to say that wouldn't sound accidentally patronizing, so she keeps her mouth shut. Whatever nasty magical headache Cora woke up with must be ten times worse for him.

They take the stairs one at a time up to the front door. Xavier tries the handle, and it pushes open easily. While that's not unusual where Cora's from, an unlocked, seemingly-abandoned house in the underworld has infinite potential to be a literal trap from hell. And after the way Jack reacted to Xavier's shenanigans in the Hunting Hall, she's on high alert.

But there aren't any monsters or vengeful spirits in the living room as far as she can tell. It's mostly exposed brick, unfinished timbers, and stuffed bookshelves. There is, however, an oversized sofa that seems like an ideal place for Jack to rest. She helps him to it, and he sinks gratefully into the cushions.

"Xavier, stay here with Mister Jack," she says in a low voice. "I'm going to look around to make sure we're the only ones here." Jack's face contorts with concern, but she heads him off. "I'll holler if anything happens, and then you can come running in to save the day. Until then, stay put. I'll be right back."

The living room takes up the entire front half of the house with two doors leading further in. Ignoring Jack's muffled protests, she slips through the right-hand door into what turns out to be the kitchen.

And what a kitchen. Like the garden, it seems to have been designed by syphoning ideas from imaginary blueprints of Cora's dream house. The mix of ultra-modern appliances and bohemian decor is messy but somehow works. A quick listen and look tells her there's no one in the immediate vicinity, and she takes a moment to snoop. Glass-fronted cabinets reveal heavy ceramics and fine crystal. Cast iron and copper-bottomed pots and pans hang over a butcher's block island in the center of the room. Drawers boast elegant flatware, hand-carved utensils, and a complete absence of Tupperware.

When she opens the campy seventies-style fridge, she's surprised to find it fully stocked with her favorite things. She reaches in to nab a handful of sour cherries but carefully puts them back as she remembers Jack's vehement warning about food. The story of Persephone drifts through her memory to back him up. But while she can pretend she's not hungry for a long time – practice with the depression diet comes in handy sometimes – thirst is something else. The pitcher of lavender lemonade is calling her name. Surely one glass can't hurt.

She's already set three tall drinking glasses on the counter before the reasonable voice in the back of her mind speaks up.

Maybe you should check the rest of the house before you get settled in.

Fine.

Cora takes a quick peek out of the picture windows overlooking the backyard, where the creek runs through the property, then pops through the door at the side of the kitchen into a wide corridor. Three more doors reveal a small bathroom done in all black, a storage room filled with unmarked cardboard boxes, and another entrance to the living room. When she pokes her head through the latter door, Jack half-rises in expectation, but she smiles and waves him off.

"So far, so good," she says. "I'll scope out the upstairs just to be safe, but the place seems pretty perfect."

She ducks back into the hall before he can argue and heads up the cherry-varnished stairs to the second floor.

The first floor was something; the second practically has her in tears. The art hanging in the hallway is all chaotic collages and framed poetry. The library is floor-to-ceiling shelves groaning with books. The studio is a treasure trove of art supplies. All the details she's designed a hundred times in her mind as little oases of pleasure are here.

But it's the bedrooms that do her in.

Where the living room encompasses the entire front of the house on the lower level, the master suite does the same on the second floor. There's hand-carved furniture, a walk-in closet the size of her room back home, and a bathtub deep and wide enough to accommodate two people. Everything is decorated in rich shades of crimson, silver, and mahogany. Peeking through the door, Cora's heart flutters with the thought of rolling in the luxurious covers of the four-poster bed with someone who can't get enough of her.

She has to forcefully remind herself of her companions waiting downstairs to tear away from such a gorgeous sight. However, that resolve totally evaporates when she discovers the completely decorated child's room across the hall. She's never allowed herself to admit any desire for children, even to herself, but this is exactly the room she's secretly fantasized her someday-son would inhabit. Her hand shakes on the doorknob as tears sting her eyes. Only sheer stubbornness enables her to drag herself from the doorway. The door closes with a soft click, and she leans heavily against the exposed brick of the corridor to catch her breath.

She's never been here, not even in a dream. That much she knows for sure. But every shade of paint, every piece of furniture, every design choice has been plucked from the quiet recesses of her mind. It's like walking through a floor plan she hasn't drawn but always hoped would be real someday.

Decades of her waking imagination created it – the perfect home, tailored to her whims.

Cora's never believed in any of the traditional afterlife options, but if living in this house for eternity turns out to be a choice, this is exactly where she wants to end up when she dies.

But that's not today.

The thought burns icicles into her mind, making her shiver. She scurries back down to the kitchen, away from the unspoken wishes lingering upstairs.

When she returns to the living room, Cora's carrying three tumblers of the lavender lemonade from the sumptuously-stocked fridge. Xavier bounces over to greet her; Jack pulls himself upright, now marginally less haggard than when they arrived.

"I know we're not supposed to eat, but I figured we could probably all use a drink." She casts a dramatic look at Jack as she gives him a glass. "Unless you want to smack these out of my hands, too."

The look he gives her in return is somewhere between unfocused annoyance and distracted thought. "It should be fine," he says. A trace of doubt lurks in his voice, but she doesn't push it. It seems ridiculous that they'd have to go without food *and* drink.

Cora plops down on the opposite end of the long, blue couch, and Xavier climbs up between them, little legs sticking straight off the cushions. Silence, comfortable and calm, pools around the three of them as they sip their drinks. The sun has started to set outside, casting delicate pink and orange light into the living room. Cora watches the shadows lengthen and distantly wonders how long they've all been running. It feels like years since they left the Garden. She glances at Jack, who's staring thoughtfully into his empty glass as he rolls it between his palms. She looks to Xavier, his eyelids heavy, about to dump lemonade into his own lap. It's enough to provoke a huge yawn, the need for sleep settling over her like a down comforter.

"Maybe we should get some rest," she suggests. "All the bedrooms are upstairs, and we can lock up down here. Should be safe enough for a few hours. We can get a fresh start in the morning."

Jack casts a glance around the room. It's gotten dark enough that she can't read his expression, but if she had to guess, he's calculating risk percentages or danger probabilities. Subtle as a brick, this one.

Eventually he says, "It should be sufficiently secure for four to six hours. However, the natives will be able to scent our location well before that. One of us should stay on the first floor in case of a breach."

He gets resolutely to his feet, stands there momentarily, then wobbles and sits back down. Cora puts a hand to her mouth to muffle an escaping giggle. It's cruel to laugh after he's been so weakened by the experimental jump, but you don't get to see an angel off his game very often.

"Let me get Xavier to bed," she offers, "then I'll come back and not help you whatsoever to get up there yourself. I'll sleep on the couch to keep watch, if that makes you feel any better."

Cora stands and scoops up Xavier, handing off his glass to the grumbling Jack and carrying the boy upstairs.

It's easy enough to get him tucked into the child's bed. He hardly weighs anything. She eases him under the train-motif covers fully clothed and flicks off the overhead light. The door's almost closed behind her when there's a rustle from the bed.

"Miss Cora?"

"Yes, sweetie?"

"I got you a present."

"Oh, really?" She crosses back and sits on the edge of the small mattress. "You didn't have to do that."

Xavier wordlessly produces the ugly fork he picked up from the feasting table in the Hunting Hall. Pride shines from his face as he hands it to her.

She takes it carefully and turns it over in the blue glow of the nightlight. It's a rustic design, maybe four inches long with three iron trident points like something you'd use to toss hay. Had she come across it herself, she'd have thrown it away as a piece of junk, but as a gift from this beautiful boy, it's a treasure.

"Thank you, little man," she coos. "It's awesome."

"You can use it to chase away bad guys." His voice is already drifting easily back into sleep and soon his blue eyes are hidden again.

Cora leans over and kisses him on the forehead, pausing for a moment to let the scene sink in. Her heart swells to be there. She sighs happily, then slips the fork into the pocket of her jeans. Easing the door shut behind her, she heads back downstairs to fetch the other man in her life.

FOURTEEN

"This would be way easier if you'd let me help you."

"I'm perfectly capable of doing it myself."

"Whatever you say, dude. I can't promise I won't laugh when you fall."

Jack's refusal to accept Cora's arm has made his move from the couch, up the stairs, and into the master suite take twice as long as it should, but she lets him win this one. While she may feel fine after a little downtime, he still seems to be fighting to stay conscious. A clenched jaw, hyper-focused eyes, and the occasional deep breath are what he lets her see; she can only imagine what he's dealing with that doesn't show.

Cora darts ahead of him and turns down the bed. The green paisley summer linens are freshly laid out, but she smoothes them anyway. As she fluffs the pillows, she notices that she's nervous, which strikes her as odd, but she shakes it off. Not like she's planning to do anything untoward here. Sure, they've bonded over Xavier and being in mortal peril and even had a knock-down fight. But still. Getting involved with an angel would be weird, right?

Jack clears his throat behind her. She starts and turns to face him with an overenthusiastically fluffed pillow in one hand and her ears turning pink. It's the first time she's really had a chance to look at him – a moment free of danger and running. He's paused to lean against the doorjamb, his spare frame strong despite obvious exhaustion. Dark eyes and hair give him the air of a brooding philosopher, and Cora wonders what he's thinking as he looks at her. Her eyes trail down to the dark scars on his chest just visible under the open leather jacket. She imagines what they would feel like against her skin.

"You're staring," he says simply.

The blush creeps further up her ears, and she averts her eyes quickly. "Sorry. Must be all that divine radiance."

He doesn't smile although it seems like he wants to. What he does do is straighten and take three long strides over to the plush throw rug at the side of the bed. There's uncharacteristic warmth in his face that Cora doubts he means for her to see. On the other hand, she hasn't known him to do anything without express purpose. Maybe this is what he's like when he's not on duty. Maybe it's exhaustion. Maybe it's her.

She shoves down her curiosity before it gallops

away with her and moves to the far side of the room to give him some privacy as gets ready for bed.

"How's Xavier?" he asks from behind her.

"All tucked in. Drifted off faster than I could've under the circumstances."

A boot hits the hardwood floor. "He's a resilient kid."

Cora nods and runs her hands over the massive cherry wood dresser, admiring the craftsmanship. Photographs in matching silver frames line the top but none of them show people; they're all vaguely familiar landscapes. You'd think whoever lived here would keep family photos or something.

A thought occurs.

"Hey," she says. "How did you get saddled with this kid-escorting gig, anyway? I get the impression you're not exactly low angel on the totem pole. Were all the newbies on vacation or something when it came up?"

"Not quite. In a rare case like Xavier's, the roster of escorts capable of using the interworld doors is extremely short."

"How short?"

"One."

Cora almost turns around to ask why that is, but the sound of his other boot hitting the floor reminds her to keep her eyes forward. Not that she's a prude; more that she gets the feeling he is. She absently pulls out the top drawer as she waits for him to finish undressing and finds it divided between the sort of practical underthings she's familiar with and the fanciful lingerie she would never admit to drooling over in magazines. This does nothing to ease her earlier sense of awkward excitement, and she shoves the drawer home.

When she turns to check Jack's progress, he's climbing into bed fully clothed. She stops him short.

"Oh no you don't. Whatever you did in that jump wrecked you, at least temporarily. You need some real sleep." She steps to the bedside, hands on her hips the way her mother stands when asserting her authority. "Either get your clothes off or I'll strip you myself."

The accidental entendre thickens the air between them. Cora freezes in wide-eyed embarrassment, willing herself to disappear, and she braces for a detached or sarcastic response, a clear rejection of something she didn't intend to offer.

But Jack laughs. It's a genuine laugh that reaches every part of his face and diffuses the tension instantly. It's a strange sound coming from him, like the baritone ring of a bronze bell coming from a fax machine. It's infectious for its rarity, and Cora can't help laughing, too.

"Well, then, Miss Riley," he says, smile still on his face, "given my current reduced state, I may have no choice but to ask for your assistance."

She squints at him. "Are you making fun of me?"

"Certainly not. Have I made a single joke since we met?" His dark eyes sparkle with what Cora can only interpret as amusement.

"...did you just make a joke about not making jokes?"

Jack laughs again, a deeper, softer sound this time. Then he stands, holds out his arms and waits, looking for all the world like a clean-cut punk scarecrow.

She wants to pass out. Between her surely dangerous heart rate, the shakiness of her knees, and the breakneck speed of her thoughts, she can feel her whole system trying to shut down.

We can't take much more sexual tension, Captain! We need more sanity!

Indecision calls up her reasonable voice, but it comes from far away through rose-colored fog.

This is crazy, right? Am I falling for someone I barely know? Am I even ready for this kind of thing? Is it a trap - an underworld trick designed to make me forget my quest? Do I care?

Jack studies her face but doesn't say anything. His arms are still out wide in a purposely-vulnerable pose that makes Cora's resistance soften further. It's a question, an offer – not a demand. If this is a trap, she reasons, whatever is going to happen would've happened already in a flurry of action and reaction like everything else since the moment they met. He wouldn't be standing and waiting like this.

She thinks about the house. About how perfect it is. About the comfort and safety of this place. About the way Xavier looks while he's sleeping. About how lonely it would be to lie in the four-poster all alone. She takes a deep breath to calm her pulse, but the scent of foreign spices and oiled leather so close makes her shiver.

Cora decides.

She steps forward and slides both hands under the open edges of Jack's coat. Radiating heat from his skin presses against her insistently. She eases the jacket down over his shoulders. It drops to the floor next to his boots, leaving him with nothing but his khaki pants. He looks down at her, over a full head taller than she, but Cora doesn't meet his gaze. Her hands move to the exposed scars that bisect his chest, her fingers delicately tracing their path from collarbone to bottom ribs. Something awful must've happened to him, but she doesn't ask. She simply touches in thoughtful silence, feeling the hammering of his heart matching her own.

When she does summon the courage to lift her chin, the expression on his face startles her. He's always so carefully guarded, a constant vigil against his own emotions. He probably thinks she hasn't noticed. She doesn't know where the struggle came from or why it's so important, but here in this moment, he's lost the fight. There's an open mix of desire and tenderness and curiosity lighting up his cautious smile.

Cora's reasonable voice tries to point out that she may not be the only one affected by the perfectness of the house, but she strangles it into silence. This is not the time for reason.

Especially not as Jack takes hold of the hem of her shirt. His shirt. "I believe this still counts as my clothes," he says. There's a question there, an unspoken request for permission.

She nods.

Slowly, too slowly for Cora's taste, he lifts the black T-shirt and peels it away, dropping it on top of the growing pile of discarded clothes. He brushes against the white Oxford shirt underneath, the one of Jeremy's that she wears to remind herself of what she's lost, and she holds her breath. Then, one deliberate button at a time, he opens the shirt to reveal ever more of her pale, freckled skin. Ancient pressures evaporate as it loosens, like he's releasing her from a straightjacket. There isn't anything to grieve anymore; it's time to stop carrying around her lost love and her lost life and move forward. Every nerve ending in her body tingles with sweet anticipation as the last button's undone.

But her reasonable voice makes one last desperate play before he can slip the shirt from her shoulders, and she gently stops his hands.

"Are you sure this is okay?" she asks. The words come as easily as breathing underwater. "I wouldn't want you to get in trouble with your divine supervisors or anything." *Or hurt me. Or leave me. Or trap me.*

He raises a hand to her face and strokes her cheek with his thumb. She can't help leaning into it. "There's nothing to worry about from me. I know my mind," he says, voice reassuring and steady. "But if you have doubts..."

The kiss is happening before Cora realizes she's moved. She has to push herself up on her toes, but she connects with enough force to rock him back on his heels. He tastes of pomegranates and saffron. Surprised only for a second, Jack steadies himself by throwing both arms around her waist and kissing back with a hunger of his own, pushing her shirt to the floor. They stand locked together at the bedside, pressing urgently against one another, the slow beginning quickening to a fever pitch. Hands finally allowed to roam free run through hair and across bared skin, fumbling with buttons and zippers and laces, as much as can be undone without breaking apart.

Jack is the first to come up for air. He smiles at her, eyes shining, and presses his forehead to hers. They breathe deeply as one person, riding the waves of shared desire as if they have all the time in the world.

Time.

The icy thought slices through Cora's hot mind. She tenses under his hands, and Jack pulls away with a concerned expression.

"What's wrong?" he asks. "Do you want to stop?" The hoarseness of his voice does nothing to hide his disappointment.

"No, I..." She sighs. "I'm worried we're running out of time."

He nods and trails his hand along her bare shoulder, making her tremble. "I don't want to sabotage your quest with my foolish desires," he says. He kisses the top of her head and whispers into her hair, "Tell me if you want me to let go. You deserve to have your second chance at a happy life."

She closes her eyes to relish the lovely, strange sensation of him against her skin that's burying the cries of her rational voice screaming about deadlines and distractions.

"Maybe this is my second chance," she says.

And then she's pushing him backwards into the thick mattress and peppering kisses over his face, his neck, his chest. He puts up token resistance and even that melts away when she slides her hand over the raised mark on his lower back. The resulting tremor and gasp pushes them both over the edge of reason, and she forgets her protests.

The last vestiges of their clothing fall to the floor unnoticed. All that matters now is skin and hands and lips and sweat.

FIFTEEN

Thin sunlight filters in through the crimson curtains and washes over the tangled nest of sheets. Jack's inner clock tells him it's 6:17 am. He's been half-awake since the first hint of dawn and is trying to hang on to pieces of the dream he'd been having. Something about a sharp suit and the number 97, then a blue-skinned woman chasing him through a forest, then a clock with spinning hands. It's all running together and slipping away the more he rises into wakefulness. Soon it's gone, leaving behind nothing except a vague sense of unease.

Cora murmurs in a dream of her own. They've drifted apart in the night, and Jack slides an arm around her waist and pulls himself against her back. The warmth of her skin against his both tempts him to drift back into sleep and to wake her. He chooses instead to take a rare moment to enjoy just being here. He buries his face in her mussed ginger hair and breathes her in. Cotton, leather, blueness, the faintest hint of exotic spices - their mingled scents make his heart swell.

But his ever-active mind only allows him a handful of empty seconds before it starts to spin.

The last time he let someone get under his skin this way, he'd been a much younger man. Certainly a much different man. That romance disintegrated in spectacular fashion, requiring months of physical, mental, and emotional recuperation that left him scarred in more ways than one. "Enchanting" isn't just a synonym for a pretty face sometimes. He swore off intimate entanglements after that. Maybe that's why it was so simple to shut down when the time came; without passion or affection, all his other emotions deflated easily. It worked so well that he didn't miss them.

Until her.

Somehow she's cracked his carefully built shell. His breakdown last autumn began the excruciating process of stripping away his defenses against his own humanity; her kiss marked the glorious, successful end to the work. It's both disturbing and a relief. Now there's no reason to keep leaning into his old persona, the one ruled solely by logic and duty. The question is how to go forward from here.

Cora stirs. It occurs to Jack in a distant way that there's something he should be doing besides lazing in bed with a beautiful woman, but then she rolls over to face him with a smile, hooking a leg over his and drawing them closer together. It's more than enough to silence his wandering thoughts.

"Hey," she says sleepily. "I wondered if you'd still be here when I woke up. Thought it might have all been a dream."

He rests his forehead against hers. "I'm afraid you're stuck with me."

"Oh no, whatever shall I do?" she says in a mocking, damsel-in-distress tone.

She grins and raises her face to catch his mouth in a kiss that ignores the perils of morning breath. He returns it with equal enthusiasm. Their hands begin to roam beneath the paisley sheets, tracing the edges of one another in growing familiarity. The promise of a repeat of last night's adventure hovers between them. He presses himself to her and is rewarded with a soft, encouraging gasp.

But when her hands shift to the small of his back, Jack can't keep himself from squirming. Cora studies him for a moment, then deliberately runs a finger over the raised tattoo there. She laughs sadistically when he fails to suppress a shudder.

"What's that all about?" she asks.

He grits his teeth against the sensation so pleasurable it borders on painful, trying to keep his breath even. "What's what all about?" he tries. Maybe if he denies it the question will go away.

It doesn't.

"The tattoo? On your back? The," she strokes it again and smirks, "interesting reaction you have?"

The second wave threatens to push him over a wild sensory edge, but Jack grabs her hand with deliberate control and gently moves it back between them. He pours his excess energy into another kiss, biting her lip playfully, taking both her hands in both of his. It's as much a gesture of self-defense as tenderness. Curiosity still shines in her eyes, though, so he has to say something.

"It's just sensitive, that's all," he says lamely. "Call it my soft spot."

His chest tightens even as the words come out. There's more to it than that, isn't there? He's had the green triskelion for nearly a decade; it's significant, a milestone, but for some reason he can't recall when or why or how he got it. His logical mind is rankled by the dissonance of knowing he should know and not being able to remember. It feels vital that he tell her the story. Where's the memory?

Cora doesn't seem to notice his internal struggle, however; she simply shrugs and lays her head in the hollow of his shoulder. As he gazes down at her, feeling the comfort of her presence wrapped in his arms, the urgency of trying to remember melts like ice in hot coffee. There's no rush; it'll come to him eventually. He settles onto his back with her against his chest and squeezes her reassuringly.

"So, what now, Mister Angel Man?" she asks, mischief in her eyes.

He gives her a quick kiss on top of her head and says, "I'm sure we can think of something. Though I imagine Xavier will be waking up soon."

Cora pouts. "Damn kids. Always ruining my fun."

"Don't blame him. We'll just have to make up for it later." He grins and nips the top of her ear .

"You are *so* going to pay for that," she murmurs.

"I intend to."

She pulls him down and kisses him with a ferocity that makes him regret the lack of time, then scuttles out of bed, giggling her way toward the shower.

Jack stretches his long limbs and sprawls across the mattress like a Persian cat after a big meal. There's nothing he needs to do, nowhere he needs to be, no one he needs to please except himself. And Cora, of course. While emotion has managed to reassert itself into his life, this contented stillness is particularly foreign. He distantly wonders if he's ever had it before or if he's always denied it could exist. The kiss Cora plants on him as she goes to check on Xavier convinces him it's the latter.

The door closes behind her with a soft click, and he's alone in the bedroom.

Jack realizes that apart from a bleary half hour in the living room last night, he hasn't had a chance to investigate the house properly yet. He stands and walks the room without bothering to dress. The place is comfortable and inviting enough with its large windows and wood furniture, and Cora seems to feel right at home. But now that he's poking around, the meticulous, highly trained part of his mind says something's off. He flips back and forth between feeling like he's prying and knowing there's something he needs to see.

It's the picture that draws his attention. It's a modestly framed photograph in the center of the collection on top of the dresser. Most are standard vacation fare of smiling strangers on a beach or crowded together in a living room, but this one stands out. He picks it up in both hands and stares.

A smiling family stands in front of a large house. The woman looks up lovingly at the man, his arm around her shoulders, and their son sticks out his tongue at the camera. The short woman with red hair. The thin man with tan skin. The dark boy with blue eyes. The house with lilacs and rose bushes in front.

Crushing understanding followed by a wave of guilty nausea nearly makes him drop the picture. He should have seen the signs, been stronger than this, taken more care. Questions and possibilities rush to suffocate him, but he rallies quickly, pulling himself together with speed born of experience. He replaces the photo, then tugs on his rumpled clothes before rushing down the hallway. There's no time to lose.

She's facing the stove as he enters the kitchen, and Xavier is perched on a tall stool at the center island, kicking his feet impatiently.

"Cora...," Jack begins, keeping his voice level to avoid spooking her. He can't be sure what will happen if she panics.

She turns around, a spatula in one hand and a frying pan in the other, and beams at him. "Hey! You're just in time for pancakes. Pull up a chair, and I'll get you a plate."

He silently takes the empty stool next to Xavier as she dishes up the boy's breakfast. Now that he's looking for them, he can see gossamer strands of energy connecting Cora to the house like a spider web. They anchor her to the floor, the ceiling, the furniture. Neither she nor Xavier seem to be aware of the threads, and Jack fears it might be too late for him to intervene.

"Cora, I need to tell you something."

"What's that?" she says, going back to the stove.

As soon as her back is turned, Jack moves the plate of pancakes out of Xavier's reach. He starts to protest, but Jack puts a finger to his lips for silence and the boy thankfully obeys. This is going to be hard enough without tying Xavier to the house, too.

"Can you turn off the stove for a moment?" Jack says to Cora. "It's important."

The concern in her face as she turns to face him tears at his determination. He folds his hands and grips them together tightly, anything to alleviate the discomfort of upsetting her. He can see there's going to be no easy way to explain the situation. Best to dive right in and deal with the consequences.

"I think we've accidentally stumbled into your heaven," he explains. "This is where you're meant to be. The house is trying to absorb you by using your belief. If we're to continue on our missions, we have to leave here as soon as we can, before it's not possible to leave at all."

Gray eyes stare in confused silence. Jack waits for the information to sink in, praying that whatever lucid part of her remains can hear him. He's not prepared for what she says.

"What are you talking about, 'missions'?"

His hope slips, but he keeps trying. "We've been working together to get through the worlds of the doorfield. You're looking for Door Thirteen so you can win your second chance; I'm escorting Xavier to his proper heaven." He glances at the large clock over the sink. "And we're both running out of time."

"A second chance at what?" She gestures around the kitchen. "This is the home I've always dreamed of. It's absolutely perfect. Why would I leave?"

"That's the problem, don't you see? It's *too* perfect. It's designed that way." He stands and rounds the island to her side, his voice taking on an edge of urgency. "This is an incredibly rare afterlife, Cora. I've never been here before. I couldn't see what was happening. What it did to you." He hesitates. "And to me."

She takes a step back, hurt blooming in her cheeks. "So, what happened last night...?"

"It's complicated. There's something here, but I can't say how much is real and how much is the house until we get away from it."

He tries to take her hand, to reassure her that it's not like that, but she pulls away, her expression changing from confusion to angry disbelief.

"'Something'? Is that all?" She backs up another step, widening the gap between them. "This is our *home*, Jack. We're a family – you and me and Xavier." She points to the boy staring at them with scared eyes over his plate of untouched pancakes.

"Xavier and I don't belong here," Jack says, "We're not affected by the house the same way you are."

A fat tear leaps down her right cheek. "Why would you say that? Don't you want us to be together?"

Jack sighs bitterly, forcing down the building desire to give in, to stay here forever as an integral part of Cora's afterlife even if it means he never goes back to the real world. He can feel the house attacking his resistance, reminding him of the sweetness of their time together and of how good it feels to be wanted for something other than efficiency or obeying orders. Almost-invisible silver threads brush his arms seeking purchase as Cora's eyes plead with him to not say what he's about to say.

"Cora, I have to go. If I don't get Xavier to his heaven soon, he'll never be able to join his family." Every word rings dully in his skull, every word a death sentence.

Xavier's small voice breaks the ensuing silence. "Mister Jack, I'm bored. Can we go home now?"

"Yes," he replies, eyes still on Cora. "I'm ready if you are."

She's crying in earnest now. Sobs shake her compact frame and redden her face. When Jack moves to lift Xavier from his seat, he expects her to start screaming or to try snatching the boy from his arms, but she doesn't move from the center island.

He's pushing open the door to the living room when she finally speaks, her voice barely above a whisper.

"Please don't leave me."

It almost works. The urge to rush over and

comfort her twists his stomach into knots. He stops in his slow retreat, heart in his throat, tears that haven't been shed in ten years stinging his eyes. But the damage has already been done. His duty must come first, no matter what he feels or how badly he wants to let the house win. He closes his eyes to avoid seeing his betrayal mirrored in Cora's.

"I don't want to. You have to believe that."

"Then don't! Stay here. With me," she pleads, her genuine anguish coloring the air. "Please."

Jack clenches his jaw to stop himself from making promises he can't and shouldn't keep. Nothing he's saying is getting through to her. Anything more and he might lose his own fight. Wordlessly, he walks into the living room. She follows with tears streaming down her face.

As he puts his hand on the doorknob to leave the house, Xavier looks over his shoulder and says, "Miss Cora, come on! It's time to go."

Jack holds open the front door, leaving the offer hanging there. To his surprise, she rushes across the room and throws her arms around his waist. She squeezes hard enough to force a breath out of him. And several tears. He hugs her back with his free arm, kissing the top of her head.

"Come with me," he breathes. "Don't let this place take you."

But all he sees is fear and sorrow in her face, no understanding. His heart creaks with the effort of holding itself together as he breaks away and steps out of her reach onto the porch.

"I promise I'll come back as soon as I can," he

says. "I'm not going to let you go without a fight."

It takes every last shred of his willpower to walk away from her as she sinks defeated to the floor. His footsteps are matched by the sound of her hitching breath and repeated pleas for him to stop, to stay, to let her right whatever wrong she's done to him. Xavier starts crying, too, but Jack doesn't stop.

The further he gets from the house, the more his rational mind reasserts itself. He lets the old, familiar programming take over for a while, telling himself that forsaking his new, more human self is only temporary. It's the only way he can summon the courage leave Cora behind and complete his duty to Xavier.

He's somewhat consoled by remembering the hints about her true nature that have cropped up. Her unique gray eyes, finding the door in the Hunting Hall, and the powerful energy transfer all strongly support his theory about her. It's possible she'll already be gone when he comes back for her, although he's not sure how he'd feel if he arrived to find an empty house.

Maybe he should go back and tell her. Maybe that would be enough to break the spell.

But he has a job to do and only another day in which to do it. It goes against everything his heart's screaming at him, but he'll have to trust that things will work out.

Jack walks on, guided by the energy signatures of the next doorway, wishing not for the first time that he'd never taken this assignment.

SIXTEEN

Once upon a time, there was a chubby little girl with red hair and freckles who thought the world was a magical place where anything was possible. Her daddy taught her to believe in faeries and to see what's really there. Her mommy taught her that everyone has something special about them and that she could grow up to be whatever she wanted. She played outside with her friends, did well in her studies, and daydreamed whenever she got the chance. She was strong and fierce and trusted that everything would work out fine even if she didn't know how.

Everything did not work out fine.

As she changed from little girl to grown woman, the world also changed. The magic gradually drained out of her life. Faeries were for children. Lovers consumed her thoughts. Career choices loomed. And when Death knocked at her mother's door, she decided not to leave her small town. Her dreams of traveling the globe to experience the vast riches of life evaporated.

The woman settled down with a suitor who wanted the things she knew she should want. He bought her flowers, had a good job, and was loved by her parents. He made sure she never wanted for anything. They planned a life together. She grew comfortable in their love and in the soothing routine of their life.

Then one day, the woman realized that she'd let thirty years slip past. None of her childhood dreams had come true. She wasn't the special star she'd always believed she'd be. Her life had become monotonous and painfully average. She wondered where the magic had gone and if it was too late to find it. The more she noticed that it was missing, the sadder she became, and the further she drew into herself.

Her lover didn't understand. When she asked him for help, he selfishly turned away and rejected her. Now she would have to face the world alone. To her surprise, this didn't upset her as much as she thought it would. He was a good man but not good enough.

Perhaps things would work out fine, after all.

And so she packed her things and drove away from her home in search of the missing magic. She didn't know where the road would take her, who she would meet along the way, or if she would find what she was looking for. All she knew was that the time had long passed for her to have an adventure.

She never expected to die. She never expected to fail her quest before she even began. She never expected to forget her own story.

Eventually there aren't any more tears for Cora to cry. She sits half on the porch and half inside, leaning against the open front door of her house, staring at the imaginary trail of Jack and Xavier's departure. They left hours ago, judging by the sun, but she can't bring herself to move in case they come back.

They're not coming back. They've abandoned you here. They don't need you.

Her heart clenches at the thought, but she doesn't have the energy to fight the acid voice anymore. Besides, it's true – they did abandon her. Left her here like a crazy stranger keeping them from their destination.

How could Jack ruin everything like this? It's the suddenness that hurts the most. Or maybe it's the desperate way he pleaded with her to go with him. Or that it wasn't enough to leave, he had to take Xavier, too. After all this time together, in this perfect house with this perfect family, she can't wrap her mind around any of it.

Cora's eyebrows crease as part of the thought snags.

"All this time together..."

Memory isn't her strongest sense by a long shot, but she should remember how long she and Jack have been together. How long they've lived in the house. How long Xavier's been with them. Those seem like simple, incredibly important statistics she'd be able to recall at will, but they're not coming. She knows with unshakable certainty that it's been a long time; she just can't pinpoint how long. It's possible she's too exhausted to call it up after everything she's been through this morning.

The somewhat familiar sound of a single chime gently requests her attention. She turns to locate the source, grateful to drop her discomfiting train of thought, but there aren't any clocks in the living room. Curious, she takes a deep breath and pushes herself up to standing. She casts one last hopeful glance across the yard before going inside to investigate as the chime rings again.

Repeated stops and starts at the behest of the mysterious sound lead her from the living room to the kitchen to the hallway. She opens the door of the storage room to look at the pile of cardboard boxes, waiting to hear the chime again, but it doesn't come. This must be the end of the line.

It's weird to her that none of the boxes are marked. She's always been meticulous about that in the past. The detail adds to her growing sense of unease, but she waves it aside. Maybe there's something in one of these boxes to jog her fuzzy memory. There has to be a photograph or a letter or something concrete to tie her back to Jack and Xavier and the start of their life together.

Cora randomly selects a box at the top of the pile and pulls it open, then lets out a delighted squeal.

The box is filled with paraphernalia from her childhood, things she thought she'd lost. There's a fat yellow bird, a blue monster with too many arms, and a ragged teddy bear missing an eye. Under those is a music box with a ballerina inside. She takes out each of the beloved objects and hugs them to her. Oddly, there's no coating of dust or musty storage smell, like everything's been put away recently.

The further she digs into the pile of boxes, though, the less interesting the contents seem. The next one contains winter clothes. The next is filled with important-looking papers. Her search becomes more frantic. Disappointment seeps into the cracks of her heart. Where are the pictures of their family? What happened to the love letters and adoption papers? Boxes are torn open and thrown into the narrow corridor behind her one by one. They should be here. Why aren't they here? Did Jack take those, too? Why would he destroy the memories of their time together? What did she do to deserve this kind of punishment? Frustration and anger make her growl.

When she gets to the last box, she sighs and pushes it away, then stands to leave. There's no point. There's nothing in here that she needs or wants anymore. He's gone. They're both gone. She's alone here in her perfect house, and she needs to accept that. Better to leave the memories where they are and not disturb the past. She doesn't need to remember.

Except...

It doesn't feel like her thoughts. The voice and the words are familiar, the same as she always hears in her inner monologue, but there's a hollowness to them. They're edged with a defeatism that raises her hackles like a cat being rubbed the wrong way.

She stops halfway out the door of the storage room and goes back to the lonely box at the back of the room with her suspicion rising. There's nothing special about it; it's like every other one so far. But the way her mind conjured up all those reasons not to open it makes her want to open it even more.

Cora drops to her knees and slowly peels back the tape. The texture of the air around her changes as she folds back the flaps, and she finds herself holding her breath.

Inside is a single black scrapbook.

She lifts it out carefully, as if it might burst into flames or disintegrate, and sets it on her lap. The cover is unnaturally heavy, and she has to put effort into opening it. Pressed inside are newspaper clippings, letters, photographs, ticket stubs, stickers, and hand-written notes. It seems to chronicle her entire life. This is exactly what she's looking for – why was it so hard to find?

Seated on the polished hardwood floor, she scours the scrapbook for anything about Jack or Xavier or this house, systematically turning and scanning each page. But rather than finding relief, she only uncovers more unease. Every memory she's confronted with makes it harder to turn the pages.

An article about the arrest of James Underwood for sexually assaulting Sarah Fox. A round-trip airplane ticket stub for New York City. A letter from the University of Missouri proudly announcing her acceptance. A cancer ward wristband in her mother's name. A much-folded napkin with a phone number and "Jeremy" scrawled on it with eyeliner. A set of car keys.

Shock taps new reserves of tears that sting her already raw eyelids. These are all her stories, the most intimate parts of who she is, yet she doesn't remember any of them, like they happened to someone else. The disjointed feeling of being two people at once puts a fresh stranglehold on her heart, making her chest ache.

And the thing she was looking for – the reassuring evidence of her relationship with Jack and Xavier – isn't here. She shakes the book violently, hoping the pages are stuck together. A single large picture slides out and lands face-up on the floor.

None of the people staring at her from the old-fashioned sepia image are Jack or Xavier, but she does recognize every single person there.

Henry Adams. Rebecca Coulter. Sarah Fox. The Graves twins.

And Cora Riley.

She gasps as memory finally rushes up to meet her.

I left home. I drove away, and there was an accident. I died, and the Mistress gave me a quest. I met Jack, and I came here, and...

A tickle on her arms makes her glance down. Fine silvery threads climb along her, weaving themselves into a spider's web around her as she sits on the floor. An overpowering urge to fall asleep right here, right now rolls over her as more threads gently anchor to her skin. The scrapbook slides from her fingers, and her eyes flutter closed.

Everything is fine, nothing to worry about. She's perfectly safe here in this house designed specifically for her. There's nowhere she needs to be, nothing she needs to do, no one she needs to please.

The familiar chime sounds again, cutting through her sleepy haze, followed by the sensation of an egg being cracked over her head. Warmth oozes down through her scalp, and a far-away voice whispers in her mind.

You swore an oath to me, girl. Do not fail now because you are too weak to succeed on your own.

Shame flares in Cora's cheeks, and she furiously stands to her feet, snapping the threads that held her to the floor. She can't help shouting out loud, "I'm not weak!" but her voice falters. "I just don't know what to do. I can't think straight."

Find your own way. Be who you were meant to be.

"What does that mean?" she shouts at the air. But the voice fades like an echo in a cave, and there's no answer.

Patient as tree roots, the translucent spider webs creep their way up her legs to rebind her.

Stay here, the house says, *you belong here.*

The powerful urge to flee rises up in Cora's throat. "No!" she screams. "I have to find the door!"

She growls with fury – at herself, at the voice, at the house, at Jack – and yanks the threads from her skin and clothes. They become more substantial as she flees the room, tripping her in her flight toward the door. Her hand dives automatically into her pocket and fishes out the fork Xavier gave her. Two quick slashes and she's free again.

Her progress is agonizingly slow. Every time the silver tendrils touch her skin, she wants to give in, to lie down and stay forever. It would be so much easier. So much more right. This is her heaven. This is where she belongs.

Then she remembers the scrapbook and all the dreams it represents, the still-unquenched desire to understand what makes her special. Failure means losing her last chance to leave her mark on the world – and possibly the wrath of a goddess or two.

Fresh resolve powers Cora through the living room. She leaps through the open front door as the silver threads, now thick and solid as snakes, shoot after her. The jump clears the porch, and she lands heavily on her hands and knees on the springy lawn. Without turning to see what might be reaching for her, she sprints past the rose bushes and wooden fence in a wide arc. Every step takes her further from her perfect, beautiful house and the sweet afterlife she deserves. It tugs cruelly her heart to abandon it like this, but she's not ready for eternal rest. Not yet. There's still so much to live for.

She doesn't dare stop running until the last hint of the house has disappeared under the horizon. Out of breath, tears, and ideas, Cora sinks to the ground in the middle of what looks like someone's back forty. There don't seem to be any other houses in the area, which seems odd after the communal nature of the other afterlives she's visited. Maybe this heaven is for loner introvert weirdos who don't want any neighbors.

She leans against a felled tree to contemplate her predicament. She's exhausted and alone, and her safety is questionable at best. Is the house the only hazardous place for her? Do the fields want to trap her, too? At least her mind is clear for the time being; what she needs right now is an escape plan.

No matter how hard she tries to focus on getting out of here, though, her mind inevitably leads her into thinking about Jack. Sitting here by herself and out of reach of the insidious house, she wonders how much of what she feels for him is real. Sure, there's the flutter of butterflies when she recalls his hands along her back, the taste of his skin, the intensity of his eyes, but how can she trust what she feels? Or what he feels? There's too much room for doubt.

And not enough time.

Squinting at the setting sun, Cora tries to work out how long it's been since the Mistress shoved her through the first door. Two days, maybe? She wonders if she would have been able to escape the house if the quest's deadline had passed. And she can't stop wishing she'd been strong enough to go when Jack begged her to leave with him. He said he'd come back for her, but how long could she wait?

A speck of treachery fires in her mind: Will he even come back at all? It's possible, even probable, that he'll finish his assignment, drop off Xavier, and then go wherever it is angels go when they're done with work.

I'm not going to be a damsel in distress, waiting on some guy to save me. I'm the hero of this story, goddammit. Time to start acting like one.

Cora forces herself to her feet and starts pacing in tight circles while she thinks. The only way out is through one of the invisible doorways. Jack seemed to think she could find the door out in the Hunting Hall, and she sort of did, but he was there to open it. Even if she could manage to locate a portal on her own, she's not sure how she'd get through or where it would take her.

As she wears down the grass around the fallen tree, she gradually notices the mild buzzing sensation in her stomach. She dismisses it as hunger, then as romantic hormones, but the buzzing grows steadily stronger until it's vibrating through her entire body. It jangles her nerves but doesn't hurt. In fact, it feels kind of nice, like the beginning of an orgasm.

She's settling into the feeling when there's a short, insistent tug behind her navel. Then another. And another. Panic quickly gives way to curiosity, and she follows it forward. Two more tugs, two more steps. The electric tingling in her body intensifies the more she follows along. By the time she steps in front of a barbed-wire fence, the sensation is so strong she feels like she could shoot lightning from her fingertips.

She waits a moment to see if there are any other directions, then she reaches out and puts a shaking hand on the barbed wire. There's no spark or shooting pain, just a quietly certain sense of *yes*. This is the doorway, she's sure of it. Turning her head and putting the spot in her peripheral vision, she can even see the boundaries superimposed against the background.

"Great job, Riley. You found the magic door. Now what?"

Snippets of information, things Jack's said and done mixed with tidbits of myth and legend, scurry to piece themselves together to form an instructional picture.

Of course. Easiest thing in the world.

Cora closes her eyes and takes a deep, grounding breath, then another one to get the jitters out. Remembering the way she transferred her energy to Jack in their last jump, she pushes and pulls the electric tingle in her body until it's focused into her sweating hands. She holds them out over the fence, feeling for the edges of the portal. The instant her fingertips contact the boundaries, power erupts from her, forcing her eyelids open and sucking the breath from her lungs. Ripples of blue energy crisscross the air as the half-real, half-transparent doorway outlines itself in front of her.

The whole process takes a mere seconds, but by

the time it's over, she feels like she's run a marathon being chased by a lion. She bends over with her hands on her knees and waits for the scenery to stop spinning while she catches her breath.

Easiest thing in the world, huh?

Once she's recovered enough to look up without barfing, she lets out a little squeal of excitement and follows it up with a happy dance in front of the doorway. Not only did she not need some guy to gallop in on a white horse to rescue her, she just opened a magical portal to another dimension all by herself. It would take two of her to be more proud.

If that isn't special, she doesn't know what is

Biting her lip to keep from blurting out any more excitement, she steps up to the section of fence that appears to be a reversed image of itself and steps through. There's the feeling of careening down the first big drop on a rollercoaster. She opens her mouth to scream with glee, but the sound's whipped away in the rushing wind. Flashes of color whizz by her too fast to identify. Then there's a soft *poomp*, and she's there. Her first jump – all alone and completely under her own power.

Cora's about to do another celebratory booty dance but stops mid-grind when she sees where she's landed.

Impossibly blue skies stretch out in all directions; the only clouds she can see are making up the entirety of the ground she's standing on. She turns in a slow circle to take in her surroundings and realizes there isn't a single rock, tree, car, house, or valkyrie in sight. What she does see is an enormous pair of spit-shined golden gates as high as the Empire State building. She can faintly make out a square speck at the base of them, topped with a glint of silver.

Huh, she thinks as she walks toward the speck, *turns out there is a capital-H heaven after all.*

SEVENTEEN

Despite never attending church a day in her life, Cora's received more than her fair share of exposure to the idea of fluffy-cloud, harp-playing Heaven from living in the Bible Belt. She'd probably be excused, therefore, for expecting the angel in front of the Pearly Gates, which are actually gold, to be statuesque and to exude the sort of holiness she'd never admit makes her cry. That's what angels are supposed to be: an awe-inspiring presence to wow the recent dead upon arrival.

The squat man huddled over a book so large it defies physics, however, looks like he should be driving the 2AM downtown bus. A silvery halo hangs over his balding head and downy wings do sprout from his back, but he's also wearing stained, wrinkled robes and incredibly thick glasses.

When Cora approaches, he makes a point of ignoring her and scratching in the book with a long-feathered quill. She tries waiting, then clearing her throat politely, then waving, then runs out of patience.

"Hello?" she says loudly, knocking on the wooden podium. "Excuse me? A little help?"

The man gives a mighty sigh of annoyance and peers over his glasses. "Yes?"

"Are you Saint Peter?" It's a pretty safe guess.

He straightens a little with self-importance. "What do you think?" he says, pointing to a name badge pinned to his robe.

Sure enough, it reads *Saint Peter*.

"Really? How come you're all," she gestures vaguely, "dumpy?"

Another annoyed sigh says he's gone through this too many times. Once was probably too many, Cora muses.

He narrows his eyes, bunching his bushy white unibrow and glowering at her. "What do you want? State your business or shove off."

Cora bristles. "Hey, how do you know I'm not here as a new resident?"

More glowering. "I'm Saint Frickin' Peter." He taps the tome in front of him with the pen. "And you're not in the book."

Right, the book. If Jack successfully delivered Xavier, the boy's name should be written in there. She pushes herself up on tiptoe and tries to read upside down, but the angel leans over the enormous pages protectively, so she backs off.

"Actually, I'm here to see someone who *is* in the book." That earns her a guardedly curious glare. "A little kid from New Orleans, about six? Freaky-blue eyes? First name, Xavier?"

He gives her a sidelong glance then runs his finger down the open page, muttering to himself and scratching his dingy beard. Cora's ears pick up something about "pushy frickin' spooks." She's not sure whether to giggle because an angel's trying to swear or be offended that he called her a spook.

"Ah yes, here he is," he says eventually. "Xavier Cornelius Banks. Admitted this morning."

"Great! Can I come in to see him?"

"Absolutely not."

"Hey!" she protests, genuinely surprised. "I promise I won't be long or bother anybody else. I've been traveling with Xavier and his handler for a while, but we got separated." Her voice wavers toward the end, the wounds still a bit too fresh.

The angel leans forward, face suspicious. "Handler?"

"Yeah, Jack Alexander. Tall dude? Says he's the only one who goes on these lost-soul missions." She waves a hand at the book. "Look him up. I'm sure he's on your payroll or something. My name's Cora Riley; he'll vouch for me."

Saint Peter doesn't take his eyes off her as he digs around in his side of the podium. A thin grey booklet titled *Angel Directory* is produced, and he flips through the entire thing before pressing a finger to his right ear, his focus softening.

"Brenda? It's Peter. There's a young lady out here named Cora Riley asking to see someone named Jack Alexander." Pause. Huff. "Yes, of course I looked him up in the directory. He's not there. Why else would I call you?" Pause. "Well, if he's not in the system, then we might have ourselves a serious problem. Lady's saying this Alexander person delivered Young Master Banks. Either she's lying or we missed something." Pause. Eyeroll. "Fine."

He lowers his hand and slots the directory back into place. "Brenda says they'll see you in Central Services," he says, all fussiness and bother. "But whoever this Jack Alexander guy is, he's not ours."

The angel plops gracelessly off his stool and waddles away toward the titanic golden gates. They sweep inwards soundlessly, and Saint Peter stumps through without checking to ensure she's behind him.

Cora's feet move without help from her distracted brain. What does he mean, Jack's not theirs? What else could he be? As she follows the grumbling gatekeeper, her heart can't decide if it wants beat her ribs so hard they break or simply stop forever.

"Honestly, Mrs. Banks, I couldn't possibly. But I'm sure Xavier would be more than happy to take up my slack in the cake department."

"Okay, honey, but you'll never get any meat on them little sticks you call bones if you don't eat. Ain't no lady wants a man she can snap in half."

"I assure you, ma'am, that's not a problem."

"Whatever you say, Skinny. Here, baby doll, you

have Mister Jack's cake. He wants to waste away into nothin'."

"Don't do that, Mister Jack! You can't disappear!"

"I'd like say that I won't, but you never know exactly what might happen."

Four sets of eyes stare at Jack as the too-serious reply settles over the living room in the Banks' heavenly home, heavy as the hummingbird cake on Xavier's plate. Jack winces inwardly at having said the wrong thing. Again. One of these days he'll get the hang of garnishing the truth enough to avoid upsetting people.

Mrs. Banks appears unruffled, however, and she gives him a playful push in the shoulder that almost tips him over. "Now don't be like that, Mr. Alexander. All scarin' people and such. We're together now, safe and sound, and it's all thanks to you."

"I'm just doing my job, ma'am."

"And a damn fine job you did, son," rumbles a broad-shouldered man at the end of the couch. "Last report we got from one of those clipboard fellas was that you all'd been too long and wouldn't make it." The woman next to him inhales dramatically, and he wraps an arm around her. "Maybel and I thought for sure our grandson'd be lost forever. Good thing you come along."

Xavier's grandmother nods. "You sure you won't stay and celebrate with us? The Joneses next door and the Greens across the way are comin' over after the children head to bed." Her dark eyes sparkle mischievously.

"No, thank you. Now that Xavier's been returned, it's time for me to head home myself."

Jack hoists himself out of the deep recliner and makes his way around the room to shake each person's hand. It never fails to amaze him the effect Cloud Nine has on its occupants. Whatever they looked like in life, whatever personality flaws they'd accumulated, it all gets washed away when they cross the threshold. The hands he shakes are no older than his own, the faces filled with so much gratitude are unmarred by the weariness of human life. This isn't his resting place, but Jack's admiration of that healing gives him hope. Maybe some of it will rub off on him.

When he gets to Xavier, the boy's sapphire eyes are already filled with tears. Jack kneels down and lets him throw chubby arms around his neck, not minding the sticky smear on his shirt. They sit that way for a while, comforting each other in front of the family without caring. It's been a hell of an assignment, given one thing and another, and it's mildly disconcerting how attached he's grown to his charge. They train you to disassociate from the work, but look where that got him last time.

"You've been a brave boy, Xavier," Jack whispers. "I'm proud of you." He gives the boy one last squeeze then lets him go.

Mrs. Banks walks him to the glass-paned front door of the bespoke mansion. She blows her nose loudly into a lace hankie then tucks it up her sleeve and engulfs Jack in a bear hug so tight he sees stars.

"God bless you, Mr. Alexander!" she wails as she plants a huge, wet kiss on his cheek, making him pinken with her sincerity. "You come back any time you want, you hear?"

He gulps a lungful of air after she releases him and manages a smile and nod on his way out the door. The instant it closes, a joyful cry goes up and a stereo's turned on full blast, the bass reverberating the house's windows.

His polite smile grows into a proper grin as he makes his way at his usual quick pace to Central Services to wrap up the paperwork. A job more than satisfactorily done. When he took this assignment, he hadn't been sure he was ready to come back. There's no other work he's ever wanted to do, and the enforced time away felt like an eternity, but he didn't know what to expect. A lifetime of being careful had made him leery of the man he'd become over six months away, and he feared being ruled by the messy emotions he'd previously set aside. But despite all the entanglements and confusion he's had to navigate, the way Xavier's case has unfolded reassures him that he's not completely been undone.

Jack's practically swaggering by the time he rolls into the lobby of Central Services where he's greeted by the rustle of feathers and ring of footsteps in the busy halls. A few angels wave or call out hellos as they spot him, and he waves back. It's definitely good to be back in the swing of the job, even more so now that he can let himself enjoy it.

"Oh. My. God!" exclaims the woman at the front

desk. Her Bronx accent fills the room as it climbs an octave. "Is that you, Spooky Baby?! It's been so long!" She bounces to her feet to greet him, stretching her small pinkish wings.

"Hello, Brenda," he says, kissing her politely on both cheeks. "It's nice to see you again, too."

The thin silver halo atop her brown hair jiggles as she inspects him top to bottom. "Ooh, but you look good. You been working out?"

He snorts a laugh and starts searching a floor-to-ceiling block of cubbies crammed with identical clipboards. "The opposite, actually. Six months at home doing nothing but eating peanut brittle and watching *Lifetime.*"

Brenda practically purrs. "Oh really?"

"No. But close."

The administrative angel pouts dramatically and plunks herself into her desk chair. She's about to snark something back at him but is interrupted by a call. She holds up one pink-manicured finger to signal Jack to be quiet and taps her other hand to her ear. Jack continues to pull out clipboards and puts them back as he searches for his paperwork.

"You've reached Central Services, Brenda speaking, how can I help you?" Pause. "Never heard of him. Didja look him up in the directory?" Pause. Huff. "I dunno, maybe you wanted to hear the sweet sound of my voice. It's awfully lonely out front from what I hear." She laughs at her own jibe. Pause. "Lemme check the computer. Just a sec." Clickclickclick. "Nope, nothing." Pause. "Could be a scheduling problem or somebody in payroll fricked it up? Send her over and see if Garren can sort it out without having to get the Big Guy involved."

Jack makes an "aha" noise then turns to the high counter on the side of Brenda's desk to fill out Xavier's release forms.

"What's that all about?" he asks. But his mind is already elsewhere, his usually careful handwriting progressively deteriorating as he ponders what happens next.

If Cloud Nine was the next jump, the house must be in row three. Stepping back should be easy enough, although the lateral moves might take some time. If she's even still there…

Brenda rolls her eyes dramatically. "Peter's got his panties in a wad again. Some dead broad that doesn't belong here is down at the gate asking for somebody called Jack Alexander. Figured I'd get her over here before Az hears about it."

The middle of Jack's signature scrawls wildly off the page and onto the countertop, leaving a long black streak. "Did you get her name?" he asks sharply.

"Cora something? Hey, where you going?"

But he's already gone, pen clattering to the floor, clipboard abandoned, speeding off down the long hallway toward the Ombudsman's office.

"How many more times do you want me to tell you the same thing?" Cora leans heavily into her palm and sighs dramatically.

The angel on the other side of the desk shuffles

the same pieces of paper he's been fiddling with for the last fifteen minutes. "I'm sorry to press you, Miss Riley, but your story is confusing at best. We have no records of anyone in our employ named Jack Alexander or of this thirteenth door for which you claim to be searching. Management requires that I record each detail to ensure a proper inquiry should one be deemed necessary."

"Wait, an inquiry?" She jerks up straight in the uncomfortable chair. "Exactly how long are you planning to keep me here?"

The tips of his wings twitch defensively. "Only until we can determine that you do not present a clear and present danger to Cloud Nine. The circumstances of your arrival are highly unusual, you must admit."

Frustrated, she snatches the brass nameplate from the desk and brandishes it at him like a cudgel. "What else could you possibly need to know, Garren, Executive Assistant to the Ombudsman? I've told you everything from beginning to end five motherfucking times!" He flinches, and she's quietly pleased by that. Pointless bureaucrats should be shaken up every once in a while. "Is there a real angel I can talk to?" she asks, purposely replacing her improvised weapon in the wrong spot. "Someone who actually understands English, for example?"

To his credit, the angel doesn't rise to the bait. He probably can't, which takes some of the fun out of it. He quietly moves the nameplate back where it belongs then fiddles with her file a bit more, re-

reading the contents. Precious minutes drain away as she drums her chewed fingernails on the tabletop in the cramped office.

"Hrm...," Garren eventually says, eyes still glued to the folder.

Cora exhales loudly. "There are few things more annoying than someone 'hrm'ing to themselves when they're trying to get someone to ask what they're thinking."

"Hrm..."

"Ugh. Fine. *What*?"

He raises his purple eyes to meet her gray ones. "I notice that none of your paperwork gives a description of this alleged guardian angel. Perhaps telling me more about him would fill some of the gaps in your story." The feathered tips of his off-white wings flick pensively, like a cat's tail as it waits for a mouse to appear. "That is if he actually exists."

"He exists! Geez, you're seriously making me doubt my sanity here, dude."

Cora takes a long breath and steels herself. While she does want to find Jack, if only to strangle him for leaving her behind, calling up his description pulls too many heartstrings at the moment. This bureaucratic angel is probably screwing with her for being rude, but she can't chance not giving him what he asks for. It could be her only ticket out of here.

She takes another breath and closes her eyes, drawing the man from memory in that private darkness.

"He's really tall – maybe six and a half feet? Closer to seven? Dark skin, dark hair, dark eyes. Really skinny. Dude needs a sandwich. But he must work out like a maniac 'cause he's got these abs..." She trails off for a moment, the blush tainting her cheeks, but she powers on. "Some kind of scars on his chest like he got attacked by a bear or werewolf of something." She furrows her brow. "And a green curlicue design on his back."

She opens her eyes to see that Garren's blushing as badly as she is. She laughs nervously and looks away quickly.

"Well, uh, that description is quite thorough, Miss Riley, thank you," he says with only a hint of embarrassment. "And I believe I am acquainted with the individual you have been referring to."

Relief floods every cell of her body. "Thank freaking God!" she exclaims, slumping back into the unyielding office chair, breathing a happy sigh. "I guess he's using a pseudonym or something when he's out on missions. Who is this guy?"

"Your assumption is an astute one. The person you have described is commonly known here as –"

At that moment, the door to the tiny room slams open with so much force it throws the framed Lord's Prayer to the beige carpet in a spray of broken glass. Garren rises to his feet in indignation, and Cora spins in her seat, ready to dress down the intruder. But the angry words dry up on her tongue.

Jack, or whatever is name really is, stands in the doorway, panting slightly. He a ragged breath, then straightens in the most awkward movement Cora's ever seen him make. His long legs make quick work of the room, and he leans against the assistant's desk in what he must think is a nonchalant manner. With his back to Garren, he locks her gaze and smiles as best he can.

"Hello again," he says. "Fancy meeting you here."

EIGHTEEN

Gray eyes aren't the only thing Cora inherited from her father. Her righteous temper flares, concentrating the bizarre emotional rollercoaster of her last several hours into a white-hot blowtorch of rage. She springs to her feet and grabs two fistfuls of Jack's leather jacket. His startled face is only inches from hers as she screams at him.

"You abandoned me in that hellhole, you fuck! You weren't even looking for me, were you?" She doesn't wait for a response. "The house was eating me alive! I could've been stuck there forever, and you wandered off like I didn't fucking matter!" Tears of frustration wet her cheeks, and she releases his lapels to wipe them away. "You were supposed to help me," she murmurs, voice softer but retaining its edge.

Jack steps forward to touch her arm, but she pulls back and holds the distance, more for his protection than her defense. He drops his hand with a bitter sigh and lowers his head.

"I had to get Xavier to his heaven before it was too late," he says. "If we'd stayed much longer, his resonance would have been too weak for it to accept him. He would've been forced into the Void." The muscles in his jaw tense. "I couldn't let that happen."

"But you could let me get sucked into oblivion without a second thought."

His head snaps up. "No! Never. My hand was forced, and I had to fulfill my duty to Xavier first. He couldn't survive without my help." He tries again to step forward, and this time she allows it. "But I was confident that you could."

Cora lifts her chin to stare imperiously at him, every inch of her challenging his story, her grey eyes an icy thunderstorm. She trusted him, and he walked out when she needed him most. Just like Jeremy. She wants to hate him for it.

But before he can draw a breath to continue his defense, her glare dissolves and she blinks several times as the light of understanding dawns.

"You knew," she says in an awed whisper. "You knew I could find the door and get out."

Jack gives her an approving smile. "I had my suspicions. You caught my attention in the Garden, and by the time we left the Hunting Hall, I was nearly certain." He takes another unchallenged step forward. One more and they'll be touching. "The ability is remarkably rare, however. I've never met anyone else who has it."

Cora's eyes narrow as she steps out of his reach. She'll buy that he knew she'd be okay but leaving her to fend for herself isn't the only questionable thing he's done.

"Don't try to get all sweet with me, mister," she says. "Even if I am some kind of rare mutant, that doesn't explain why nobody here knows you." She nods toward Garren, still frozen in indecisive anxiety behind his desk. "They keep saying you don't exist, that you don't work here, that you're not a guardian angel. For all I know, you're some kind of magical compulsive liar who gets off by leading people into perilous situations and rescuing them."

He winces as if she'd slapped him, but she pretends not to notice. A hundred questions poise themselves to leap from her lips. And, of course, she has to ask the hardest one first.

"Who *are* you, Jack?"

He meets her hurt-filled gaze for a moment then says over his shoulder, "Garren, could you give us a moment?"

The administrative flunky seems more than happy to oblige. He sweeps up the contents of Cora's dossier from the desk and hustles out the door without another word. Rustling feathers disappear down the hallway, leaving Jack and Cora facing each other in the tiny office.

Jack inhales deeply once they're alone and sits in the nearest chair, waving a hand at the other to offer it to Cora. She drags it over slowly, maintaining a wary buffer between them, then perches on the edge of the seat, arms still crossed in front of her.

"Well?" she says.

He leans forward and rests his forearms on his thighs, his hands clasped and head bowed. He takes another deep breath and, in a quiet, steady voice, makes his confession.

"Jack Alexander is my real name, but I haven't used it in almost a decade. I'm not a guardian angel, although I'm sometimes called on to fill that role because of my abilities. I'm a special agent for a classified department of the Federal Bureau of Investigation. Most recently, I've specialized in the retrieval and protection of underage persons of interest, although I have also done significant work in homicide and what you might call 'foreign relations.'"

"Show me your badge."

His brow furrows. "What?"

"You heard me. If you're really an FBI agent, you'll have a badge. I want to see it." She holds out her hand.

There's a flicker of annoyance on his face as Jack digs in his back pocket to produce a flat black square which he drops into her waiting palm. Cora runs a forefinger over the smooth brass shield embedded in the leather. There's no decoration or design – just a simple, engraved letters and numbers.

SCD FBI No. 97

"What's the acronym?"

"Supernatural Cases Division," he says, sitting back in his seat.

Cora hefts the badge lightly, considering the idea. "Like *Men in Black*?"

"Something like that, yes – but we don't deal with aliens."

"How come I've never heard of you guys before?"

There's a faint smirk on his face as he says, "The SCD is tasked with overseeing and managing the interaction of the supernatural with the mundane. The two worlds overlap in significant ways, and we ensure there's as little impact as possible on the mortal population. Covertly. Too much exposure could cause mass panic on either side."

"And that means...?"

Jack considers this for a moment. "Do you want to know everything, or do you want to know what's important right now?"

"Whatever. I get the feeling you're not going to tell me the truth anyway."

"I'll tell you anything you want to know," he says, the hurt clear in his voice, "but it's a lot to take in at once."

She softens slightly. The fiery anger she felt is all but burned away, leaving behind only a cherry coal of curiosity. Everything he's said so far makes a sort of fucked-up sense, and after discovering she's got super powers and that there's a magical police force, nothing short of full disclosure will slake the rest of that fire. If anyone else had suggested that she couldn't handle the truth, she'd probably kick him in the shin. Right now, though, the bigness of it all is starting to get to her. She has to admit he's got a point. Sort of.

"Tell me what you think I can handle right now."

Jack gives a little laugh. "I'm absolutely confident you can handle anything I throw at you, Cora. You've more than proven that. But we may not have time for me to explain everything in as much detail as you may like."

"That's okay," she says. To her surprise, she actually means it. "I just want you to stop lying to me."

He nods. "Fair enough." He scoots his chair forward until their knees are almost touching. "You already know humans aren't alone. The SCD keeps an eye on the other beings that share our reality. Deities, folk heroes, and vampires are some familiar examples, but we also monitor spontaneous human abilities." He gestures to himself, then to her. "Like opening the doors between worlds."

"Is that good or bad?"

"Possibly both. The ability is considered a high-level threat because of the implications for security and risk of abuse, but it's so rare it's estimated only five users ever existed. For reference, telepathy occurs in one out of every thousand humans."

"Damn. I'm sort of impressed with myself."

He laughs warmly. "As you should be. You've seen what the ability can do here, but that's only a fraction of what's possible. Once we get you back to the world, I'll see to it that you receive the training you need to make good use of your power." He smiles and puts a hand on her knee.

She inhales sharply, suddenly too aware of the promised future in his words and the eerie intimacy of his touch. The memory of stolen moments in a perfect house spools out around them, quickly making the air too hot to breathe.

Jack carefully retracts his hand. "Cora, about what happened..." he begins.

"It's okay," she says, shaking her head dismissively. "Forget about it. I know it wasn't real." But a note of suppressed doubt leaks into her voice. "Right?"

"Not exactly," he says slowly. "The house can't manufacture anything on its own."

She winds her fingers around each other as if that could exorcise her guilt. "So, everything that happened there... I did that?"

He drops his gaze to his shoes. "We both did," he says. "You brought me inside, so the house accepted me. It drew on our mutual desires so it could build an ideal afterlife for you. Whatever we felt for each other was – is – real, but the house magnified and accelerated it to make it useful."

The silence that follows is broken only by the hum of the fluorescent office lights as they sit with their thoughts. Some part of Cora knows she should be overwhelmed by the new information and complex emotions fighting for her attention. But she isn't. In fact, the whole peculiar business makes more sense to her than the last thirty years of her "normal" life. There's comfort in the insane nonsense of it all, a feeling of being alive she's missed for so long that she thought she'd never find it again. Whatever bullshit she and Jack have been through these last couple of days, maybe it was worth it.

Eventually Jack raises his head, apology in his face, but her serene expression stops him short. There's no blush in Cora's cheeks when she locks eyes with him. She reaches over and gently takes one of his large, soft hands in her small, rough one.

"I don't know exactly what the house did to us," she says, steady voice barely above a whisper, "but I do know I'm not going to forget about it. You said it drew on something real. I'll admit to that on my part. And if it found something inside of you, too..." She squeezes his hand. "Maybe we should take it from where we started before the house and see what happens. You know, without all the magical interference."

Jack smiles lopsidedly and squeezes her hand in return. "That sounds like an excellent plan."

An abrupt knock at the door shatters the moment.

"Yes?" Jack calls out, making no effort to hide his annoyance.

A harried-looking Garren eases open the office door and pokes his halo through. He's holding a much thicker stack of paperwork than what he left with, and his face is markedly pale.

"Management would like to see you both," he says. "Right now."

He doesn't wait for a response, just turns on his sandaled heel and strides off in a rustle of feathers and robes.

Jack and Cora stare after him, and then Jack shrugs, stands, and waves her toward the door. She gives a small, disappointed sigh. Whatever else they need to say to each other will have to wait.

Garren manages to stay several paces ahead of the pair as they follow him through the bustling hallways of Central Services. The building reminds Cora of a corporate version of the Mistress' castle – all identical doors and bland décor. Angels of every description file past with a hand to an ear, talking insistently to other members of the heavenly host about deadlines, meetings, and quotas. Pudgy cherubs zoom overhead carrying mail to unknown destinations. Cora can't help grinning a bit. She can think of at least a dozen church ladies back home that'd die of scandal if they found out that Heaven's full of cubicles and TPS reports.

When they reach the end of a particularly long series of doors, Garren punches an elevator button and waits. His eyes flit around the lobby, his attention anywhere but at the two humans accompanying him.

Cora raises an eyebrow at the angel but decides not to push it. She turns her back to him and says to Jack, "Management is exec-speak for capital-G God, right?"

He shakes his head. "He doesn't see anyone in person anymore. The way they've got the Host set up these days, he doesn't need to. Assuming nothing's changed since I've been away, 'management' refers to the archangel choir. I'd imagine our guide here is taking us to the upper decks to meet with Michael or Gabriel."

Garren does a good job of disguising his flinch as

a sneeze.

"Bless you," Cora says.

The elevator dings its arrival before they can get any more digs in at Garren. They all shuffle into the metal box, which is large enough for several humans but the angel's massive wings force the three of them to get exceptionally friendly. Cora's face is buried in Garren's armpit; Jack is somewhere behind them both. Badly-executed harp music tinkles down from overhead speakers. No one says a word.

This must be a special circle of hell, Cora thinks. *One reserved for tailgating drivers and people who talk at the theater.*

Her nose is so full of angelic B.O. she only notices they're descending when the elevator stops moving. The silver doors slide open, and the three squeeze themselves out into an empty, chilled hallway with one fluorescent light shining over a solitary door at the far end. It's more like a tomb than an office basement. The stark contrast with the brightly-lit floors above gives Cora the willies and makes the fine hair stand up all over her body. She lets Garren lead the way and moves closer to Jack, who's holding himself on taut wires, chin lifted and nostrils flared.

Cora elbows him. "What are you doing?" she asks in a harsh whisper.

"Figuring out where we are."

"By sniffing the air? What are you, some kind of bloodhound?" She snorts sarcastically, but when he doesn't respond, she arches an eyebrow at him.

"Wait, you're not, are you?"

"Werewolf, actually," he says distractedly.

She stares at him, eyes bulging in disbelief. "Shit, really? How did you end up with two sets of powers? That hardly seems fair."

"It's only partial. I'd be happy to tell you the whole story later. Right now, though, we need to focus. We're about to be in serious trouble."

As she's about to ask why, Garren stops them in front of the lonely office door. He knocks timidly, producing a hollow, metallic sound that rings out and dies away in ripples along the corridor. When the sound is gone, there's a click and the door swings inward, accompanied by an overpowering smell of mildew. Garren nods his head toward each of them in dismissal then scuttles back to the elevator.

Cora watches him go as the sensation of being trapped tightens in her gut. "What's that all about?" she says to Jack.

He simply points to the engraved silver plaque on the door:

Azrael
Archangel of Death
By Appointment Only

NINETEEN

He came when Dad died. He didn't think Jack could see, but he could, his deep brown eyes keen before they knew what they were looking for. The darkness in his angry mind took a shape that leaned over his father's mouth and inhaled without sound. He didn't cry or call out. He simply watched, a serious boy becoming a serious man too soon.

He came when Jack lay helpless and healing in the infirmary. He opened his eyes to see the formless form hovering over him the way it had over his father twenty years before. It ran its wisps over the sucking wounds in his chest like a question mark. He didn't cry or call out. He simply told the specter to leave, a dying man fighting to stay alive.

Cora's concerned eyes are on Jack as he stands poised to enter Azrael's office, but she doesn't ask what he's thinking. Instead, she cautiously pushes the metal door open and peers into the gloom. But there's nothing to see. No windows, no lamps, not even a residual glow from the naked bulb in the hallway; it's an orchestrated, careful black. She raises a questioning eyebrow at Jack. He rolls his shoulders, then his neck, and nods to her. They step over the threshold together, every muscle between them tensed for a fight, and the door swings silently shut, plunging their light-sensitive eyes into complete darkness. The air is so still that all Cora can hear is the rush of blood in her ears. She nearly screams when a withered voice hisses in front of her.

"Welcome."

A match flares into life with near-blinding brightness. It's touched to a candle wick that casts dim illumination over an ancient desk supporting a closed, hand-sewn book larger than Saint Peter's register. The buttery light grows into a small pool that stops before it reaches Jack and Cora, heightening the sense of entombment rather than alleviating it. Cora's eyes snatch at shadows, trying to picture the room and its occupant, but the pieces slip away before she can fit them into the puzzle.

There's a rustle of rough fabric and two thick, grayish hands protruding from a black robe fold themselves on the book's cover. Cora takes an involuntary step back when she notices that each fingernail of those hands is a lidless eye. They move individually and focus intently on her, seemingly unimpeded by the utter blackness.

"Welcome," the voice says again with layers of harmonics that strain Cora's ears.

Jack's hand on her back eases them both up to the edge of the light. She can see him keeping his eyes averted from the ten on the desk. She follows suit and glues her eyes to her boots.

"We've answered your summons, Azrael," he says. "What can we do for you?"

"You can do nothing for me, Jack Alexander. You are simply here as a matter of convenience and are free to depart whensoever you choose. It is with your companion that I wish to speak."

The snakelike voice orients itself in Cora's direction. "Attend to me, girl."

She risks a glance at Jack who nods. Inside, the terrified animal part of her is clawing at the door to escape, but she contains it enough to steady her voice.

"Yes?"

"Cora Leigh Riley, you have committed grievous sins against the accepted laws of the Otherworlds and Cloud Nine. For this you are brought to me for final judgment."

Indignation miraculously overrules fear. "I haven't done anything wrong. The Mistress gave me a quest. I'm allowed to be here."

The insinuation of a hood appears in the circle of light on the desk, right at the edge of Cora's downcast vision. "Which she gave unwillingly after your selfish demand. You have no rights within the Otherworlds aside from passage to your assigned afterlife."

"The rules say I get a quest if I ask for it. Isn't that all that matters?"

A low chuckle. "Only in the beginning. And now that you are near the end, there are other rules that must be obeyed."

"Like what?" The level of sass in the question earns her a prod in the ribs from Jack. She alters her tone to a more respectful one but only just. "I mean, what are these other rules?"

"I am given dominion over all souls who pass through these lands. The privilege and responsibility of your quest became my purview once you stepped through the Gates." A wet clicking noise comes from inside the hood. "While I cannot countermand the Mistress' poor decision, I can enforce the remaining laws of order."

"That's not an answer," Cora says. She takes a small defiant step forward that has her almost touching the desk. The roving eyes in Azrael's hands dart all over her, making her skin crawl, and she raises her gaze in disgust.

It's a mistake.

A low rumble, somewhere between a growl and a hiss, emanates from the hood. Cora tries to lower her eyes again, to apologize before she's eviscerated or willed out of existence, but she's locked in place. A face forms in the darkness beneath the outline of the hood, and she's forced to watch it develop like a Polaroid. Hundreds, thousands of tiny eyes blink back at her from a grinning, bare human skull.

Azrael's many-layered voice reverberates in Cora's mind like a boulder crashing into the sea.

"You will show me proper respect, you miserable wretch, or there will be no parley!"

Behind her, Jack swears in a language she doesn't understand, and then he's at her side, slamming his hands down on the desk.

"Even you must obey the laws, Azrael!" he shouts at the archangel. Sweat stands on his forehead, and his jaw is clenched so hard Cora's afraid his teeth will crack. "You cannot deny her right to the Choice!"

Silence slides around them as the terrible face and hands melt away from the guttering candle. Jack sways dramatically, and Cora unlocks in time to keep him upright. The effort required to shout down an archangel must be immense. He shakes himself a couple of times, making gestures that he's okay, then she turns her focus back to the desk.

"Tell me what you want," she says.

A low hiss precedes the archangel's response, sending a shiver up her spine. "Cora Leigh Riley, your crimes are thus: You have transgressed against the laws of order by insisting upon the Mistress' quest. You have transgressed against the laws of death by abandoning your rightful afterlife. And you have transgressed against the laws of Cloud Nine by transporting earthly possessions into the realm." The hands reappear on the vast book's cover, all ten eyes pinpoint-focused on Cora. "Within the terms of your agreement with the Mistress, I am unable to enforce punishment for the first two crimes. The third, however, is at my discretion." One of the fleshy grey hands turns over, revealing a palm comprised entirely of a milky eye with no iris. "Relinquish the object to me, and I may be merciful."

Cora's brow furrows. What did she bring here? She absentmindedly pats her various pockets until she finds something solid.

Oh. That.

A fond smile touches the corners of her mouth as she remembers Xavier, and she draws the crude fork from her jeans to hold it up in the candlelight.

"Is this what you're looking for?"

"You know that it is."

She turns it over in her hands, admiring the shoddy craftsmanship. "What could you possibly want this for?" she wonders aloud.

"No earthly possessions are allowed in the realm of Heaven. This is common knowledge."

That seems true. But as she continues to examine the fork, it occurs to her that if she were writing this story, this is exactly what would happen if a villain were trying to steal treasure from the hero. Reasonable explanations, subtle use of authority, bullying, temptation. And besides, this is the Angel of Death; it seems incredibly petty of such a powerful being to force a shitty eating utensil from her if it weren't important.

She lowers the fork and settles her eyes on the repulsive hands on the desk; it's as much defiance as she can manage at the moment.

"And what happens if I don't give it up?" she says.

"You must. It became mine the moment you

came here."

"Azrael…" Jack warns.

A gritty sound of irritation slithers from the black hood. "Child of God, you are blessed with free will – a divine birthright denied to the Heavenly Host. You must utilize that gift here before me now and endure the consequences of your choice as is your God-given right."

"That sounds fair. What are my options?"

"You must turn over the object to me or keep it for yourself."

"And the consequences?"

The wet clicking noise sounds again, and Cora can't stop herself from picturing the eye-covered skull and its horrible smile as Azrael says, "No mortal is allowed knowledge of their fate. Ignorance is the price you pay for free will."

Jack intervenes angrily. "She's asked; you have to tell her. Those are the terms of the treaty. If you continue to attempt to circumvent the laws, I will not hesitate to begin your investigation myself, right now."

"Yes, law-man, I understand," the archangel snaps, making the candle flame dance precariously close to extinguishing.

To Cora he says, "Should you relinquish the object to me as keeper of this jurisdiction, I will allow you to safe passage to return to your intended afterlife. Should you keep the object for yourself, I will cast you from my sight and no other may help you leave this realm or fulfill your quest."

He offers his eye-palmed hand again. "Choose."

Every scrap of common sense tells her that something underhanded is going on. Azrael said she was near the end of her quest, and he clearly doesn't want her to continue. It seems like he's determined to sabotage her with rules and bravado, trying to coerce her into doing what he wants without question. Maybe there's more to his reticence than he lets on. Could he be in bed with the Mistress, conspiring with her to ensure she fails? Well, she's not having it. Whatever choice needs to be made, it's going to be made here, by her, fully aware, or not at all.

"I've visited my heaven," she says, "and I'm not quite ready to give up my second shot at a meaningful life for that, nice as it is." She grips the fork in her left hand, feeling its comforting weight. A tingle seeps through her fingers, reminding her of the reason for her journey and her newfound power. "And, you know, I don't think you're allowed to hurt me or stop me as long as I'm under the aegis of the Mistress' quest. So, I think I'll take my chances and keep it." She tucks the fork safely back into her jeans pocket. "Besides, the terms were that I turn over anything I find to *her*. Not her minions."

The defiant proclamation is buried as shrieks of unbounded rage pile into the room, boring through the soft tissue of Cora's mind, layer after layer of voices screaming in unison as Azrael's hands form claws that swipe impotently at her. Tremors shoot through the floor that threatens to crack open and swallow them whole. The two humans fall to their knees, fumbling for one another and covering their ears against the auditory onslaught. Jack's large frame easily shelters Cora, but neither of them can move until the archangel's fury is spent long minutes later.

When the cacophony subsides and the ground is stable again, Cora peels her hands from the sides of her head. A little blood is smeared across her palms, and fears of permanent damage flash momentarily through her imagination, but there's no time for that. Jack is already pulling her to her feet. The single candle has been thrown from the desk, leaving no clue as to the direction of the exit.

"What now?" she asks into the dark.

"I'm not sure. Azrael doesn't give up on his prey under normal circumstances, and you've been more resistant than he's accustomed to."

"I'm not sure if I should be proud or sorry."

"For what it's worth, I've never known anyone to be so calm in his presence."

"Hey, you were pretty damned impressive yourself," Cora says. "I thought for a minute there you were going to take a swing at an archangel."

There's a chuckle in the darkness. Then he says, "Whatever his reasons for disappearing, he's bound by the Otherworlds' laws to keep his word, so it's possible he's left us to our own devices."

The humor drains out of her as quickly as it rose up, replaced with a sharp grasp of the situation. "Which means we have to find our way out of here," she says. "Then I have to figure out how to find a door everyone's telling me doesn't exist." She sighs. "Great."

"You don't have to do it alone, you know," Jack says.

"Sounds an awful lot like I do. Azrael said no one else could help me. Besides, you don't exactly have a stake in this mission anymore. You can go home."

"Do you want me to go?"

"Do you want me to want you to go?" She immediately shakes her head. "Sorry, that was stupid." She takes a deep breath and tries again. "I can't ask you to keep babysitting me. This is my quest and my responsibility."

"I've never thought of it as anything less than that." Pause. "The 'your quest' part, not the babysitting part." Pause. "What if I accompanied you in my official capacity? Between what you've told me so far and some of the things Azrael alluded to, it sounds like the agency may benefit from recon on what's happening at the castle."

"That could work," Cora says slowly. "Is that the only reason?"

"No."

The scent of Old Spice rises up as Jack moves nearer. Her pulse and breath quicken and catch by turns; she's mildly surprised that the room doesn't catch fire based solely on the temperature of her face. She reaches out in the darkness and feels for his hand. It slides easily into hers. Rather than pulling him to her and rifling through his clothes the way she wants to, though, she simply shakes his hand, a physical reminder of their pact back in the Garden.

"I'd be glad for the company, Mr. Alexander. Welcome to Team Lost Cause."

He returns the gesture, but before they break apart, now-familiar electric buzzing tugs on Cora's consciousness.

"Do you feel that?" she asks.

"I do. But I'm having trouble locating the source. Take a look."

Cora closes her eyes redundantly to focus on the sensation, letting go of Jack's hand and holding out hers like a pair of dowsing wands. Her consciousness creeps carefully around the room until it latches onto the energy signature. Clearly outlined in her mind's eye, right behind Azrael's desk, is a doorway.

"The door," she breathes.

Jack sounds troubled at the information. "There shouldn't be one here. Part of the treaty with the Otherworlds includes negative zones for interdimensional travel. The only way in or out of Cloud Nine should be outside the Gates."

"I don't know what to tell you, dude. It's right there." She reaches back and takes his hand again. "Maybe it's our ticket out."

Hands and minds outstretched, the pair pick their way around the massive wooden desk until they hit a bookshelf on the back wall.

"May I?" Cora says.

"Be my guest."

Power builds up in Cora's fingertips as she brushes them along the leathery spines of the books to search for the doorway's edges, which she finds almost immediately. She traces the outline to demarcate the door, and it glows blue as it transforms. Thankfully, the drain on her system is significantly less dramatic than last time; she feels invigorated rather than spent once it's fully open. Perhaps it's because this door is so much smaller than the others – a perfect square at floor level, no more than four feet high.

Jack sighs. At nearly seven feet tall, it'll take a fair amount of folding for him to pass through.

"What, too good to get down on the floor?" she chides him. She grins and gives a short salute. "See you on the other side," she says.

And then she's gone.

TWENTY

It's not right from the start. The way she opened the door, the kaleidoscope passageway, the easy landing – none of it should happen like that, especially not for someone without a second of training. Raw talent. Jack scans the deathly silent grassland of the doorfield unsure of whether to be impressed, concerned, or jealous.

"Awesome, right?" Cora says breathlessly.

He turns around and sees her flushed pink face, her proud grin, and her shining grey eyes, and he can't help smiling. Ego aside, he's quietly glad to share his strangeness with her.

"Very," he says, crossing the room.

The swollen orange moon, riding low in its velvety, too-close sky, watches over the pair as they take in the rows of white rectangles standing patiently with their backs turned to them. The great, hulking shadow at the far edge of the doorfield's horizon can only be the castle. They look in every direction but only see more acres of brown grass stretching away into the disappearing distance.

"I'm not seeing an extra door, are you?" Cora says.

Jack shakes his head, eyes glued to the moon. There's a lonely tug in his heart at seeing it that he has trouble shaking. Damned lycan infection.

She doesn't seem to notice his staring. "I sort of imagined there'd be a huge gold door in the middle of the field after the other ones ended," she continues. "Maybe with a sign saying, 'Congratulations! You found the secret thirteenth door!' and Vanna White showing off my new car."

"That sounds highly unlikely."

She scoffs. "It's a joke. You know, for laughs?" A little sigh. "You really need to either learn about sarcasm or watch more TV."

Jack lets this slide. She's probably right, but the calculation his mathematical mind has churned out demands immediate attention. He double-checks the skies and his inner clock to be sure, but when it comes to time, he's never wrong.

"Cora," he says carefully, tearing his eyes from the seductive moon, "we've only got two and a half hours left."

Her eyebrows slam together as her expression shifts from playful to near panic in an instant. "That's so soon." She spins around to face the vast field, but there's nothing there to see except more high grass. She whips back to the rows of doorways, and her eyes narrow thoughtfully. "What if we walk back to the castle? The Mistress said I'm supposed to go through Door Thirteen, but would she really know if I didn't use it?"

Without waiting for an answer, Cora strides purposefully toward the back row of doors. Jack barely has time to take a step to follow her before there's a resounding *bong,* and she's bounced to the ground. She picks herself up, swearing and angry, and then tries again – more slowly this time – but with the same results.

Curious himself, having never been on this end of the doorfield, Jack reaches out and tests the space between Ten and Eleven. The air forms a bubble around his hand like pushing through plastic wrap, but it doesn't tear when he puts his weight into it.

"Fuck this shit!" Cora screams at the space between Eleven and Twelve. Tears of frustration shine in her eyes as she turns to him. "Now what?"

Jack's gut twists. He doesn't know. For a man used to having all the answers, the last three days has been a series of confusing, tangled moments of borderline insecurity. He's never not known what to do so many times in such a short period. The vicious voice of his old self, so recently shed, purrs alluringly, reminding him that operating on the cold comforts of logic avoids such problems. But the voice is weak now; it's easier to shake it off. He takes a deep breath, the scents of dry grass and cotton and leather grounding him back in the moment.

"Outsiders are only allowed to port into and out of the underworld from the castle and Door Twelve. I've never been here before," he admits. Cora's face falls, and the twisting inside him tightens. He pushes experimentally on the elastic space between the doors again. "If we can't go back the way we came, then I suggest we head out into the field to search for the exit."

"Can't you tell if there's another door nearby with your magic woo-woo powers?" She waves her hands vaguely at him.

Briefly, and neglecting to mention she can do it herself, Jack closes his eyes and stretches out his consciousness. All that comes to him is the background static of the Otherworld. When he opens his eyes, he can see she knows it's pointless without being told. She turns to gaze out over the empty grassland, and for a long moment he's not sure if she's going to break down into tears or take off running. He certainly wouldn't blame her for doing either. But as he watches, she sets her jaw and lifts her chin, transitioning smoothly from lost little girl to determined fighter. Good.

"Okay, let's do this," she says. "If I'm going to run out of time and get stuck out here, I want to get as far away from the castle and those goddamn doors as possible. At least then I won't have to be reminded of how bad I fucked up for eternity."

He manages to catch her elbow before she marches off. "Wait. Let me show you something before we go."

Cora quirks an eyebrow but stops. Impatience

ripples under her skin strongly enough he can feel it through his fingertips.

"It'll only take a second," he reassures her. "We're not close enough to a usable portal to sense it yet, but you can channel your energy into a sort of extended radar. It picks up much smaller signatures to guide your search." He holds out both hands palms up and invites her to lay hers over them. "Fair warning: I've never had to teach anyone this before. The explicit description isn't clear to me, so I'm going to go through the process, and you should be able to feel how it's done so you can do it yourself."

Cora nods and gives him her hands, sending a delicate tremor through him that has nothing to do with magic. Eyes half closed, he draws up his consciousness into a thin circle that hovers around his midsection like an invisible hula hoop. He inhales deeply, and the hoop expands. Again. And again. It pushes past Cora with a hint of resistance, and he feels her shiver as she's enclosed within his energy. More breaths and more expansion. Steady, careful, precise. Within half a minute, the sensor circle is extended a hundred yards.

He opens his eyes and lets Cora's hands fall. "Now you."

She nods again, and there's an immediate burst of blue energy that forces him backwards. It takes single-digit seconds for the circle to reach her limits. When it stabilizes, her forehead's glossed with sweat and her eyes are bright.

"How was that?"

It takes him a moment to collect himself, but eventually he says, "Good. Solid and functional, if messy." Her disappointment at the critique doesn't deter him; if she's going to get through this and be trained, praising her for everything won't do her any good. "Do you think you can hold it?"

"Yeah, if I concentrate. It feels weird – like trying to rub your stomach and pat your head at the same time." She sniffs confidently. "But I'm sure I'll get the hang of it."

He gives her a small, encouraging smile. "You will." He gestures to the waiting field. "Shall we?"

The burnt-pumpkin light of the sinking moon lends the high grass a sinister aura as they slide through it in silence, precious minutes ticking away. Occasionally, one of them looks over a shoulder to keep their bearings straight with the rows of doors. Jack sneaks a glance at Cora now and then to see how she's fairing with holding the sensor circle. Every trainer, mentor, and teacher he's ever met has assured him that he's an oddity, even in the supernatural world. Watching Cora acclimate so quickly to her new reality calls up a tiny speck of hope that they're wrong. Even from a dozen feet away, he can see the change in her gait and lightening of her expression; it's already getting easier for her to use her powers.

It seems to be on Cora's mind, too.

"So," she says, eyes still searching the skyline for the mysterious thirteenth door. "You want to fill me in on this whole door-opening business while we're wandering aimlessly in hell's half-acre? Seems as good a time as any for a magic lesson. I'm hoping there's a proper name for it, for one thing."

"I've always referred to it as 'sidestepping.' Some people call it 'planeswalking.' A more scientific term might be 'interdimensional quantum teleportation.'"

"Sidestepping." She says the word as if tasting it. "And you said you've never met anyone else who can do it? How'd you find out that you could?"

Jack shrugs. "It just happened one day. I was fifteen, out on a walk around my neighborhood, and went through the chain link gate at the park like usual. I came out on a black beach on a black ocean and had no idea how I'd gotten there. It took me six days to get home – also an accident, if a happy one."

"Weren't your folks worried about you?"

"Not really. There was a lot going on that week."

It's a lie by omission – his favorite sort. She doesn't need to know that Dad had died or that Mom didn't get out of bed for a month after or that Emma stayed at boarding school instead of coming to the funeral.

"Well, didn't the government come to investigate? Like, whoever had your job back then?"

"From what I understand, they didn't have the technology to track my sort of activities at the time. It's one of the projects I've spearheaded at the agency since I joined."

"Huh," she mutters. "Did you do anything with your powers after you figured it out?"

"In small ways. I ended up in New Orleans for

college, which put me in touch with various resources that helped me understand what I was doing. Studying physics also helped. Once the SCD picked me up, though, I received proper training."

Cora sighs wistfully. "Lucky you got started young," she says. "You didn't have to worry your whole life about growing up to be a bland nobody."

"True."

She gives a little laugh, eyes combing the grassland ahead. "You know, as many times as I imagined what would make me special in the world, I never once pictured getting super powers. I kinda hoped I'd be a bestselling author or invent a perpetual motion machine."

Jack nods. "You were looking for meaning and risked eternal purgatory to find it. You got your wish, even if it's not what you expected. It's been my experience that many people who manifest supernatural abilities aren't so lucky or willing to embrace them."

The bitterness in his voice is accidental, and he mentally berates himself for letting it escape, but it's too late to hide it. Cora, being bright and curious, picks up on it immediately.

"Jack..." she starts. He silently hopes she'll let it go. If she asks, he'll have to tell her, and he's not sure what he'd say. Pride wrestles with honesty right up until she says, "What happened to you?"

Honesty wins.

He takes a deep breath and throws his gaze across the high grass as the memory replays. "My last assignment ended badly. A teenaged girl found out she could grant others magical abilities through tattoos – a high-level threat. I failed to bring her in after initial contact, and when I caught up with her later..." his voice wavers, "she was dead. She'd tried tattooing herself and the mixed resonances overloaded her system."

"Holy shit."

He doesn't reply. What can he say?

They walk a few more minutes with the story dissolving in the swishing grass. But Jack knows he hasn't actually answered her question.

There isn't anything to be ashamed of, he reminds himself. *It's past. Things are different now.*

Eventually he continues. "I put myself on disciplinary leave," he says, "and promptly had a nervous breakdown. I realized I'd become more machine than man – no emotion, only logic. I'd trained myself to be the most efficient agent possible, but the tattoo case broke me. It took six months locked in my apartment to dismantle myself enough that I could understand why she'd choose death over going into custody." He smirks without humor. "By the time I came back to work, hardly anyone recognized me."

Cora stops walking and says, "*Are* you human?" She points to his chest. "Because if that's werewolf-related, that usually means no."

His hand goes automatically to touch the scars that cross his torso. The question catches him off guard, a rare experience, but it's clear why she'd ask. "I am, and it is. That's another story for another time, though."

Time.

The word stops their conversation dead. Jack glances over Cora's shoulder, and she turns to follow his gaze. A thumbnail edge of moon barely peeks over the horizon, and the field around them glows softly with its own light. There's no sign of a useable door anywhere.

"How long?" she whispers.

"Just over an hour."

Her shoulders shake as she starts to cry.

And then he's holding her. Before he has time to talk himself out of it, before he has time to wonder if it's the right thing. When she turns in his arms to face him, he almost breaks away for fear he's crossed some unspoken boundary, but she folds herself against his chest, and he relaxes. She doesn't make a sound as tears course freely down her cheeks onto his shirt. He rests his chin on the top of her head, one hand in her ginger hair, not knowing what to say and avoiding the insipid platitudes most people resort to in moments of uncertainty. All he can do is hold her and hope it's enough.

When she presses herself closer, there's a dull jab at his thigh. He leans back and says, "Is that a fork in your pocket, or are you just happy to see me?"

He meant it to be a joke, but she leaps away from him with a gasp. So much for working on his sense of humor.

Despair apparently forgotten, Cora frantically digs in her jeans pocket and produces the fork she's carried with her since the house. Jack raises his eyebrows at her, openly confused at her sudden excitement.

"Remember how badly Azrael wanted this?" she says. "Didn't that seem weird to you? I mean, why would he care unless it's important?" She gives a laugh that's almost giddy and waves the utensil like a baton. "The Mistress did seem super eager to make sure I gave over whatever I find. Maybe it's a divining fork or something."

Even as she says it, there's a faint tug at the edge of Jack's awareness that trips his sensor circle. Cora's startled expression says she's picked it up, too. As she lifts the fork to examine it more closely, the tug on his mind turns into a pull, then a yank – the sort of psychic progression he's familiar with closing in on a doorway. But he's not moving.

"It's getting closer," Cora says apprehensively, eyes half-lidded in concentration. "I can almost reach out and touch it."

Now there's an idea.

Jack closes his eyes and reels in his spread-out consciousness in increments, feeling for the precise edges of the signal. He slowly stretches his right hand out into space. It connects with something solid, making a hollow knock on contact.

"Whoa," she whispers.

When he opens his eyes, they're standing in front of a door twice the size of those in the field behind the castle. The paint is divided precisely down the center, half glossy white and half matte black. A silver number plate declaring this to be

Door Thirteen perches over a massive lock decorated with intricate scrollwork.

"How is that even possible?" Cora breathes.

Jack shakes his head. "It shouldn't be." His eyes narrow at the key in her hand. "Someone's playing with the rules."

"The Mistress?"

"Possibly. But I suspect it goes beyond her."

"Meaning...?"

"Let's find out." He gestures for Cora to step up to the door. "Ladies first."

She rolls her eyes at him and steps forward to grasp the doorknob. There's a faint click as she turns it, then she pushes, but nothing happens. She puts her shoulder to the door after a moment's pause and grunts in an unladylike way as she tries to force it open. It doesn't budge. Wordlessly, she turns to Jack and points angrily at the door. But his efforts come up short, too, no matter how much pressure he applies.

"Useless fucking thing," Cora swears at the fork in her hand.

Jack takes a step back as she starts to pace and examines the details of the unmoving door. Something's not right about it, aside from the unusual paint and the fact that it found them instead of vice versa. Diagrams of the rest of the doorfield unfold in his mind, offering themselves up for comparison.

"Can make an imaginary door appear out of nowhere," Cora says, still muttering at the fork, "but can't bother to unlock it for us. Worthless piece of shit."

Jack seizes her arm mid-swing as she winds up to hurl the offending object across the dry grassland.

"Hey!" she shouts. "What the hell, man?"

Letting go quickly, he says, "It's a key." He points at the elaborately decorated keyhole under the knob. "None of the other doors have actual locks except this one."

She squints at the door, face screwed up with doubt. He waves her forward and touches the three tiny holes barely visible inside the scrollwork under the knob. She glances from him to the crude eating utensil in her hand to the ornate lock, then she shrugs and slides the tines of the fork into the unusual keyhole. It fits perfectly. A delicate chime rings out across the field, followed by a soft click. She pushes experimentally on the door, and it swings silently inward.

The musty scent of confined paper and ink spills out of the revealed room and into the open landscape. Oil lamps burning on high tables illuminate the floor-to-ceiling bookshelves ringing the room. Neither Jack nor Cora moves for a moment, their bodies tensed to slam the door shut should anyone call out or attack, but no one comes. When she seems satisfied that it's safe, Cora slides the fork-key back into her pocket and tiptoes inside. Jack takes one last glimpse back at the doorfield, then steps through, pulling the strange thirteenth door shut behind him, leaving the two of them standing in what appears to be the castle's library.

"Do you know how to get to the throne room?" Cora whispers.

"I've got a rough idea, but I get the impression things have changed since the last time I was here. Check the map."

"Map?"

Jack walks to the library's normal door and taps on a framed poster beside it. Cora chuckles as she inspects it.

"I had no idea the nerve center of the underworld was basically a mall," she says. "Apparently, we're here at this big red triangle, and the throne room is here in section 4A. Pretty straightforward."

"Given that the Mistress is expecting you, and there's roughly half an hour on your clock, I don't think we need to be concerned about sneaking around guards."

Jack unceremoniously pulls open the door and steps into the hallway, already drawing their route to the throne room in his mind. But Cora tugs on his jacket before he gets too far.

"Not yet," she says. "There's someone I have to see first."

TWENTY-ONE

The uneventful walk from the second floor library down to the dungeons is enough to worry Jack. Eerie emptiness cranks up his danger sense until he's practically twanging. Under normal circumstances, the castle's halls are filled with the bustle of underworld management, but now they only echo with the sound of two pairs of feet. There's no sign of the minor demon staff, the weights and measures crew, or the lesser angel interns. No sign even of the orcs Cora's said to watch out for.

He's fairly certain he's done a good job of disguising his annoyance at the detour. She didn't bother to fill him in on the details, even after he reminded her of the precious minutes they're wasting going so far afield. They've entered the castle through an unapproved route, meaning an intruder alert has gone off in the head office; the Mistress already knows they're in the building. Guards could be hunting them down right now, or worse, planning ways to delay them until the clock runs out. Cora's lack of concern chafes his need for efficiency, but he keeps it all to himself. It's her quest and her fate; he's just along for the ride.

As they round the final corner before the entrance to the dungeon, the acrid stench of unwashed lizard skin stabs into Jack's sinuses, throwing his trained agent mind into the control seat. He raises his arm to stop Cora and presses them both against a heavy tapestry on the corridor wall. She raises an eyebrow in confusion, but he puts a finger to his lips for silence.

Two seconds pass, then soft voices float toward them.

"I dunno, Terry. Seems like a waste of time to me. I mean, why bother puttin' her in prison in the first place? Seems like it'd be easier to lop her head off and be done with it."

"You sayin' you know better than the Mistress what to do with her hostages?"

Jack peeks one eye around the corner to assess the threat. A pair of squat guards in full plate mail lean against the barred door to the dungeons, spears propped casually against the wall. Challenge rating: One, easily neutralized. Options for attack compile as he watches.

The orc on the left waves his hands defensively. "Ain't sayin' anything of the sort! Just thinkin' out loud, Kevin. No need to get all shirty about it."

"Thinkin's risky. Remember what happened to Steve?"

Terry groans inside his helmet, sounding like a constipated bear. "Poor guy can't catch a break. His wife must be some kinda saint, stayin' with him after that."

"Right. Best keep them thoughts to yerself." Kevin hefts his weapon onto his shoulder with a grunt. "Alright, let's head out. Hank and Larry'll be here soon enough to do their time on watch."

Jack ducks back around the corner as the guards stump their way down the hall. He tenses, ready to spring if they're discovered, and Cora tries to suck in her gut to make herself less visible. But Terry and Kevin pass right by them, chatting inanely about who can eat the most whole chickens. Jack counts to ten over a slow exhale, letting the battle tension drain away before giving Cora the all clear.

They pad over the flagstones and together manhandle the thick wooden crossbar out of its brackets and onto the floor. Jack hauls on the heavy door to let Cora slip through, his inner clock ticking ever louder. He estimates they've got five minutes before the new shift arrives. And ten before Cora's time runs out.

A rustle from the drafty bowels of the dungeon immediately catches his attention as they enter, and he sniffs the air furiously, trying to pick out the source from under the rotting hay and stagnant water. He throws out an arm to stop Cora from bolting into the half-lit gloom, but she's already past him. Muttering curses under his breath and pulling the door closed, he follows her to a cell in the center of the aisle.

"You came back," someone is saying to Cora.

It's a voice that makes Jack jump with its familiarity – a voice he'd never have expected to hear in this place. He strides to the cell, startling Cora out of the way, his eyes searching the darkness inside as he grips the rusted bars.

"Lady Hel?" he says.

There's another rustle in the dirty hay, then the black and white goddess is standing in front of him. His eyes widen at the sorry sight of her filthy rags and matted hair, but her bearing and icy blue gaze are regal as always, giving him some small comfort. She slips her cold hands over Jack's and smiles.

"Agent," she says warmly.

"Hel? Like, hell-Hel?" Cora says to the woman. "Huh. All that stuff you said about being the most called-on ruler of the underworld actually makes sense now." Then she crosses her arms and shoots Jack a dagger-filled look. "And you guys know each other."

"Of course," he snaps. It comes out too sharply, and she flinches, but he's too unsettled to assuage her. He can apologize to Cora later; Hel's situation needs to be rectified now.

There's the barest touch of the goddess's mind on his, a gentle knock asking for permission to enter. He allows her in, knowing what she'll see. Tendrils of thought turn over his memories since she's seen him last, lingering too long over a glowing rosebush, a ruined apartment, a bloody statue, and a too-perfect house. Her eyes narrow as she disengages.

"You have changed, my friend," she whispers. "Devotion of many kinds has wrought strange things in your heart."

He manages to resist the urge to glance at Cora, but his palm twinges smartly where he cut himself in the Hunting Hall, making him wince to remember Ishtar's claim on him. Willpower alone keeps him focused on Hel. Time is far too short to bother with his petty stories since they last met.

"How did this happen to you?" he asks.

She lowers her eyes. "I was off guard and distracted by my hunger – it was so strong when she played her hand. She had insinuated herself into my house as a guest, and by the time I realized her intention to seize my throne, I was too weak to resist. I fought valiantly, but belief was on her side. More souls trust in the power of chaos than in the rule of law, it seems." The goddess laughs bitterly. "She overwhelmed me and discorporated the majority of my host. I have been slowly deteriorating in my own dungeons for the better part of a year."

Jack's jaw clenches in anger, not at the Mistress, but at himself. If only he'd been here. If only he hadn't stopped taking Otherworld assignments after the werewolf attack. If only he hadn't been so weak as to break down the way he did. If only.

"I'm sorry, Lady," he says. "I should have been here."

"There is nothing you could have done, Agent. Her machinations are greater than one man can handle alone, no matter his skill."

"I'll be the judge of that," he growls. "Tell me her name."

She lifts her chin and squeezes his hands. "It is

the Lady Eris."

Silence.

A thousand thoughts speed through his mind in short seconds as he cross-references information, projects possibilities, and commits details to memory.

Eris. Goddess of chaos. On SCD watch for felony mortal intervention, repeated trespassing attempts, and conspiracy to commit Otherworld treason. Known to attract minor beings that have lost their way. Graves threat rating: Eight.

Jack blinks slowly and takes a deep breath to focus. "What's she planning?" he says as calmly as he can.

"Many details are hidden from me, but I have discerned some things from her impassioned interrogations."

Her gaze slips around Jack's side to Cora. "You brought it?"

Cora steps up to the bars and holds out the rough fork. "Yes, ma'am. I figured it was important after people started trying to take it away from me. It unlocked the thirteenth door, but I don't think it'll open a normal lock like yours." She lowers her eyes. "I'm sorry."

Jack watches curiously as Hel reaches out and closes Cora's fingers around the object. A gentle breeze swirls around the two women, and there's a localized flash of ruby-red light that forces him to squint, but it fades quickly. When Cora opens her hand, there's a large, ornate wooden key where the ugly fork used to be. Even Jack is momentarily surprised.

"Eris seeks my key – this key, the one that opens all doors," Hel says, turning her focus back to Jack. "I used the last of my power before I was imprisoned to spirit it away and prevent it falling into her hands. However, your companion has helpfully retrieved it and brought it directly to her." She stares meaningfully into his dark eyes. "It will open the Gauntlet."

The phantom smell of burning magic slams into him, compounding with gut-wrenching vertigo as visions of falling walls and churning bodies riot through his mind's eye. The Gauntlet crashing down, all protection lost, the worlds colliding, everything gone to ruin and waste.

He swears loudly enough to invoke an echo over the stone walls. Cora's eyes dart around in anxious confusion and even Hel blinks in surprise. There's a long, pregnant moment as they all listen for the pounding of armored feet coming down the hall, but there's nothing.

"What the hell, Jack?" Cora says accusingly, letting out her held breath.

He rounds on her, knowing his intensity is frightening but unable to modulate it. "We can't let Eris have the key, Cora," he says. "Give it to me – I'll sidestep away and take it somewhere safe." He holds out his hand expectantly.

Cora shrinks back from his outburst at first but then rights herself, squaring her shoulders and shoving the key back into her jeans pocket. "No way. I promised to turn over whatever I find to the

Mistress, or Eris or whatever the fuck her name is, otherwise I fail the quest and get stuck here forever." Hurt creeps into her proud expression. "I thought you wanted to help me get out of here."

"I do. But she's the goddess of chaos, and there's no guarantee she'll honor her end of your bargain." He takes a step toward her, casting a looming shadow in the flickering torchlight. "You don't understand what will happen if she uses it to open the Gauntlet. This is so much bigger than your quest."

"Then take it back from her later! If I'm so naïve and still managed to bring it all the way here, surely you can use your wonky secret agent powers to steal it back from her once I'm done with it. Easy, right?" When he doesn't budge, she backs up protectively. "Don't do this," she whispers.

The angry tears in Cora's eyes and the pleading harmonic in her voice make Jack hesitate before simply overpowering her to seize the key – for her own good, for the good of humanity as a whole. It's only a moment's pause, but it's long enough that Hel can grab his elbow from between the bars of her cage.

"No, Agent," she says in a low voice. "The girl has oaths to fulfill. If she fails those tasks, her role in what is to come will unravel. While your impulses are noble and otherwise correct, all will fall to naught in the days to follow if you do not let her proceed."

He spins around to face the goddess with the bile of frustration rising in his throat, but magical wind whips her hair around her face and silences his angry protests. Power crackles along her skin, dancing up his arm where she holds him in her cold grip. The divine blaze in her now-red eyes dwarfs his own righteous fire, and he lets it die with reluctance, torn between the duty he's sworn to uphold and her prophetic declaration. He knows better than to argue with whatever it is she sees, but he doesn't have to like it.

"Fine," he snaps.

The breeze dies down, and Hel sags as her aura fades and Jack backs away from the bars. Cora's eyes prickle his skin, but he refuses to look at her until his indignation dies down and takes the urge to fight away with it.

"Keep it. Do whatever it is you think you need to do," he says to Cora. "I'd suggest starting with releasing Lady Hel. But you've got four minutes before you're overdue at the throne room."

Or rather, she had four minutes.

As Cora steps to the lock, a gruff voice shouts, "Hey, you!" from the top of the staircase.

Jack snaps his head up to see a pair of guards hovering at the entrance to the dungeon. His annoyance at being forced to stand down leaps gratefully from brooding to action. Cora starts to fumble with the lock on Hel's cell, and he pushes past her to buy them some time. If they can free the goddess, there's a chance that everyone can get what they want.

"Gentlemen," he says, a wide, sadistic grin on his face as he sets up the distraction. "How can I help you?"

Jack stretches his arms out wide to intercept the orcs as they clank down the stairs and try to plow past him toward Cora. He easily hooks the taller of the two with a long leg, sending him crashing to the cobblestones, but the other guard ducks out of Jack's slippery grasp on his breastplate and continues charging. Jack spins around to re-engage, cursing himself for letting his battle reflexes get so rusty, but the guard is already securing Cora's hands behind her back. She shoots Jack a wan smile and shrugs as best she can; Hel's cell door is still firmly shut. Then she gives him a surreptitious nod downward; following her gaze, he sees her slip the key into her pocket.

He sighs and lifts his hands in grudging surrender. "You'd better be taking us to see the Mistress," he says to the guard that's picking himself up off the floor.

"Shut up, you!" barks the prone orc. Then he says to his partner, in what he probably thinks is a whisper, "How'd he know that, Hank?"

Jack rolls his eyes at the blatant incompetence and starts walking toward the hidden entrance at the opposite end of the passage. The guards have to jog to catch up with him, Cora in tow.

Hank darts ahead before Jack can climb the stairs and glares over his shoulder. "You lot stay here while I announce your presence," he says as he disappears into the throne room.

Two minutes to go.

Jack can smell the heady fear rippling off Cora as

they wait, her only chance at freedom hanging precariously in the air. He looks down to see her grey eyes shining up at him under brows furrowed with questions. It's enough to evaporate the last dregs of his righteous anger. They've been through more in the last three days than most people go through in a lifetime – or afterlifetime. Whatever happens next, whatever fate Hel sees coming, he's not going to let Cora face it alone. Duty is one thing, but it's time to live for something more.

"Cora, I'm sorry," he says quietly. "I've always been a difficult person to get along with, but I'm on your side." He locks eyes with her, pouring as much sincerity as possible into his gaze. "I promise you that we're getting out of here together."

Her eyes narrow and, for a moment, he's eighty-two percent sure she's going to tell him to go fuck himself. But then she smiles.

"Together," she nods.

At that moment, Hank pokes his head back through the door and scowls at them.

"Get a move on, Larry. Mistress is waitin'."

There's an odd sound on the edge of Jack's hearing as they're prodded up the stairs to the throne room. It sounds like the chime of a bell.

TWENTY-TWO

The fire that warms the cold flagstones of the throne room roars off to the right. The medieval arms and armor gleam over the massive mantelpiece. The candle-filled chandelier sways over the plush carpet leading up to the enticingly empty golden throne. The orc guards leer from their positions around the room. Everything is exactly the same as the last time Cora stood here. If she didn't know better, it'd be easy to think she'd lapsed into a recurring dream, starring her as a clueless lost soul back at the start of the quest.

But while the room may be the same, there's no denying the change in Cora herself. Rather than allowing Hank and Larry to bully-march her into the audience as she dodges shadows, she strides ahead. Jack's presence behind her bolsters her to a degree – it's always a good idea to have backup – but it's not what sustains her. Newfound power strums her nerves, charging her with an electric confidence she'd never imagined in thirty years of aching to be more than a boring, average girl with a boring, average life. What she's learned about herself in the last three days has made her eager for this final judgment. The dreams are real; her power is real. She's ready to get back to her world and set it on fire.

Chin lifted, shoulders squared, feet sure, she comes to a stop at the foot of the dais and calls out to the absent Eris, "I'm here. Let's do this."

In response, a grandfather clock that isn't there rings out thirteen times, signaling the end of the quest. The rest of Cora's entourage parks itself a respectful distance behind her as she waits through every sonorous chime. As the last echoes die away, the space over the throne shimmers with golden sparks, and Eris comes into focus, one element at a time. Dress, legs, shoulders, arms, neck, head, crown, face. Cora crosses her arms impatiently through the process, making a show of being bored.

"That was a little melodramatic, don't you think?" she says once the transformation is complete.

If the usurping goddess hears the snark, she doesn't let it show. She opens her arms wide in greeting as she picks her way down the dais stairs, casting the scent of apple blossoms ahead of her. The smell gives Cora an instant migraine. Funny – didn't it make her swoon before?

"Welcome back, dear one," coos Eris through a sickly sweet smile. "I must admit that I expected you to have been lost in the Void before the end of the first day. You have done superbly well in your adventures."

She reaches Cora on the plush carpet and has to bend nearly double to slide her thin alabaster arms around Cora's shoulders, pulling the returning hero to her with as much warmth as an arctic sea. Cora allows the embrace but stands rigid until it's over rather than reciprocating. Eris then holds her out at arms' length like a long-lost niece and scrutinizes her face.

The knocking sensation in Cora's mind isn't unexpected. But this time, rather than letting the goddess rifle through her thoughts and memories unchecked, Cora resists, intuitively channeling her energy into a protective shield. It must be visible to everyone else because she hears Jack *hrm* appreciatively behind her, and Eris breaks her faux-affectionate hold to step back in alarm.

"You have grown strong since last you stood before me," Eris says. Her voice is still sweet, but there's a note of hostility that doesn't escape Cora's notice. To be fair, she'd be pissed if someone resisted her attempts to break into their brain, too.

"I like to think so," Cora says. "And now we've got some business to resolve, I believe."

"We do."

Eris slinks to the side as if she's going to start circling Cora but stops at the zenith of her arc, directly in front of Jack, placing herself between the two of them. She peers at him with her elegant eyebrows raised, spending an inordinate amount of time sizing up this new mortal and practically undressing him with her eyes. The fine hair on Cora's arms and neck stand to attention, although she's not sure if a danger response or simple jealousy.

"This is a fine specimen of manhood, girl," Eris purrs. "An excellent offering."

"He's not for sale." It comes out in a borderline growl.

The goddess shrugs delicately. "Alas." She lets her gaze linger on the thin, dark man then turns her attention back to Cora. "What else have you brought me, sweetest heart? You arrived within mere moments of your appointed time, which entitles you to the precious second chance for which you have bargained, but I sense you have discovered more than a handsome companion in your adventures."

"There's this one thing," Cora says.

She retrieves Hel's oversized, carved wooden key from her jeans pocket and holds it up for Eris to see. The hunger that flashes in the goddess' black-on-black eyes makes Cora's breath catch in her throat, and she takes a protective step back.

Eris seems to remember herself and fluffs the crows' feathers around the collar of her dress with rehearsed casualness. "You remember the terms of your quest, I trust. Anything you have found in the doorfield is forfeit to me."

"I remember."

Eris' porcelain hand opens in the air. There's no request, just the assumption of acquiescence.

But the scene in the dungeon short minutes ago makes Cora hesitate. The way Jack and Hel reacted to the idea that this woman – this trecherous deity – would get hold of a key that opens any door put a fast-growing seed of doubt into Cora's heart. If she hadn't met Jack and had blindly turned it over when (if) she returned, what would've happened? And what will happen now if she refuses to give it up?

There's another brush against Cora's mind as she thinks. It's not a blatant intrusion this time, more like a stone skipped across the surface of her thoughts. It bounces more heavily on each landing, straining Cora's crude mental shield with its ripples – once, twice, three times. The shield trembles as Cora tries to route more energy into it, but the weakness it produces in her body frightens her into cutting off the power entirely. On the fourth skip, Eris' attack breaks through the barrier, and icy fingers latch onto Cora's dark, hidden places. She wobbles with vertigo as her memories and desires are churned up with alien interest.

Eris turns her pupilless eyes to bear down fully on Cora. Their endless blackness shines with flecks of golden glitter, and she can't not stare into them. Her resolve melts away in sheets as the sun-warmed tones of the goddess' voice wash over her.

"There could be a place for you here at my side, Cora Leigh Riley. The minor talents you have discovered are nothing compared to what I can bestow upon you. Out there, the best you can hope to become is a pawn in a bureaucratic game. Here, you will be loved and feared as the sovereign of worlds within worlds. Your superiority will be unquestioned, your power ever-growing." She leans forward until her sculpted nose nearly touches Cora's. "Relinquish that which you have brought to me, and you will have your seat amongst the gods."

Sweet apples fill Cora's senses, further silencing her inner voices of protest as visions of unbridled power rise up in sharp focus. Every decision and whim changing reality. Life and death in the hollow of her hand. The ultimate fate of every soul on Earth completely up to her. Eternal beauty and immortality. All she needs to do is surrender an insignificant piece of wood.

The key is halfway to Eris' open palm when, from what seems like a million miles away, someone calls Cora's name. There's a brief scuffle that starts with a piggy grunt of surprise but ends with a metallic click and a guttural chuckle. A curl of a smile touches Eris' red lips, and she breaks her gaze momentarily to glance over her shoulder.

"A valiant effort, Mister... Alexander is it?" she says. "But this girl and I have a pact, and you will not interfere with its resolution."

Eris swings her attention back to Cora, but the brief respite is all she needed to come back to herself. Reality crashes back in as the fantasy of being an all-powerful goddess disintegrates, replaced by indignation at being so easily tempted. It throws gasoline on her dimmed yearning to secure her second chance. She screws her eyes shut and shakes her head, as much to clear it as to express her disdain for Eris' tricks.

"No," she says.

It comes out so quietly even she doesn't quite hear it, but it gets the goddess' attention.

"No?" Eris repeats with a hiss.

"Yeah, I said 'no.' I don't need what you're offering – not anymore. And even if it wasn't on the table, this key isn't yours. I should be handing it over to its rightful owner, not to you."

"What makes you imagine you have a choice in the matter, stupid girl?" Eris' cruel smirk is clear even without Cora seeing it. "You agreed to the terms of your quest. You must fulfill what you have sworn."

Cora opens her eyes but keeps them trained on the wooden key gripped inside her white-knuckled fist. The clarity that comes with anger is slowly collating pieces of information – myth, experience, rumor – into a plan.

"Why don't you take it if you want it so badly?"

Eris scowls, and behind her Jack says, "The terms say you have to give it up willingly; she can't take anything from you by force."

Cora grins smugly. "That's what I thought." She takes a step back, widening the gap between her and the goddess. "I don't have to give you anything if I don't want to. This isn't your territory. You stole the throne from Hel, and I'm pretty sure that means you don't have any real power here. You can't punish me, Lady Eris."

A crackling aura of white-gold sparks erupts around the goddess, momentarily blinding Cora, and a hot, dry wind fills the cavernous room as Eris howls her fury.

"You have no understanding of the law, foolish child!" Eris seizes Cora's wrist, forcing her to look up. "You may have learned my true name, and you may question my claim to this realm, but you have made an oath to me and it is inviolate." She squeezes, grinding Cora's bones together until she nearly drops the key from agony. "You must relinquish that which is mine or suffer the consequence of failure." Cruel humor curls her lips. "Both the key and your companion."

Every limb, every nerve, every cell of Cora's body freezes. "What?" she manages to croak. "You want Jack, too?"

"You found him in the course of your quest, did you not? And you used his skill and knowledge to navigate the doorfield, correct?" Eris laughs haughtily. "Not only does he fall under the terms of our agreement, but you have cheated Azrael's binding to prevent other assistance, as well. Your stubborn ignorance has made his life forfeit."

Cora manages to wrench herself from Eris' iron grip and twist around to face Jack. "Is that true?" she asks.

He nods gravely, fists clenched at his sides. "You swore to her. It's the terms that matter, not where she is or what she claims to be."

Cora turns back to the triumphant Eris, fight draining out of her and mind overheating as she tries to reason her way out of the trap. The options are so stark. Hand over the key and her friend in return for her precious second chance at life? Refuse to give them up, be obliterated for breaking the oath, and have them taken anyway? Or...

"What if," she says, voice treacherously shaky, "what if I give you the key, but you let Jack return to the real world with me? Will that work?"

"Cora, no!" Jack cries out.

Amusement trickles into Eris' face. "It is far too late in the game to play that card, silly girl, although I applaud your tenacity." She leans down, forcing eye contact with Cora and whispers, "You must pay everything you owe."

The bottomless gaze bores into Cora's mind again, and she knows she can't withstand the strain a third time. She only has a split second to act before the goddess of chaos makes it impossible for Cora to choose her own fate.

There's only one way she can think of to save herself and prevent whatever miserable fate Jack and Hel have foreseen.

Snap.

The quiet sound builds up echoes over the throne room walls before dying away in a pool of silence. The next sound is the *click-click* of the two halves of Hel's magical wooden key hitting the naked stones of the floor. The third sound is the faint chime of a silver bell that only Cora can hear.

For what seems like an eternity, no one moves. No one speaks. No one breathes.

And then everything happens at once.

A shriek like a jet engine crams the room with noise, building in intensity with Eris' screams of wrath and inciting the terrified orc guards to scatter from their posts. Somewhere behind Cora, Jack is shouting her name. She wants to run to him but a burst of impossible black light over the throne stuns Cora into stillness. The goddess sneers at her hesitation and uses the moment to snatch a spear from a fleeing guard. Taloned hands spin the weapon around with effortless grace. Cora steels herself for the fatal impact.

But the blow doesn't come.

A sonic boom erupts from the swirling darkness over the throne, the immense shockwave throwing Cora onto her back and knocking the wind out of her. She tries to scramble to her feet, but animal fear locks her muscles as Eris dashes toward her, murder in her eyes. She hears Jack bellowing curses nearby as he rushes forward to intervene.

It's too much. Cora's system overloads, collapsing her fully to the floor where everything is quiet and dark.

"Vitals look good. Miss Riley, nod if you can hear me."

What was that light? Where's Jack? Where am I?

"She's waking up! Get the doctor!"

"Cora? Cora, baby, can you hear me?"

Nod.

"Oh my god, Dan, she's awake!"

But I'm not done. I left him there all alone.

"Oh, shit, she's crashing."

"Don't go! Baby, stay here – don't leave us!"

I have to go back. I still have work to do.

Color seeps back into the world as Cora opens her eyes to stillness. She twitches a finger experimentally and finds she's not hurt. Facing the dais, she pushes herself up to sitting, the details of the room coming into sharper focus.

Where the throne held a swirling vortex of black light before, it now holds its rightful owner. Cora stares, marveling at the difference between the small, filthy woman she bargained with in the dank cells and the towering, radiant goddess of the underworld sitting before her. Hel's black and white skin glows softly, her blonde hair is sleek, and her rags have been replaced with a flowing black robe. Eyes like flame rubies are trained on a point over Cora's shoulder.

She turns to follow the gaze and nearly screams as she comes nose-to-point with the bloodstained spear clutched in Eris' hand. The goddess' face is twisted with hate, the weapon poised in mid-attack inches behind Cora, her free hand flexed into a vicious claw. But she isn't moving.

Slowly, willing her heart to calm itself, Cora slides backwards and gets to her feet. She turns back toward Hel, whose face is a mask of concentration, and realizes that she's keeping Eris in stasis.

"Time is short, and I am still weak," Hel says in a faraway voice. "I can only hold her for a few moments more before she breaks free."

Cora nods, "Not a problem, my lady. Happy to oblige." She calls out into the throne room. "Hey, Jack, let's blow this pop stand."

No answer.

"Jack?"

Still nothing.

Lead weights of dread drop into her stomach as she hesitantly steps around the frozen goddess. The dark part of her heart knows what she'll see there, and she doesn't want to look. But she does.

A pained groan escapes her lips as she dashes to Jack's side and falls to her knees.

He's lying face-up, eyes closed, in a growing pool of blood, a gaping hole straight through his leather jacket, his thin shirt, the muscled wall of his side. Cora presses both hands to the wound, not feeling the rise and fall of his breath. She doesn't try to stem the tears that leap down her face onto his chest when she puts an ear to it and hears nothing.

"No, no, no," she wails, voice rising with grief. "This wasn't supposed to happen. You said we'd go back together, goddammit!" She lets her forehead rest over his heart, her hands covered in his blood, her hot tears soaking his shirt. "Why'd you do it, you stupid bastard? I'm not worth this."

"He seemed to think that you are."

Cora rolls her head to the side to look up at Hel. Tears and hope crack her voice. "Can't you...?"

"No, child," Hel says. "I cannot interfere in the twists of his fate, and my powers are yet reduced from my imprisonment." She learns forward with an air of urgency. "The window for your escape closes swiftly. If you wish to return to your world, you must go now and alone."

There's regret in the goddess' voice, but it doesn't matter to Cora. All she hears is that she's lost him, that he gave his life so she could have another chance at hers. An animal growl rumbles through her and spills out between her clenched teeth. She pounds the stone floor, sending a dark red splash into the air and bruising her fist. She curses herself, Eris, and even Jack for making it end this way.

But her quiet, reasonable voice manages to break through her grief: *You can't stay here. There's nothing left to stay for.*

Brushing away her angry tears, Cora takes a deep, shuddering breath, then bends over and presses her lips to Jack's forehead. The residual warmth there rips another hole in her heart, but she stands and whispers, "Goodbye." Trembling legs carry her automatically back to the dais to stand before Hel.

"What happens now?" she asks in a weary voice. "I broke the key. I lost my friend." She hangs her head, shoulders rolling in dejectedly. "I've got no energy left to look for a door if I wanted to."

"Come here, my girl."

Cora shuffles up the shallow dais steps until she's practically touching the goddess' tall knee with her shoulder.

"You are more remarkable even than you have discovered on this journey, Cora Leigh Riley," the goddess says. "You have fulfilled your oath to me and restored my kingdom by refusing to choose chaos over virtue. You believe. And for that, you have my gratitude." Hel's enormous black hand reaches out and gently lifts Cora's chin. "There is more to your story than this ending, child. Remember the lessons you have learned here; you will need them in the days to come."

A pair of hot tears course down Cora's cheeks as she gazes into the divided face and feels her strength returning. "I will," she whispers, wiping away the tears and snot.

Hel smiles softly and waves her white hand. A wash of red light appears, solidifying into a freestanding cottage door. The brass number plate says "zero."

"Go. Be who you are meant to be."

Cora nods, her grey eyes meeting Hel's red ones for a brief moment, then steps gingerly down from the dais to the door and puts her hand on the knob. A pang of guilt demands she looks back, if only to cement Eris's mad expression and unforgiveable crime into her memory for later; her own power isn't the only thing she needs to remember. But she doesn't turn. She can't bear to see Jack's broken body again.

Then she takes a steadying breath, turns the handle, and pushes the door inwards on silent hinges. Blinding white light pours out. She steps through, and falls forever.

PART III
YOU CAN'T GO
HOME AGAIN

TWENTY-THREE

I didn't want to come on this assignment. I insisted that the terms of one I'd just completed, the one that led me to her, were fulfilled and I was officially in debriefing. I argued with Agent 99 that my transgressions from the Steeltown incident had compromised my functionality and that I haven't fully recovered. Logically, someone else should be sent for her retrieval. I tried quoting regulations – more reflex than excuse – but he wouldn't hear it.

He said tough shit. It's my job, and I've had enough time to deal with my personal problems. I'm the one who got her into this; I have to be the one to clean it up.

So I came. And I waited.

I've been watching over her for a full day of almost-rousing and dipping vital signs, but she's yet to truly wake. The silence gives a man a lot of time to think. I thought I'd had enough of that during my self-imposed suspension, but the chaos she's brought into my life has served as the vital piece of data that allows the pattern to emerge.

As a hotheaded young man, I was on the receiving end of a breathtaking number of disciplinary actions, reprimands, and near expulsions from the force. Superiors don't like hearing their rookie has bloodied a third suspect or tipped off another sting operation or disappeared into Faerie without a trace. But that was me. I wanted – needed – to be at the center of every investigation and every new assignment went right to the core of me. I sympathized, empathized, excused, and identified. I hadn't learned how to distance myself from a case. Too much heart, not enough head.

I knew things had to change when my behavior landed me in the hospital for three months battling lycanthropy; a situation that could've been easily avoided if I'd followed orders instead of my still-underdeveloped instincts. Emotions were the problem, so shutting down the unreliable, messy system seemed like a clear choice to keep my career and my sanity intact.

But I pushed too far – the dangers of a finely tuned mind turned to grim purposes. No one should aspire to out-logic their desktop computer. No one should tell their mother that her crying on the anniversary of her husband's death is pointless. No one should watch a young girl die at her own hands in desperate fear of their pursuer – of you – and not be able to shed a single tear. Human beings aren't meant to function without emotion. I can see that now, these five years distant, although as much progress as I've made in reclaiming my humanity, maybe I'll always be something of a mechanical man. Even nothingness leaves a residue.

She stirs in her sleep, and I manage not to flinch at how loud the rustle of bedclothes is in the silent room. I watch her shift and settle, pushing down the hope that this time she'll open her eyes.

When I arrived yesterday to inform the hospital of the SCD's involvement with her case, they said she'd been comatose for four days and showed no signs of recovering. It took an hour of checking and crosschecking my credentials before they grudgingly allowed me to exercise my authority. I had her moved to a private room, dismissed her care staff, and sent her parents home to wait for further instructions.

She started stirring an hour after I took up my armchair vigil. The doctors are thoroughly confused by the change, but it's fairly simple. She's not in a coma; she's a sidestepper who got lost on her way back.

It's easy enough to do – it happened to me the first time I made a big jump – but I should've been there to ensure it didn't happen to her. I gave her my word that we'd make it back together and didn't follow through. I was reckless in confronting an armed deity and reaped the consequences. A bit of a flashback to my old self, I suppose. If only she'd waited the five more minutes for me to regain consciousness. Not that I blame her for leaving or for missing the nearly imperceptible healing of the wound. Had I been conscious, I certainly would've told her to go without me, regardless. Her quest, her life. But watching her struggle now, knowing the terror of being lost in the shades between worlds where I can't reach her, I can't help wishing it had gone differently.

Regret isn't an emotion I've got a handle on yet, despite wallowing in it for weeks following the breakdown. You can't drown it in alcohol or blind it with darkness. I tried. You can only pretend it doesn't exist and move on. But it's so much easier to give into self-loathing and let the past consume everything. I allowed it for a while, losing most of thirty-five to denial, guilt, and substance abuse. I'm still unsure exactly what brought me out of the spiral, but as I sit here in patient anticipation, I'm relieved that it did.

Sometimes, this re-education process is unbearably cliché.

She stirs again. It's merely the twitch of a finger, but that's more than enough to grab my attention. I get the unsettling feeling she's responding to my brooding, although it's more likely that I'm merely attributing meaning to coincidence.

I sigh at my own ridiculous behavior and nervously adjust my sunglasses. They're not there; I haven't worn them since I left Steeltown nearly a year ago. But I need to do something to alleviate my building unease, so I unfold myself out of the ridiculously uncomfortable armchair and pace the small room while smoothing the wrinkles in my suit like a hormonal teenager outside his prom date's door.

To keep myself focused, I haul my thoughts back to the job. I ran through the scenario a hundred times over the long trip from headquarters to her beside. I'd appear at the hospital, dig in for surveillance, wait for her to revive, debrief her, present her options, and then transport her back to the agency. The same procedure I've followed for years.

Inevitably, though, memories of our time in the underworld keep insinuating themselves through the professional litany. The way she carries herself with such confident curiosity. The strength of her hands and her mind. The smell of her skin so close to mine. And then I'm off imagining things as illusory as the events in that house.

I wonder what she remembers. Will she know who she is? What she's capable of? What she fought so hard to accomplish? The Otherworld? Xavier? Me?

Us?

I shake my head. There is no *us*. Even if she does wake up and remember everything with perfect clarity, we had an agreement. While I can't deny an attraction even before the house, I also can't forget what happened there.

The voice of my old self, of Agent 97, rises up at the edge of my thoughts as if on cue, diminished now but never truly gone.

It does not matter what you feel – what you think you feel. You are foolish to think you could ever be ready for such a thing, foolish to believe she would understand. This is another embarrassment at the hands of enchantment, at the hands of another woman who doesn't know her power. Let it slip into the past and forget.

Maybe he's right. Looking at it objectively, I know I should keep my distance, stay professional, do my job, and let it go. Let *her* go without complicating things further. She's young and ambitious with her whole second life ahead of her; I'm worn and broken, likely having outlived my share of chances. There are far too many scarred places in my psyche to be worth anyone's investment.

The heart monitor jingles behind me, breaking the logic spiral, and I fight down the urge to run to her. This is it.

I cross the short distance from the window to the bedside in one step. She's struggling to surface. Ever the fighter. I can clearly picture the bright corridor she's walking, her hand grasping for the edge of the portal, the desperation to make it through this time. I start to close my eyes against my own memory of the place then snap them open again. A nurse will arrive any moment, and I need to see her wake for myself. That first look will tell me everything I need to know.

Her nearly invisible eyelashes flutter and catch the harsh fluorescent light, refracting it into something beautiful. Then slowly, as the door creaks open behind me, her lids open in a bloom of thundercloud grey. Her eyes flick around the room, getting her bearings, adjusting to the light. I hold my breath. The nurse bustles to the end of the bed and tries to bully me into moving, but I stand silent and steadfast. I need to know if she's still there.

Then her eyes focus on me.

"Hey," she whispers. "Fancy meeting you here."

The nurse has had enough of my interference within the ten seconds it takes Cora to speak, and I'm muscled away from the bedside with linebacker skill. But the entire hospital staff have already been briefed as much as needed – which is to say gruffly and hardly at all – and I'm in charge, so she doesn't demand that I leave. There's a haze of questions rising in Cora's eyes, but she doesn't have time to speak again before the solid woman in white starts fussing over her. I swallow hard to douse the twinge in my gut and resume my vigil from the armchair. I can wait a little longer.

"Good morning, Miss Riley!" the nurse chirrups in a clipped accent. "Glad you decided to join us! We were worried about you for a while. I'm Cherry. Now let's get you set up here. There we go."

The bed is levered into a gentle sitting position as Cora undergoes Cherry's ministrations. While her body has lain motionless for the last five days, her spirit has been aggressively pushing itself to exhaustion. So long apart makes it difficult for body and spirit to rejoin, and her limbs are as yet unresponsive to her commands. She snarls in frustration at needing assistance to wash her face and brush her teeth while lying in bed. Her hands shake as she raises them; her skin is nearly translucent; her features are drawn from the effort of healing her body while she slept. So different from the strong woman who fought by my side in the Otherworld. But she catches my gaze whenever Cherry forgets to stand in my way, and her eyes are still bright. I make an effort not to smile, doing my best to appear professional and detached. It should be easy after so much practice, but I find it difficult to maintain since meeting her.

Several minutes pass as Cherry calls for the doctors, then double-checks Cora's vital signs and removes the tubes and monitors. There's a hushed conversation between the two of them about her physical and mental condition after nearly a week in a coma following her accident. She asks about solid food and coffee. A change of clothes is brought out. Visitors and parents are mentioned. Eventually, I realize the nurse is stalling. I can't blame her for being spiteful – I did usurp her authority quite effectively – but I have no patience for this kind of inefficiency.

I rise from the chair and firmly take hold of the nurse's elbow. "Thank you, Miss Cherry. I will inform your superiors of your admirable dedication to your patient." I half-walk, half-march her away from the bedside. "You will be notified should your assistance be required again." She almost gets her fingers caught in the door as I close it against her protests.

And then we're alone.

TWENTY-FOUR

I stand at the door for a moment and let Cora examine me. The starched black suit and tie is a harsh contrast against how she's used to seeing me, and I'm sure my official approach with the nurse is strange, too. It's been ten years since anyone's seen both my work and personal side – how long has it been since I had a personal side? – and I'm not sure how quickly she'll adapt to it. Valkyries and goddesses are one thing; mortal reality is another. There's so much she still needs to know.

"So, uh, you ran off the nurse before I could put on real clothes," she says, half a smile on her face. "Guess who gets to help me with that?"

I look from the pile of neatly folded clothes at the foot of the bed to her somewhat amused expression, my heartbeat accelerating. This seems like a terrible idea given the potential tension between us, but she's still unsteady from having so recently come around and the doctors won't arrive for approximately thirteen minutes. It would be cowardly to refuse her request.

I cross the room, wishing for the protection of my tinted lenses to avoid her seeing any traces of emotion in my face.

We don't speak. She extends a hand to me, and I help her shift her weight to the edge of the bed. The hospital gown bunches around her thighs as we work together to swing one leg and then the other over the side. Her feet dangle a few inches from the ground. I unfold the clothing, which turns out to be a blue summer dress and nothing else. I'm not sure if I should be relieved or disappointed. She takes the dress, brushing my arm unnecessarily, and starts to remove the hospital gown. I turn around to give her some measure of privacy, and she laughs softly at my discomfort. There's a whisper of fabric, then a tap on my left shoulder. I turn back to see her fully clothed. She smiles, holding out both hands to me. I wonder if she notices the tremors in mine as I take hers. She flexes her lean arms and carefully lifts herself from the mattress. The slight weight of her body is nearly too much for her weakened legs. I easily hold her up when she wobbles, keeping her from falling either back into the bed or against my chest. She smiles as she steadies herself. I don't, still trying to hold the façade of professionalism in place, trying to honor our agreement, trying not to give in to the impulse to kiss her.

Once she's stable, I step away. The smile slips

from her face and is quickly replaced with mild confusion. But her heady scent of cotton and leather and blue is distracting me from the duties I'm here to perform, and I need to put some space between us to keep my head clear.

"Miss Riley..." I begin, smoothing the front of my jacket.

"Jack..." she says.

We both stop and start at the same time.

"You can't call me that here," I say hurriedly.

"It's Cora," she says, an edge of ice in her voice.

An awkward silence dominates the room as we stare at one another. I don't know how to fill it, but she does.

"What's going on here, agent?" she asks, putting acid emphasis on the formal title. She crosses her arms and sits heavily on the edge of the bed. "Doesn't seem like you're here for a friendly visit in your shiny shoes and sharp suit."

This is already not going well, and I haven't even officially begun. I start again, gathering old confidence from the routine of the job and willing it to show in my face.

"Miss Riley. My name is Agent 97." I retrieve my badge from the inner pocket of my jacket and show it to her. She rolls her eyes. I put it back. "It appears that you have manifested high-level supernatural abilities as a result of trauma. My duty as an agent of the Supernatural Cases Division of the FBI is to debrief you on the paranormal incident you experienced from the twelfth to seventeenth of July."

Cora huffs and waves a hand at me. "Fine. Debrief away."

As much as I want to drop the secret agent mask and behave the way she's used to seeing me, I can't. I need to put distance between whatever feelings I have and the assignment. Getting too invested in the end result of this conversation could be devastating if it doesn't turn out the way I choose to trust that it will.

I take a quiet breath and reel in my energy to ground myself before continuing.

"At twenty-three fifty-eight on July twelfth, you departed from your parents' home headed south on rural route BB, travelling approximately fifty miles per hour. Your vehicle lost traction due to gravel on the roadway and crashed at the roadside. No other motorists were involved in the accident. Emergency services arrived to find that you had lost consciousness due to severe blood loss from various wounds on your neck, head, and torso. You were rushed here, to St. John's Hospital, where trauma surgeons repaired your external injuries, but you did not regain consciousness – a fact that doctors were unable to explain. Your loved ones took shifts watching over you for four days. You appeared to rouse several times, but you did not fully wake until today.

"My department became aware of the supernatural aspects of your case after receiving post-assignment documentation regarding Xavier Banks. Your ability to locate and utilize Otherworld portals classifies you as a nine point three on the

Block scale and a level five threat to national security, requiring mandatory investigation and detention."

The last word gets her attention. She already had tears in her eyes from the description of her accident, but they seem to evaporate as she sits forward, suddenly keenly alert.

"What the fuck are you talking about?" she says.

How I manage to keep my voice calm, I'm not sure. "All subjects with a Block rating over seven must be taken into custody as standard procedure. This ensures a thorough understanding of the subject's abilities, as well as allows the agency to establish a tracking and safety plan going forward."

She narrows her eyes. "So, what you're saying is that I literally went through hell to get my life back – which you helped me do, let's not forget – and now you're going to arrest me for being a sidestepper and implant a tracking device in my brain?"

The memory rushes up before I can stop it. Sitting in a diner across from a wild girl with black hair screaming her defiance when I told her the same thing. My words, my inhumanity, my rigid execution of duty filling her with fear so strong it killed her. I've lived the moment a thousand times, playing out every possible scenario in which it could've gone differently for both of us.

I can't let it happen again.

She flinches when I move, drawing back as if I'll snatch her up and force her into handcuffs at any moment. I hold out my hands for patience. Slowly, I unbutton my suit jacket and shrug it off, hanging it neatly over the chair next to me. The belt is next, snaking out of its loops to free my sidearm, which I lay on the cushion. I undo the tight knot of my thin black tie and let it fall onto the pile. All the trappings of my authority are removed and set aside. If I'm honest, I've done it more for me than for her – Agent 97's costume is too familiar and stiff for the person I need to be right now. He can't help me anymore.

"Cora, I'm sorry," I say, hands still raised in supplication. "That's not what I'm here to do at all. They sent me to collect you because of everything you went through. Your talents, the quest – it's so far beyond anything we're used to dealing with. But I promise I'm not going to hurt you. Or let anyone else hurt you."

I take a step toward her. She doesn't recoil this time, although there's understandable suspicion in her eyes. My heartbeat roars in my ears as I wait for her response. I've already broken her trust once; I can't do it again right before I ask her to make the biggest decision of her life. Her grey eyes carve me up like lasers as she takes my measure. It's like we've never met before. I suppose we really haven't until now.

"How did you survive what happened in the castle, Jack?" she says.

The question surprises me, making me feel even more foolish than I already did. It hadn't occurred to me she'd want to know. Perhaps all she needs is an explanation to settle her reservations. I lower my hands and chance another step toward her. There's about a foot of empty space between us now. It feels like a mile.

"I heal fairly quickly, especially in the Otherworld. One of the benefits of surviving a werewolf attack." I smile faintly. Her serious stare doesn't change. "But I didn't wake up until you'd already gone. I helped Hel secure Eris and then stepped back to DC. I didn't find out where you were until after I filed my reports on Xavier and the underworld coup. Even though it's out of my jurisdiction, I was asked to debrief and collect you because of our...," I fumble with the words I want to use and opt for something more innocent, "time together."

Micromovements in her shoulders and face are my only indicators that she's buying any of it. Agent 97's voice rises in my mind, pointing out how little I'm accomplishing in terms of the assignment. I know he's right, but my own voice, as rusty as it is, reminds me that the job isn't everything. If I let 97 take over after fighting so hard to win back my humanity, I may not be able to push him aside again.

"I waited here," I point to the uncomfortable armchair, "thinking about everything that happened. I spent a lot of it trying to dissect the past and what it could mean for the present. But now that you're awake, it's time to think about the future."

Cora's eyes narrow, and I push on, ignoring the compulsion to slip back into professional armor.

Nothing will make this next part any easier.

"There are two options. The first is that you accompany me willingly back to the agency in DC, where you'll be evaluated as a potential asset. Given what I've seen of you in the field and the level of your abilities, I'm confident you'll be admitted."

She raises an eyebrow. "Meaning?"

"We'll make you an agent."

Her eyebrows furrow. "What? Really?" she says. It's almost a laugh, it's so incredulous.

"Really," I say. "It's part of why we bring in high-level subjects. Where do you think we get our operatives?"

Cora smirks unselfconsciously as she considers what I've said. Even that small hint of acceptance lightens my spirits. This conversation never goes well, but it was going so badly – and I admit I have so much invested – that I'd started to plan for the alternative arrangement.

"What's the other option?" she asks.

"You refuse to come willingly, and I take you into custody anyway."

"Wow. That's not much of a choice, is it?"

I shake my head. "No. But the agency views resistance to cooperation as evidence of antagonism, which would make you ineligible for training, to say the least. Regardless of any other circumstances in this situation, I have to complete the assignment."

A deep breath. There it is, everything out on the table. Now it's up to her to choose which path we both take from here.

Cora peers at me from the edge of her hospital bed. Her face is blank, but I try to read it regardless, searching for anything that tells me what she's thinking. She lets nothing slip through, though; she's better at this game than I am. I watch with growing impatience as she carefully stands and crosses gingerly to the pile of my things on the armchair. She rifles through my jacket until she finds my badge. The buzzing overhead lights make the mundane bronze shield look vaguely magical as she inspects it.

"What happens if I take the second choice?" she says in a far-away voice.

"You'll be placed under arrest and transported to Washington under my supervision. When we arrive, you'll be taken to our holding facility where you'll await formal interrogation and, if necessary, reconditioning. A best-case scenario would be that you're given a tracking device after the tests are complete and permitted to return home without any modifications."

My jaw clenches as I imagine the worst-case scenario. I see her in a white jumpsuit, vacant eyes staring out from a tiny window, confused and afraid. I shudder at the thought and then move to stand protectively next to her. It's highly unprofessional, but I lay my hand on her shoulder. The warmth of her bare skin almost derails me.

"Are you sure that's what you want, Cora?" I say. "You're too powerful for me to let you 'accidentally' slip away. I'll do everything I can to protect you, but I can't make any promises if you refuse to cooperate. This is out of my hands."

She raises her chin to search my eyes. Déjà vu – I remember this look on another face. I sigh and swallow down the wave of nauseating guilt, the triumphant echoes of Agent 97 ringing in my mind. I've failed. Again.

But as I pull away to reach for my handcuffs, she grabs my hand in mid-air, taking it in both of hers.

"Oh, man, I so got you!" Her face clears, suddenly readable again, and she lets out a silvery laugh. "Of course I want to be a magical secret agent, are you fucking kidding me?" She holds up my badge as if it were hers. "Agent Riley, reporting for duty."

It's another day before we're free to leave. I take the head doctor aside at one point to explain without explaining that the battery of tests they're running is pointless, but I don't fight too hard. My authority only extends to her protection now that she's accepted the offer to join the SCD; the hospital's requirements come first. I stay out of the way, contacting Mr. and Mrs. Riley to let them know Cora's awake and phone conferencing about the case with other agents, but I maintain a constant presence in her room to ensure there's no time wasted in securing her discharge. We have a final errand to complete, and I'm anxious to get moving.

We're waiting for her release paperwork to arrive when she asks about Eris. It's the first moment we've had alone since Cherry returned with the doctors in tow, and I knew we'd need to discuss the larger picture of the events in the castle. But I'd hoped to save it for the long trip back to the Capitol.

"So," she says slowly, "it turns out I'm not dead, even though Eris said I was. You want to tell me what actually happened down there? I'm guessing being a magical freak has something to do with it."

"I'd suggest 'supernatural' as a label, but yes, it does."

I glance out the door to ensure no one is on their way to interrupt us. The hallway appears to be empty for the time being, so I cross back to sit in the armchair across from her. I'll need to be quick. The last nurse left less than a minute ago, but someone could arrive at any moment. Cora perches on the edge of her hospital bed, fixing me with expectant curiosity. I shift forward in my seat and keep my voice low to cover the unnerving ambiguity.

"We don't fully understand the mechanics of sidestepping yet," I say. "There simply isn't enough data to form solid conclusions because it's so rare. So, when you said you'd visited the Hunting Hall in a dream, I'll admit to a large measure of surprise. Dreamers of any kind are unusual. And dreamers spontaneously manifesting interdimensional travel is completely unheard of."

"What you're saying is that I'm not normal, even by supernatural standards." She actually sounds excited at the prospect.

I smirk. "Something like that. I can only draw on my own experience for comparison, however. My talents are purely corporeal – I can't visit other worlds without my body – but it seems you can step even while unconscious."

She tilts her head to one side. "Then how did I recover while I was in the underworld?" she says, touching the bandaged gash at her neck. "If my spirit or whatever goes out for a walk, doesn't that mean there's no life force to heal my body? How come I didn't just bleed out?"

My eyebrows knit together as I consider this. "I don't know. It appears that vital signs, cognition, and musculature weren't affected the way they would be if you were in an actual coma. But that's all I've been able to glean from the situation so far."

I sigh and press a hand to a tightening temple. More mysteries.

"I'm making you crazy, aren't I?" she laughs. She waves a hand dismissively. "Don't worry about it – now that there are two of us, it'll be easier to figure out."

I can't help smiling back. The thought of working together to unravel the biggest mystery in my life is more than enough encouragement to get back to headquarters as soon as possible. Once she's completed her training, it's possible I can sway Agent 50 into placing her under my mentorship...

Cora clears her throat delicately, bringing me back to the conversation. She doesn't say anything; she simply smiles and waits. I square my shoulders and sit up a bit straighter to cover my lapse in concentration.

"As for Eris' involvement, I suspect she agreed

you were dead because she couldn't actually tell. The underworld isn't her realm; it could only support her, not grant her additional powers. She likely assumed you were dead because you were in the underworld and left it at that."

"But why would she be there in the first place? Doesn't she belong in the Greek section of Pretendy Funtime Land?"

"Eris' presence in Hel's domain is completely unprecedented," I say, ignoring her flip description of the Otherworlds. "No deity has ever attempted a complete takeover of another holding; all the beings on that side of the Gauntlet have coexisted relatively peacefully until now. It's possible that Eris's belief levels fell so low that she felt she had to do something desperate to survive, but seizing another deity's realm is too extreme a move to be so simple. That she likely wanted Hel's key to open the Gauntlet is strong evidence that there's something more at work."

"So, let me see if I understand." She ticks off points on her fingers as she walks through the information. "Gods and goddesses and all the shit from myths and legends not only exist, but they're living together in a supernatural commune on the other side of something called 'the Gauntlet' and are powered by how much people believe in them. And this one goddess in particular is trying to steal someone else's territory, but you're not sure how she's able to do it or why she wants to."

"Essentially, yes."

She gives a sharp laugh and says, "Dude, that is

fucked up."

TWENTY-FIVE

Fifty-eight minutes later, I'm standing in the gravel driveway of an odd homestead tucked inside the curve of a rural highway. I would've shot right past it had Cora not pointed out the drastic turn covered by thick oak trees and marked only by an unassuming mailbox on the opposite side. A deep inhale brings me the scent of freshly chopped wood, horse sweat, tomato flowers, and a small pond nearby. I allow myself a private smile; my father would've loved it here.

A pack of miscellaneous dogs kicks up dust in the summer heat as they sprint toward the sound of my unfamiliar black SUV. They stop dead when they reach my feet and immediately sit, cocking their heads to the side in question. I bend down to pat the leader, a red chow mix, on his dense skull – approval without authority. His purple tongue lolls happily, and his pack mates, which include a Great

Dane and white goat for some reason, crowd around for their turn to be scratched. It happens more often than you'd think.

"Addy likes you," Cora says.

I straighten and turn to face her as she alights from the passenger side of the car. The midday sunlight in her red hair gives her a regal glow. During the ride, she couldn't stop talking and pointing out memories from her childhood along the route, stories about bonfires, gnomes, school days, and pixies. But now, standing in front of her house, knowing it might be the last time, it seems she's run out of things to say. It's as if the rest of the world is wide open for her to share, but she's not sure if she wants me here in her most intimate place. I don't blame her.

"Maybe I should wait out here. I met your parents when I arrived at the hospital, but they weren't exactly happy to see me. Especially after I told them to leave. I understand if you're worried about their reaction to you bringing me home."

I see her repress a smirk, then she brushes past me to open the rusted gate leading into the yard. "Nah. No matter what I say, it's still going to be a bit of a shock, what with the magical alternate dimension stuff and all."

"Fair enough," I say.

She leads me up a long, thin path worn into the grass by years of use. The dogs trail behind me until we reach the porch where they flop down on the cool concrete. Cora reaches down to her pocket, then laughs silently, and knocks on one of a pair of front doors. As the sound of hurried feet comes toward us, I realize how exposed I am standing here in my shirtsleeves without the protection of my suit. I exorcise my nerves by rolling up my cuffs to the elbow; it's something to do with my hands to keep me from thinking about being naked while I talk to her parents.

The screen door swings open a few seconds later, revealing Susannah Riley, a graceful Southern woman in her late fifties with dark brown hair and eyes. She gasps with joy, and I have to jump out of the way when she pushes open the front door to throw her arms around her daughter. I politely turn my attention to patting the Great Dane at my knee while the women stand locked together saying muffled, earnest things into each other's shoulders. The dog leans on me so hard that I have to grab the handle of the other door to keep my balance. But the knob turns in my hand, and I'm forced to let go. I look through the plate glass window, senses automatically prepared for a fight, and see someone watching me. With grey eyes.

I clear away from the door, and Daniel Riley steps out. He's on the tall side of average height with sparkling eyes in a serious face under a mess of graying red hair. We size each other up as the Cora and her mother continue to talk in their private bubble on the other side of the porch. The hair on the back of my neck prickles under his silent scrutiny.

"Agent," Mr. Riley says after a long moment. His Irish accent is well concealed but still noticeable. "I believe we owe you some thanks for bringing our dear girl back to us." The way he says it makes me wonder how much he already knows.

Mrs. Riley breaks apart from Cora and turns to me. There's a quickly hidden flash of anger in her eyes before she says, "Yes, thank you." Then she laughs a little artificially and smoothes her immaculate hair. "Oh, where are my manners. I'm so sorry – won't you come in for something cold to drink?"

I nod respectfully. "Certainly, ma'am. Thank you for offering."

I'm ushered through a living room decorated with soft shades of pink and green into a kitchen filled with the smells of living plants and baking bread. Mr. Riley offers me the seat at the end of the table, which I take, noting the placement. Cora busies herself with glasses as her parents join me.

"Agent...," Mrs. Riley begins.

"Mr. Alexander, ma'am."

She smiles briefly with a chilly edge. "Mr. Alexander. I wanted to apologize for the way we acted at the hospital. When you turned up, we weren't exactly in the right state of mind to be talking to mysterious strangers."

"It's not a problem, ma'am. I've certainly been called worse things in my life, and if it were my daughter, I can't say I wouldn't have done the same."

"It's not every day you're contacted by a member of a government organization," says Mr. Riley.

"I certainly hope not," I reply. I mean it as a joke,

but he doesn't smile.

Mrs. Riley does, though. She reaches out and pats my hand in a motherly fashion. "Don't mind Dan, Mr. Alexander. He's one of those conspiracy folks – always looking for another explanation for the totally reasonable."

Condensation already stands on the glass of lavender lemonade by the time Cora hands it to me, and the force of the scent memory stifles my reply as our time in the house asserts itself in the real world. I risk a glance at her to see an empathetic apology in her face. We smile at each other as innocently as possible, and the weight of Mr. Riley's gaze touches the entire exchange. If he's anything like his daughter, he's seen more in that moment that we want him to know. He reaches over to Cora and squeezes her hand when she takes the seat beside him.

I leave the glass untouched in front of me and clear my throat politely, slipping on enough of Agent 97 to give me some distance from the situation. The sooner I explain what comes next, the sooner these people can go back to hating me. That will make this easier somehow.

"Mr. and Mrs. Riley, I'm afraid that I'm still here on official business. There are complications surrounding your daughter's accident and recovery that initiated my involvement in her case. These complications are not one-time occurrences, meaning further steps must be taken."

Mrs. Riley stares at Mr. Riley. Mr. Riley stares at me. Cora stares at the table.

"Put simply, your daughter has demonstrated supernatural abilities," I continue. "The agency I work for oversees these manifestations, and I have been assigned to debrief Cora, which I have done. I'm not at liberty to discuss the details of her profile, but her talents are significant. This has created a rather unique opportunity for her. "

Cora seems to sense the break I leave for her in the discussion. She raises her eyes from the scarred tabletop and looks from one parent to the other.

"They want me to come work for them," she says.

There's a stretched moment as the news sinks in. Cora squeezes her father's hand as he continues his stony grey stare. Then Mrs. Riley's eyes narrow.

"What does that mean, exactly?" she asks me.

I shift my gaze from Mr. Riley to his wife. "It means Cora would be trained to use her abilities as a special agent of the United States government in Washington, D.C., effective immediately."

She scoffs and waves a hand dismissively as if shooing a fly. "Cora's a bright, wonderful girl that can do anything she sets her mind to. A little fanciful, maybe, but that's her father's doing. Traipsing around in the woods to hunt for faeries is one thing, but all this talk about superpowers and secret agents is ridiculous. Of course she's not going anywhere for any magical training."

Cora looks at her mother with an expression I don't understand but is reflected in her voice. "Mom, I already said yes."

Mrs. Riley glares at her daughter for a long

moment, then she pushes back from the table and says, "I need to go finish the laundry," to her husband with telling poison. She dumps her untouched lemonade into the kitchen sink, then sweeps out of the room and disappears down the basement steps.

Mr. Riley is the one who breaks the tension. "*Piskie*, you best go pack. I'll sit here and chat with Mr. Alexander a while."

Cora nods and stands, rubbing unshed tears from her eyes. Her father and I watch her climb the stairs to the attic in silence.

Once we're alone, he turns to me, hands clasped in front of him and eyebrows raised, as if interviewing a potential suitor or interrogating a petty thief. I indignantly straighten to my full height at the opposite end of the table. We've got about ten minutes before someone interrupts and I lose my chance to ask the questions I've been holding onto since I first saw Cora's grey eyes.

"How long have you known?" I say.

"I always suspected, but it didn't show until she moved back home last month." He twitches a smile. "She's a late bloomer."

"What did you tell her?"

"Nothing yet. I honestly wasn't sure what to say. 'Sorry, darling, you're a changeling. Have fun with that,'?" He tilts his head at me. "What gave it away?"

"Grey eyes only occur in a very specific community." I manage a brief smile of my own. "The massive energy fluctuations and opening interdimensional portals were strong signs, too, though."

His critical expression raises the fine hair on my neck and arms again. The touch of Faerie will probably always do that to me; I'll never get used to being seen through.

"You've been at this a long time," he says, "but do you know how it works?"

"I know it's genetic and incredibly rare."

"Aside from that."

My ears redden. "No. We can't detect it, so we can't study it. It's something I'm working on in what little spare time I have. We only know of five manifested planeswalkers, past and present, and they were all discovered by accident."

He nods sympathetically. "It's hard to explain. Growing up a halfling, you just *know*." One grey eye clouds over until it's totally white, gazing over my shoulder at a place I could easily sidestep to but never want to see again. "I'd hoped it wouldn't happen to her. The chances were so high against it. She grew up all those years being able to see what's really there but never showing any true talent. I was relieved, to tell the truth. But when Ma called to her in that first dream, it was only a matter of time." He falters, then his eyes return to their usual thundercloud grey. "I just didn't think it'd happen like this."

I nod and rotate the sweaty glass of lemonade between my palms. Part of me understands. Had Queen Mab called to any child of mine, I'm not sure what I'd do, either. But the larger part of me knows there's no escaping fate – certainly not for planeswalkers.

"If it makes you feel any better, she's amazing at it," I say. "Once she's trained, she's going to do incredible things."

Mr. Riley laughs softly. "Of course she will. But for whose side, I wonder?"

The sound of footsteps coming down from the attic stops us from delving deeper into that rabbit hole, but I make a careful mental note of the aside.

Before Cora reaches us, I lean in and whisper, "Come to DC with us, Daniel. Help me understand. Make a difference in both our worlds."

But he simply smiles – a full, toothy smile to cover the secrets he won't share – and lets his daughter end our talk by throwing her arms around his shoulders from behind.

"Hey, *piskie*," he says. "You all ready to run off to the big city with your secret agent lover man?"

"Daddy!" she protests, pushing him playfully. "It's not like that."

Mr. Riley chuckles knowingly. "Sure, sure, whatever you say, darling."

He loosens her grip on his shoulders and stands to give his daughter a hug so fierce it extracts a squeak from her tiny frame.

Father and daughter proceed to have a whispered conversation clearly not meant for my ears, so I slide from the kitchen chair and stall for time by running the mineral-heavy water, intending to wash our cups. I pour out my full glass in the sink. It's easily over ninety degrees in this Missouri heat, but I couldn't bring myself to touch the lavender lemonade. There are too many awkward memories to wrestle with.

But before I can start cleaning, the washcloth is snatched from my hands. I snap my head up to see Mrs. Riley beside me. She's pointedly not engaged in the exchange between her husband and daughter. Rather, she's eyeing me with intense interest. After a few seconds, she seems to come to a conclusion that she doesn't share. She presses the back of her hand against my side, and I allow her to ease me away from the sink. I stand next to her as she cleans the glasses in quick succession, then hands them to me for drying. I get the distinct impression that I'm either being tested, accepted, or both.

It's only after the last glass is safely deposited in the cupboard and Mr. Riley and Cora have moved into the secondary living room that she speaks to me. She puts her back to the countertop, craning her neck up to look me full in the face with her jaw set.

"You take care of my little girl, you hear me?"

I duck my head to her in deference. "I will, ma'am."

"And if she gets in trouble, you call me. I don't care what time it is."

"Yes, ma'am."

"And I swear to god that if she disappears, gets blown up, or ends up in some sleazy political sex scandal I will come to your house and break your kneecaps myself. You hear me, Mr. Alexander?"

My eyes widen. "Yes, ma'am. Loud and clear."

She nods curtly and then sweeps into the living room to join her family.

I stand alone in the kitchen for a while, giving them a few more minutes together. There's nothing preventing Cora from coming back once her training is complete, but I get the distinct impression she won't. The blueprints for her personal afterlife are reflected back at me from nearly every corner of this house. Memories both real and imagined will drive her elsewhere, and her parents likely won't understand the reluctance to return. They deserve time to say goodbye. I certainly wish I'd had it.

Soon Cora calls for me to join them, and it's time to go. Mr. Riley shakes my hand with a crushing grip belied by his delicate skin. Mrs. Riley simply nods. Tears stand in their eyes, but Cora's parents wave us off the porch, through the pack of dozing dogs, and across the lawn. Mr. Riley wraps an arm around his wife and pulls her to him as they watch us climb into my SUV. They only turn to go inside once we've trundled down to the end of the gravel driveway.

I lean over the steering wheel, trying to see around the blind horseshoe curve. The road appears empty, but you never know on these rural highways. I roll down the window and listen. Once I'm confident that it's safe to proceed, I lift my foot to the gas.

"Wait."

I raise an eyebrow at Cora in the passenger seat.

She's gnawing on the thumbnail of her right hand, eyes wide as she stares at the blacktop stretched out in front of us. The breeze blowing through the open window carries the unmistakable tang of fear mingled with blue-tinged cotton and leather. I don't ask her what the problem is. The story of the accident that started her down this path is playing out on her face clear as day.

The thumbnail is almost entirely gone before she says, "Okay. Let's go."

In the quickest of touches, I put my hand on her knee. "I'll go slowly," I say.

She smiles. I check the curve of the road again, then gently pull out onto the highway, gathering speed toward the interstate.

We drive together in silence for a while. No questions, no explaining. There'll be plenty of time for that later. It's a long way from mid-Missouri to the Capitol, after all. For now, it's enough to sit and be on this journey, each of us ready to start our lives over as the people we're meant to be.

And so ends the first episode of the *Forgotten Relics* series!

But there are so many
unanswered questions!

What gives Cora her powers?
What's with Jack's tattoo?
What future does Hel foresee?
What is Eris really up to?

Stay tuned to find out!
Sword of Souls - December 2014

Visit elliedi.com to sign up for
book updates and bonus goodies

ACKNOWLEDGEMENTS

I never know what to write here. There's always a tertiary person left out that'll get their knickers in a twist or a genuinely important person lost in the mad shuffle that is the wrap-up of a novel. The pressure is immense. But I'll give it a shot anyway.

Thank you first of all to the wondrous support players who worked tirelessly behind the scenes to make sure this book didn't suck. Dave La Rush, evil genius brainstorm companion. Katy Rose, content and punctuation editor extraordinaire. Zack Eskins, beta reader champion. Desiree Kern, unsung artistic genius.

Thanks to the crew at Platform 302 for helping me maintain my grip on reality by insisting I leave the house to socialize every once in a while.

Props also and ever to my husband, Lino, Photoshop Hero, who also pats me on the shoulder when I cry because the plot isn't working and listens patiently when I get too excited about a new breakthrough or stupid nerd joke I'm trying to weave into the text.

A very special "thank you" to everyone who contributed their hard-earned cash to the IndieGoGo crowdfunding campaign that paid for the cover of this book. Andy Dolph, Anne Kaplan, Beth Denton, Carol Neilson, Chrysoula Tzavelas, Courtney Harper, Darynda Jones, David Burch, David La Rush, Edward Tirado, Frank Marcelli, Heather Kedding, Helen Morris, Jasmine Jobe & Doug Clark, Jeff Dunnett, Jennifer Khang, Jessica Lee, Jo Gough, Joe Giammarco, Joy Robertson, Karen Coverett, Kari Johnson, Kathryn Hunter, Kimberly Milks, Kyeli Smith, Lauren Balazs, Lauren Orsini, Lindsay White, Lisa Marion, Elizabeth Patt, Marin Harris, Megan Fair, Melanie Kristy, Mike Bramnik, Natalie Englehart, Nick Fotache, Nicole Platania, Patricia Watkins, Rhiannon Llewellyn, Shannon Lindeman, Sharon Harris, Shelby Olrich, Shenee Howard, Shirley Myers, Steve Fisher, Taryn Pyle, Tea Silvestre, Teresa Deak, Timothy Edwards, and Zachary Eskins – you guys made it possible to up my game and changed how I think about self-publishing for the future. You rock so hard.

And finally, undying thanks to you, dear reader, for sticking with me through it all. I do this for you. Thank you for giving me continued purpose in life.

ABOUT THE AUTHOR

 Ellie Di Julio is a nomadic writer currently living in Hamilton, Ontario with her Robert Downey, Jr. lookalike husband and their three cats. Between nerd activities like playing *Dungeons & Dragons* or watching *Top Gear*, she enthusiastically destroys the kitchen and tries to figure out what it's all about, when you really get down to it. She also writes urban fantasy novels riddled with pop culture references and sexy secret agents.

Her first novel, *Inkchanger*, could easily be considered *Forgotten Relics #0*, and as such, rewards readers of the rest of the series, sort of like watching *Thor* before *The Avengers*. Her second novel, *Time & Again*, with Kyeli Smith, has nothing to do with super powers or secret agents but is very cool nonetheless.

Questions, comments, funny stories?
Reviews, interviews, guestposts?
Feel free to drop love notes/hate mail at
ellie.di.julio@gmail.com
or visit elliedi.com

OTHER WORKS

Inkchanger

Zara Carter has never fit in at in Runaway Heights, a secret community of teens hiding from their own personal hells. No one has been worth the risk of opening her heart. Things would've stayed that way had it not been for the inkpen, a device that pushes Zara's artistic talents into the realm of magic. The tattoos she creates come to life, and each design gives her a taste of her deepest desire: a heart filled with hope and love.

But power like that doesn't go unnoticed. Assigned to the classified Supernatural Cases Division, Agent 97's feelers are out, searching the decaying industrial town for a wild girl with a remarkable talent.

If only he could catch her.

OTHER WORKS

Time & Again
with Kyeli Smith

Everything is perfect the day Saffron Clovers finds out she's pregnant. Now she and her husband, Nate, can have the family they've longed for. But after a series of tragic losses and intensive heartache, their marriage crumbles. Saffron finds herself completely bereft. No children, no husband, no home.

Yet, there's hope. A strangely familiar woman on a foreign beach prophecies that Saffron will have the daughter she's always dreamed of. But how?

To find out, Saffron sets off on a cross-country journey back to her childhood home to complete the circle and begin a new story. She's not sure what she'll find there; all she knows is that it's time to go.